30 DAYS OF JUSTIS

A MICHAEL GRESHAM NOVEL

JOHN ELLSWORTH

For Adriane

CONTENTS

Chapter 1	1
Chapter 2	2
Chapter 3	17
DAY 1/30	23
DAY 2/30	44
DAY 3/30	58
DAY 4/30	68
DAY 5/30	81
DAY 6/30	90
DAY 7/30	103
DAY 8/30	119
DAY 9/30	127
DAY 10/30	134
Marcel	143
DAY 11/30	147
DAY 12/30	161
Marcel	171
DAY 13/30	175
DAY 14/30	185
DAY 15/30	192
DAY 16/30	210
DAY 17/30 (Morning)	225
DAY 17/30 (Afternoon)	232
DAY 18/30	236
Brent Massingill	244
DAY 19/30	250
DAY 20/30	265
DAY 21/30	270
Day 22/30	281
DAY 23/30	296
DAY 24/30	308

DAY 25/30   310
DAY 26/30   319
DAY 27/30   321
DAY 28/30   327
DAY 29/30   331
DAY 30/30   333
Epilogue   339

Afterword   345
Also by John Ellsworth   347
About the Author   349
Email Signup   353

1

 Dear Mister Grezam:

I need Justis. They got me in Spokane jail. Now they told a lies and say I killed a man. Please help me. It's first degree murder, they say.

Sincerely, Cache Evans.

Oh, almost forget. Millicent is my mom.

I am your daughter.

2

I'm guessing the letter found me thanks to a bit of research by someone at the jail—maybe a counselor, maybe a priest.

Whatever; the letter has hunted me down. It came to my office here in Washington D.C. I work for the U.S. Attorney. My current assignment is the prosecution of terrorists. I work out of a secluded office, and I'm guarded 24/7 by the U.S. Marshal's service. For this letter to have found me, squirreled away beyond the Washington Beltway, is a minor miracle. But here it is, centered among the piles of legal files covering my desk in my wood-paneled, windowless office. There it remains for hours.

Lunch comes and goes. By chance, I notice the letter again. So I pull it out of the envelope and re-read.

Letters like it are common. Prisoners across the country are desperate for someone to save them. This letter in the small, white envelope with its upside-down stamps looks to me like one more eleventh-hour cry for help by someone who figures she is somehow related to me. Or has a special bond with me because she read about me, or whatever.

So, I instinctively back off. It isn't the first time someone has tried to draw me in with a "lost-child" scheme. Now here we are again. A new daughter? I don't think so. I try to imagine where this young woman came from as I read it yet again. But this time I am struck by one gotcha: she knows about Millicent. My Millicent detour was nearly thirty years ago. That's a long time in reverse for a pure stranger to know about.

I re-read the crude handwriting and try to imagine the writer's predicament. But then I catch myself. First-degree murder charges are terrible cases for any lawyer and at least ten times more so for the defendant. This is compounded by the fact the police aren't out there just randomly arresting people who might have killed someone. 99% of the time they've got the goods.

I ball up the letter and toss it into my wastebasket. But that isn't conclusive enough, so I fish it out, smooth the wrinkles, then run it through my shredder. I turn back to my real work, the job that makes it possible for me to feed and shelter my real family. The same job that keeps fertilizer bombs beyond the White House fence.

~

Our usual quitting time rolls around.

It's summertime here in Washington. July 3. Tomorrow is fireworks and a picnic on the Capitol Mall with my wife and kids followed by a movie at home, a World War Two feature about stalwart submariners just after Pearl

Harbor. HBO runs it every year on July 4. The kids have seen it before—it's become our July 4 ritual. A relaxing day; a lazy, family day for this father, the wife he adores, and their three children. Plus, it falls on a Tuesday, which means most staff will take off the rest of the week. I won't be one of those playing hooky, however, because I'm a newbie here and have drawn some duty days no one else wanted.

I turn back to my chores. But the letter from someone claiming to be my daughter won't stay away. It has surfaced again in my thoughts.

What if she *is* your child? What would you do about it? I draw a deep breath and stare at the paper shredder. Too late, whoever you are.

But there is one thing I want to know about Washington State law, and so I check the Washington murder statute.

I read how a murder charge can be enhanced so a defendant will face execution if convicted. It raises the hairs on my neck to think of anyone dying at the hands of any state. These are the same governments that screw up just about every service they offer, maybe a hundred times every day. So how can they be trusted with someone's very life? It's bad enough how often they convict the wrong guys over and over until the Innocence Project hopefully steps in and makes things right. Suddenly I'm anxious. I'm disturbed and my stomach burns.

Something inside me just won't leave it alone. I swallow down a Prilosec; then I shove my regular job to the back burner. My conscience forces me to consider the letter problem with the most open mind I can muster.

Millicent, the writer's mother, was a woman I'd had a two-week thing with after my first divorce. Now someone's claiming that fortnight produced a child? Never once, I swear it, did Millicent contact me to tell me I'd fathered a child. If she had, I would have stepped up and been a good dad. But she didn't contact me; not a call, not a card, not a lawsuit for paternity—nothing.

Which doesn't surprise me. The Millicent Evans I knew had been fiercely independent. She would never marry, she swore, terribly influenced by watching her mother's abuse at the hands of Millicent's stepfather, a raging alcoholic.

I'm interrupted by Warner Johns, who mans the office next to mine. He's holding a Slurpee and a briefcase. Leaving for the week and I'm annoyed. Jealous.

"Don't let the marshals shoot anyone till I get back, Michael. Can you do that?"

"Not to worry. I've collected all their guns and locked them in my desk."

"Good on you. You want me to drop by with backyard burgers on Sunday?"

"Don't bother. Have you dared to open the kitchen refrigerators? There's enough moldy cheese in there to start a health food restaurant. I'll survive and maybe have my urinary tract infection cured."

"Funny man."

"I mean the mold. Like penicillin for infections."

He nods sadly.

"Say hi to Verona."

"Do the same with Angelina, Warner. Have yourself a grand old time."

"Later."

"Hey. One thing. What would you do if someone claiming to be your daughter wrote you a letter? What if she asked you to come save her from a first-degree murder charge?"

"I'd go. Why?"

"What if you didn't know if she was really your daughter?"

"I'd go find out. You get a letter like that?"

"I did."

"Then, go and see. You won't sleep until you do."

"How would you know if she's really your daughter?"

"Find out if she's a chronic worrier. If she is, you've got your kid."

"Right."

"Who's her mother?"

"Millicent somebody."

"What, you don't even know her last name?"

"It was a long time ago, Warner."

"Sheesh." He walks off, shaking his head.

When I knew her, Millicent was working part-time as a medical researcher at the University of California in San Diego and had a second job in La Jolla. I met her when I was taking a little get-over-it time following a hateful divorce. I was burned out, and California looked like the place to walk on the sand and listen to the waves and let my heart bleed out all its agony and pain one wave at a time. Which I did. But while I was there, settling in La Jolla, I met Millie. We spent ten of my fourteen days together.

Millie was brilliant, an engaging conversationalist, a biology theorist. Plus, she spouted the kind of wicked humor that has always turned my head. She had come to California from Mississippi, where her father was a sharecropper. He owned a team of mules and three goats, nothing more, while she was growing up. After saving every penny for a year, he bought her a Greyhound ticket, put together three lunches and three suppers that wouldn't need refrigeration, passed her five twenty-dollar bills, and kissed her goodbye. That was so long ago that Millicent, boarding the bus in Waveland, was told by the driver to sit in the rear with the other "coloreds."

Four days later, she climbed down off the bus in San Diego. She stretched and gulped down her first Pacific air, then made a vow. Millicent swore the ride from Waveland to San Diego would be the last time she ever rode in the back of any public transportation. She was free of the South, by God, and that meant she would be riding up front from then on.

It turned out Millicent had a brain—a great brain. Eight years after climbing down out of the Greyhound, she had earned a Ph.D. in microbiology. She graduated with Highest Honors. On graduation day she was plucked from the rolls of the unemployed by a startup genetics lab in La Jolla. This was way before the world was sequencing DNA to eliminate a Petri dish teeming with frightening diseases that had long plagued humankind.

So, this Cache Evans—I retrieved her name from the backside of the envelope—is Millicent's daughter? Well, she certainly hasn't learned to spell under her mother's tutelage. She wants *Justis?* Seriously? Whatever happened to spelling the word *Justice?*

Which is where I have to catch myself. I've just learned I maybe have another daughter and the best I can come up with is a critique of her spelling? For the love of—

My hands automatically dial the phone number on the envelope flap. A short burst of ringing and another. On the third ring, a voice answers, "Spokane County Detention Services."

"My name is Michael Gresham. I need to speak to a prisoner by the name of Cache Evans."

"I'm sorry, Mr. Gresham, but we're not operating a switchboard for inmates. Please call during regular visiting hours."

She is about to hang up—I can hear it in her tone. But I catch her.

"I'm Ms. Evans' attorney. I would like to speak with my client. Please let's not complicate this beautiful July day."

The line goes silent. I hope I'm on hold. But I don't know.

A voice comes on the line. A voice I've never heard before, a voice that claims to be passed down from me.

"Hello?"

"Cache Evans?"

"Who's this?"

"Michael Gresham. You sent me a letter."

"Oh, my dad." Long pause. Then, "You actually called me?"

"Evidently I did. I have a few questions for you."

"Shoot, sir."

"First off, you say Millicent Evans was your mother?"

"Is my mother. She's still alive and kicking down in California."

"Is she—is she--"

"Married? My goodness, you don't waste any time, do you? Must be where I get my hot blood. It sure wasn't my mom. She never met a man she didn't hate. I'm just the opposite. I live for engaging with the male species."

Great, she lives for men. That's just what a found father wants to hear out of the gate. Plus, there is the language. The speaker isn't someone who characteristically spells "justice" as "justis." And, "Engaging with the male species?" Who in hell talks like that?

"No, I meant to ask whether she is alive and well."

"Oh, yes, she's alive all right. I called her, but she told me she'd written me off. She's no longer willing to have me occupying her thoughts. Her words, not mine. But she is coming up to see me. Should I call you father, or dad, or what?"

"Let's take that a step at a time."

"No need. Mother has your DNA from the hairbrush you left when you ran out on her. She's done all the stuff she does in the lab. You're my dad by about a billion-to-one."

"Ran out on her? Is that what she told you I did?"

"She did not. That's what I always told myself when I cried because I didn't have a dad. I was angry at you the whole time I was growing up."

"I see."

"But the DNA has your fingerprints all over it. You're my father."

"I am, okay, well, DNA: that's the kind of thing I was going to suggest. But since it's already been done, why don't you call me Michael just for now while we get to know each other."

"We're gonna get to know each other?"

The decision is already made for me. My impulsivity has me dialing airlines as soon as we hang up.

No one can execute my child. I have become the father whose five-year-old is sent home crying by a mean mother down the street. It feels just like that. A man doesn't turn his back on a daughter in jail, I don't give a damn what she's done, and I don't give a damn about his day job, either. If she is mine—which I'm making room for inside my head—then I'm going to treat her like mine. No way would I ever leave my younger girls in a jail somewhere. They couldn't pull off a crime evil enough to cost them my love and my care. And it isn't going to happen with this one, either.

"We are going to get to know each other. I'm calling the airlines as soon as we hang up."

"Well, that's more than I hoped."

"I'm on my way, Cache."

"Goody."

"By the way, what are you in jail for?"

"What did I do or what do they say I did?"

"Both."

"Well, for one I was dating men on the street."

"As in—"

"As in selling my ass for dollars."

"Prostitution. Oh."

"Yeppers. That's what I was doing."

"Okay, so what do the cops say you were doing."

"They say I killed a man."

"Go on."

"They say I gave him HIV, which turned into AIDS, which killed him. They say I knew I had HIV when I had sex with him. But I swear I didn't, Michael. I didn't know. Besides, he forced me. This was fifteen years ago. Evidently, it became full-blown AIDS, and it killed him."

"Wait. How old are you?"

"Twenty-eight."

"And he had sex with you over fifteen years ago? That would make you thirteen."

"I was thirteen when he raped me. I lived in his house. I was his kid's nanny."

"Why were you living apart from your mom?"

"I ran away. I found out about you and hated her, and I ran

away for not telling me about you. CPS took custody of me and placed me with different fosters. I wound up in this man's home. They paid me to nanny. Then he raped me."

I've heard enough.

"You stay put, okay? I'm on my way."

Stay put? As if she's about to wander off down to the soda fountain? She's in the can, Michael. Your oldest daughter is in jail on murder charges.

"Attorney Gresham, this is the switchboard. Your five minutes are up. Cache is no longer on the line with you. Goodbye."

"Wait. Where was she convicted? What county?"

"That would be Spokane County."

The line goes dead. I can only surmise that she hung up on me. No messing around with farewells with these people.

Well. I immediately dial the phone number of our office administrator, Bruce Billars. Bruce isn't going to like hearing from me. I'm going to be his problem for the night.

Fifteen minutes later, I've delivered the bad news to Bruce: that I've been called away on urgent family business and that he is going to need to replace me ASAP. Bruce isn't thrilled, but he always has a backup plan. That's why he's the administrator.

Next, I call the court in Spokane, where Cache was convicted. I write down the names they give me from her court file. The names of her defense and appellate lawyers. I hang up, and I am stunned. My daughter is on death row. The trial judge has signed the execution warrant.

So I call Kelly Larsyn, the lead trial lawyer. He takes the call without delay.

"This is Michael Gresham, Mr. Larsyn. I've just learned I'm Cache Evans' father."

Guarded tone, but he answers, "I was told Cache had no father."

"Well, she does. She's contacted me and convinced me I'm her father."

Pause. "Well, what can I do for you today, Mr. Gresham?"

"I'd like to ask you a couple of questions."

"Ask away."

"As I understand it, Cache has been convicted of giving AIDS to her foster father. He died years later from the disease."

"So the state prosecuted her for murder. Aggravated, which earned her the death penalty."

"I'm a lawyer, Mr. Larsyn. A criminal lawyer, like you. I don't understand how she could be convicted of murdering someone by giving them AIDS when she was raped."

"Yes, Cache told me she was raped. But Cache didn't testify at trial. So the jury knew nothing about the alleged rape."

"And she didn't testify why?"

"Are you kidding? Your daughter has been working the streets for ten years. She's a common prostitute, Mr. Gresham. If a jury found that out, she'd have been convicted on their first vote."

"She was convicted anyway, Mr. Larsyn."

"Yes, but I kept the jury out for nearly three days before they got a verdict. I at least gave them something to think about."

"And you thought this outweighed the truth about her rape?"

"Cache made the ultimate decision about testifying, Mr. Gresham. You must know that."

I do. I do know that the client is always the one to decide whether to testify. With the active input of her attorney, of course.

"What's the status of the case now?"

"There is no status. There's nothing left to do for Cache. All appeals are exhausted."

"And so you're giving up? Just washing your hands of my daughter?"

"Mr. Gresham, I'm going to hang up now. This was a very hard-fought case, and I'm not going to be accused by a lawyer who wasn't even there. Maybe if you'd shown up for your kid's life, none of this would've happened."

I'm ready to bury the guy when the phone line goes dead. Washingtonians seem to hang up on me as a habit. That's two in a row.

I can only go to Washington and see my daughter. It can't be over for her. I'm one of those criminal lawyers who believe it's never over. Not until the doctor looks up from his stethoscope and confirms a death.

Goodbye to my wife and kids, then Lyft to the airport. At 7:

34 p.m. We're wheels-up non-stop to SEA-TAC, which will be followed by a Delta flight to Spokane.

As I unbuckle after a long nap, I head for the restroom, where I catch a glimpse of my face in the metal mirror. We are somewhere over Omaha. Glassy eyes; white around the lips; a film of sweat across the forehead; trembling hands not good for much except sliding the lock. Then out again, into the aisle, heading for first class. Eyes are looking up from iPads and paperbacks. They hold on my face. Everyone knows. Everyone but me.

At C3 it hits me head-on.

I'm going to be a father yet again.

Another chance at the one job that always leaves me feeling inadequate. So far I've done a passable job with Dania, Mikey, and Annie. Nothing to write home about but nobody's called the cops on me, either. They haven't missed out, and I have no regrets. But it hasn't been easy. A friend of mine in law school once said that the semester exam on property law was like being handcuffed and rolled up in chains and tossed into the North Atlantic Ocean's stormy night. So alike being someone's dad. It never fails to humble me.

Fathering children is about chemistry and biology inspired by lust.

Parenting them, on the other hand, is a whole other North Atlantic.

I am ashamed of those things I did. I know what's required. I must commit to righting the wrongs inflicted on Cache Evans as much as possible. I must go the extra mile times

ten. I acted absurdly at her conception. Now she deserves
better.

Scuttling across the U.S. at 37,000 feet, I have only myself
to blame.

My deepest wounds are mostly self-inflicted.

Enough said.

CHAPTER 3

We make Seattle six hours after takeoff from Reagan International. A thirty-minute layover drags on for hours, it seems. Then I board an eastbound Delta flight. Next-stop: Spokane and the detention center.

We land in a summer rainstorm. It's somewhere around midnight by my EST wristwatch. Local time has it much earlier, though I haven't done the math yet.

I reach to the overhead stowage and retrieve my bag then head for the door. Two men wearing cowboy hats, jeans, white button-down shirts and walking heels on their cowboy boots block my exit. They are standing in the aisle, jaw-boning, as cowboys might put it. If they turn to look, they'll see I'm pissed at them for blocking the aisle. I draw a deep breath and try to relax. The reality of my unexpected trip and abandonment of my family on the eve of July Fourth and fireworks on the Capitol Mall is wearing thin. But when I juxtapose that missed holiday celebration against the reality of a daughter whom I've never met and don't know, and the terrible reality of her incarceration, the nation's birthday pales in comparison. I am exactly where I'm supposed to be, as Verona—my wife—said I would be as I was leaving. She was right.

At last, the cowboys move on; their cowboy hats pulled low on their foreheads.

It's late, yes, but I jump in a cab and head for the detention center anyway. A strong pull—the gravity of family—is reeling me in. Tonight is the time to locate my offspring, not tomorrow. "Faster," I implore the cabbie. "Twenty bucks if you beat your best time."

He waves me off and motions that I should shut the hell up, so I open my laptop. The Detention Center's website offers an inmate roster. I pull it onscreen as we roll along. Odd thing: Cache Evans isn't listed on the roster. I have no idea why she isn't. But it concerns me, and I shiver.

I stare out at the passing neighborhoods and homes with warm yellow light escaping through street-facing windows. Jailed at twenty-eight. My eyes mist. You don't get do-overs with your kids.

Finally, we reach Mallon Avenue. I jump out and pay-off the cabbie—including an extra twenty—and trot up the sidewalk as it's still pouring rain. I get wet—I'm without a hat or umbrella—those cowboys knew what the hell they were doing after all. Droplets of water dribble from my nose as I duck inside the heavy glass door of the detention center.

Inside is a glassed-in office with three or four people milling around. One of them spots me at the window and saunters over.

"Can I help you?"

"I'm a lawyer, here to see my client."

I produce my bar card and wait while she looks it over. She turns it this way and that and finally peers up at me. "Sir, I don't know what you're thinking, but this isn't a Washington Bar ID card. You're not licensed to practice in Washington."

I smile my best smile and plunge ahead anyway.

"I'm here to visit Cache Evans. She's my daughter. In the next day or two, I'll petition the court to allow me to appear *pro hac vice*. Does that get me inside?"

Now her puzzlement is apparent. "I don't get it, an attorney on her case? There's no need for another attorney in her case. The Supreme Court turned her down."

"Uh, which Supreme Court? Washington State?"

"No, the U.S. Supreme Court. Are you sure you know about her?"

"Maybe I don't. Please fill me in."

The woman finger-combs her hair away from her forehead.

"Well, your daughter was found guilty of murdering a judge. Her case was appealed to the state courts then went up to the federal courts. Last week the U.S. Supreme Court refused to hear her case, and today we returned her to Purdy."

"Convicted of murder? Seriously?"

"You honestly don't know? Your own daughter?"

"Look, it's a long story. We've been out of touch."

"She was convicted of aggravated first-degree murder. She murdered Judge Hiram Wilberforce in Spokane."

I am speechless. No sudden plans, no lawyer schemes leap to mind when I hear the words, "Aggravated first degree murder." Though it isn't my state, Washington, and though I've never practiced law here, I know what's coming.

"So where has she been sent?"

"Washington Corrections Center for Women. It's over at Purdy."

"Why Purdy?"

"Purdy is female death row. The new governor has lifted the moratorium on executions. Your daughter is on death row awaiting her execution date, Mr. Gresham. Are you here as family or as her lawyer? Death row family has unlimited visitation days for one hour every day. That's how you can best see her if you're headed for Purdy."

"I am headed for Purdy. Where is it?"

"Small place near Gig Harbor."

"And Gig Harbor is where?"

"Real close to Tacoma. Maybe an hour from Seattle."

"So I need to fly back to Tacoma?"

"Suit yourself," she says, backing away from the window. We are evidently finished here. She turns her back and disappears offstage left. The room turns a half-turn. I am dizzy and gripping the ledge below the window.

The reality—the incarceration center, the unlicensed lawyer

—closes in on me and I panic. She's my kid, and she's going to die if the state gets its way.

Stunned beyond belief, I just stand there, holding on to stay upright, trying to accept what my ears just heard. I turn to leave and head back to the airport and, as I turn, my knees buckle, and I collapse. No one sees me fall. I roll onto my side and manage to stand although I'm still shaking so bad I feel like Jell-O in my joints. A drinking fountain gives me a place to hang onto something.

Death row.

Hold on. One more question.

Back to the window I shuffle, waving at the same woman who has now reappeared. She moves her mouth near the round speaker in the glass and looks me over again. "Yes?"

"When is my daughter's execution date?"

"She was just in court here today. Her execution date is August third. Thirty days from tomorrow. It was all over TV. Your daughter is big news here."

I numbly turn around without even thanking her this time.

August third. Thirty days until my daughter's execution. And all court petitions and motions have been turned down, according to Mr. Larsyn. My mind goes berserk, and I reach behind, grabbing at the shelf beneath the window at my back. Luckily my hands find support and stop me from collapsing again. Which scares me; I'm not the collapsing type. But it tells me I'm out of control. Just like my daughter's case.

There's no time to waste. I yank out my phone and punch Marcel's number in D.C.

His sleepy voice comes on the line.

"What's up, boss?"

"I need you in Tacoma."

"I'll be there in the morning."

"Good."

I end the call.

Marcel's my investigator. It's his work that wins cases.

So why did I call him on a case that has in all likelihood been worked to death? For one, we'll talk our way through the court file. We work well, going back-and-forth.

Marcel is also my best friend. Maybe I just need him to hold my hand while I witness my daughter's execution.

She must have family present when she dies.

As in, me.

DAY 1/30

The next morning, I wake up in Tacoma after the redeye from Spokane last night. My room is in a local hotel. The furniture is itchy and worn. Last night it didn't look so worn. I'm guessing the same is true of me. I have coffee brought to my room, shower and shave and catch a cab to the airport.

I tell my cabbie to wait in line along the loading curb outside the United terminal. Marcel will appear at any second. I cannot afford to miss him because my cases need Marcel if they're ever to gel. My eyes lose their focus, and my head swims. I feel like I'm coming down with something. It again feels like the walls are closing in; I can only imagine what my daughter must be feeling on death row.

Marcel briskly exits the terminal doors, a backpack in one hand, the other pulling his roll-along. He's looking this way and that. I lower the window and wave to him and call. He angles toward my cab.

"I'm here," he announces as he climbs into the cab.

"Thanks for coming."

"You pay me for coming. No thanks necessary."

I direct the driver, "Let's go back to the Murano Hotel. We can get breakfast while I check for messages and then head out for Purdy."

"What's this all about?"

"I have a daughter in prison here."

He is a dark man with a quick smile. But right now he's all seriousness. "You have a daughter in prison? Well, it must be someone new because Dania and Annie aren't in prison in Washington State."

"It's a new daughter. Her name is Cache Evans, and she's twenty-eight."

"Why not just hire a local attorney to handle her case? Why are you clear out here?"

"Because she's on death row."

"What?" His voice elevates sharply. His eyes latch onto mine.

"Yes, I have no idea what the facts are, but I've been told her case has exhausted all appeals with no relief. If I ever needed you, brother, I need you now. Something has to be done."

"Why go back to the hotel? Let's run through McDonald's, grab a wrap and coffee, and head for the prison."

He's right. The usual stuff can wait.

"Driver, let's head for the prison at Purdy, please. Pull into some fast food joint ASAP."

The driver nods. Marcel pulls out his laptop and reads aloud about the Women's Correctional Facility at Purdy. Next, he makes a call and finds that Cache Evans is living in a SEG area. She's in maximum security and visits and hours are limited. I hear all this over the speakerphone and give thanks that Marcel has joined me because my ability to make even basic decisions is slow coming online.

"You can see her. It's doubtful I'll get in," he says. "Let's talk about what we know."

"What we know is that all Washington appellate courts have denied her appeals and the federal courts have turned her down as well. The Supreme Court refused her case without comment. So she's run out of appeals, and she's thirty days from being executed."

He whistles softly. "All right, then. Let's have you visit her inside. Get to know her. Get her story—record her on your phone. I want to hear it firsthand. Then let's head up to Sea-Tac and fly out to—where did she go to trial?"

"Spokane."

"Fine, we'll head to Spokane and hit the courthouse ASAP. Which probably means late afternoon."

"Sounds like a plan. What specifically should I be asking her?"

His eyes narrow as he looks me over. "You're more rattled than I've ever seen you, my friend."

"I know it. I'm trying to get it together, though."

"You will. Michael Gresham is banging around somewhere inside there," he says, tapping my head. "Here, check out their website." He faces his laptop screen toward me where I read:

 Capital Punishment

Per RCW 10.95 Capital Punishment–Aggravated First Degree Murder, any person sentenced to death shall be imprisoned in Washington State Penitentiary's segregation unit within ten days after the trial court enters a judgment and sentence imposing the death penalty and assigned to single-person cells. All executions shall be carried out within the walls of the state penitentiary, and procedures for conducting executions are supervised by the state penitentiary Superintendent.

Methods of Execution

Two methods of execution are legal in Washington: lethal injection and hanging. Lethal injection is used unless the inmate under sentence of death chooses hanging as the preferred execution method. Death shall be pronounced by a licensed physician.

"There it is in black and white," he says.

"Sweet Jesus."

"Hey, stop and take a deep breath. From here on, you're onstage. Get your shit together and let's save this girl."

"All right." I take a deep breath, hold it down, and count to ten. When I exhale I can feel the normal Michael Gresham breaking through to the surface. Marcel was right; I'm back. The dizziness has vanished.

A plan surfaces. "Let's do this when I finish up inside. We'll fly back to Spokane. You hit the courthouse and copy her files while I access the federal cases on Pacer."

He smiles and shakes his head. "No need. The entire Washington case can be obtained online through a private service I've got a lead on here. It'll cost, but it's worth it."

"Also," I say, all but ignoring his resource, "I need you to call the attorneys of record. All attorneys, paralegals, everyone who's touched this case will be interviewed by us. We'll act as a team in everything. No splitting up; we need both brains concentrating on each issue one-by-one."

"What should you do about your job back in D.C.?"

I stop. Yes, my job. Putting bad guys in prison in the other Washington. The one where Washington chopped down the cherry tree. Today he would be arrested for that, ordered to pay a ten thousand-dollar fine for destroying government property, and put on probation for three years. Despite all that, he would then be elected president. That's the Washington where I work. I can only hope this one out west is very different.

"I'll call Bruce Billars. They'll have to put me on extended leave. This girl comes first."

"Thought you'd say that. I'll remind you to call."

Ten minutes later, we pull into the prison parking area. It's raining sideways across the asphalt. Marcel and I talk several minutes more. The cabbie is waiting patiently up front, arms folded across his chest. His jaw discloses he's working on a wad of gum. He looks to be in no hurry.

Out the rear door I go, sliding my briefcase behind me. Against a strong, rainy headwind, I push toward the entrance to WCCW: Washington Corrections Center for Woman.

I see signs like this and I always have to ask: Exactly how much correcting is being done here? Please, spare me.

Inside I hurry, coming in out of the rain. After the usual confrontation and threats at the front desk, I establish with the staff that I'm not going to go quietly away and that I'll get the chief judge on the phone if that's what it takes for me to see my client. The warden is finally called; she handles it with all dispatch: "Take him to Ms. Evans without delay. He's her lawyer."

With that, I am led back through a labyrinth of doors that buzz open then immediately lock behind us until we reach the visitation area.

Their notion of a visit is much different from mine. They have placed me on the visitors' side of a long sheet of Plexiglas that will keep father and child from touching. Who knows? She might want a hug, or I might want to hug her. Worse, we will have to speak through an electronic device that could very well be recording us. I don't like it one bit.

So I bitterly complain to the officer who has taken me there. I demand to be allowed to visit with my client in a conference room without a barrier between us.

He whips the comm off his belt and calls his supervisor. The answer is very clear: take the lawyer to a Conference Room and take his client there.

He replaces the comm on his belt. Without comment, he turns me around and walks me back along a new hallway until we come to an open door. He more or less pushes me inside then locks the door behind me.

Now I'm waiting for the daughter I've never met. My hands are sweaty, and my lips feel numb. Scary stuff. I hear the door lock disengage. The door slowly creaks open, and a young woman shuffles inside.

She's wearing Day-Glo orange. Her hair is two braids. Her wrists are manacled and waist-chained. Her feet are chained as well. But the face. That's what makes me almost cry out.

She looks like me. Her mother is black, so there's that, but her features are not her mother's. They are mine. Even the eyes: blue as the sky. She reminds me of Halle Berry; she is that beautiful. I ignore the neck tattoo, the Harley roses. There is no jewelry, of course; that is long gone. She clutches a fat file of papers where her hands are joined by the cuffs. She doesn't look directly at me. Instead, she shuffles to the round steel table and backs onto the bench along the wall. Then she slides her feet and legs in after her. Now she looks up. There is no recognition in her eyes.

"You're Michael Gresham?" she asks.

"I'm your father."

She tosses her head back. "I think we've covered that. My mom is a lab rat. She did the DNA thing years and years ago. Dad."

The last is said with some insolence. I want to call her on it.

It wasn't me who decided not to tell me about my child. But the adult inside me prevails. I avoid confronting her as it would serve no purpose. I want to gain her trust. I want her to tell me the truth about everything, especially the truth about herself.

"Yes, I'm Michael, and I'm your dad."

"Thank you for coming." The insolence is gone from her voice. Maybe because I didn't take the bait.

"Wild horses couldn't keep me away from one of my kids. I'm here to meet you, yes. But more important, for now, is that I'm here to help you. I'm a lawyer; I'm a criminal lawyer."

"Wow. That whole thing just blows me away."

"Yes. It's fortuitous, given what's going on."

"What's that mean?"

"It means it wouldn't help much if I were a dentist."

"Gotcha."

"So," I begin when the silence between us lengthens, "I've come here to help. What a lawyer like me needs, to help, is an accurate set of facts."

"Meaning I shouldn't lie to you?"

"Something like that, yes. What I need is your best version of the facts. We don't need to worry about whether the facts make you more or less guilty. We just need the clearest view of the facts that we can get."

She shakes her head. She drops her eyes to the tabletop. "Judge Wilberforce raped me. Then he passed me around to his friends. After that—long after—he claims I gave him AIDS. He was married. He was covering up by saying I blackmailed him. I was thirteen when he raped me. It went on for years after."

"How long have you been HIV positive?"

"I don't even know. There've been lots of faces on top of me, Michael."

"Were you ever tested for HIV before you had sex with the judge?"

"I was raped before I was placed with him. I was tested then and later. Does that help or hurt me?"

"Bear with me. Some of my questions might make no sense."

"Okay."

"Let's talk about your history. Let's start with that. When were you born?"

I'm making notes now on my laptop. She sits back and jams a finger in one ear. She studies what comes out under the nail then uses another nail to flick it away.

"I was born August 4, 1989."

"So you've got a birthday coming up."

"Call it that, but don't buy a cake. I'm supposed to die the day before. The guards promise me a cupcake in the yard if it gets delayed."

"What's the yard like here?"

"Four concrete walls with rolls of razor wire around the top. The sun gets in there around noon. It lasts for maybe fifteen minutes and then climbs out again. The floor isn't grass or dirt; it's concrete. Nice place if you're a racquetball."

"But you're not a racquetball. You're flesh and blood."

She picks at her forehead. "If you say so."

"How often do they let you bathe?"

"Once a week. My skin has turned into an oilfield, and I itch all the time. 'Hey, bitch,' the guards tell me. 'Suck it up!' So I suck it up. But there's one guard who's nice to me. She wrote the letter you got because I can't have pencils or pens because I might commit suicide by writing my story."

"How would that kill you?"

"It would bore me to death. I'm just another runaway whore."

"What about the HIV? You're taking medications?"

"Supposed to, but the prison docs haven't seen me yet. So none's prescribed."

"So you're not getting HIV medications?"

"No, I'm not."

"Sweet Jesus."

"Yeah, I was on the Atripla once-a-day plan. Now that shouldn't be that big a deal to get in here. But so far no dice."

"I've dealt with HIV in confinement before," I tell her. "If you miss even one dose of your antiviral lots of bad things happen. Missing even a few doses can allow the HIV to spread in the body by making copies of itself. Which can cause drug resistance."

She is nodding. "And drug resistance is when HIV changes and makes your medications not work. Well, welcome to my world. Aren't you glad you asked?"

"I am. We'll have a motion on file immediately to get your drug regimen going. And I'll stop and talk to the warden about it today. I'm guessing you were in Spokane Detention until yesterday?"

"That's right. But listen, because I don't get it. They're going to kill me one month from today. Who cares if I'm loaded with the virus then or not?"

"That's not the point. You've constitutional rights to certain things, including necessary medications, regardless of your sentence. We could make a federal case out of it. But I don't think we'll have to. What else are you taking?"

"Were. Were taking."

"Okay, what else were you taking?"

"I've got a forever case of gonorrhea. Two street dudes raped me and gave me a strain that nothing stops. Doctors have tried over and over. It's a new strain from Thailand. So far the old meds aren't knocking it out. So I've always got the clap. So does anyone else who screws me bare."

I'm holding up my hand. "You just triggered something. Did you have this STD when you had sex with Judge Wilberforce?"

"I forget how long it's been. It was after I was in foster at Serenity House. I ran down to the 7-Eleven for a pack of ciggies, and two winos raped me. Inder warned me. He told me not to go south of Sprague Street alone."

"Inder?"

"My old pimp. He's not my pimp now."

"Was an autopsy done on Judge Wilberforce?"

"I don't know. Why?"

"As you said, he might have this same drug-resistant STD. Maybe he gave it to you. Maybe it wasn't the winos at all. I'm making a note to check this out."

"Nobody ever asked me that before."

"Not even your lawyer?"

"Not even."

"Why didn't you testify at your trial?"

"Lawyer wouldn't let me."

"He might have done you a favor, but I would want the jury to know about the rape by Judge Wilberforce. Incidentally, did you ever tell the police you have HIV?"

"No. I tell them to wear a rubber when they fuck me. They would come back and kill me if I gave them HIV."

"The police rape you?"

She smiles and waves me off. "Come on."

"Do they have sex with you in a hotel? Anyplace we can get records?"

"No, they rape me in the backseat of their squad cars. All the girls get raped by them. It's not so bad because they're usually clean. The downer is that they're mostly Afghanistan vets. A couple of them are real head cases."

"Police rape's another case, and maybe we'll get to it one day. So how did the prosecutor know you had HIV?"

"They filed a motion, and the court made me give a blood sample."

"Did anybody talk about it at trial?"

"A witness came in and told the jury how the judge died. Natty little dude in a green tie with a red alligator on it. I'm not making this up."

"I believe you."

She smiles a sideways smile. "For a big city guy that's pretty naive, isn't it?"

"I'm not a big city guy. I grew up in a small town, and I've still got straw in my hair. Let's get back to the witness with the green alligator."

"Can I ask you something first?"

"Ask away."

"Where are you staying?"

"Davenport Hotel in Spokane."

"Oh, Mr. Moneybags."

"Mr. Anti-bed-vermin. The Davenport's got a great rep."

"Okay."

"Why do you want to know where I'm staying, by the way?"

"I don't know. I'm just curious about how you roll, I guess."

"Let's get back to this natty little dude who told the jury how the judge died. Was this a doctor, by any chance?"

"Maybe—yes. I think so. He talked about how Judge Wilber-force died."

"Did he talk about any tests he did on the judge?"

"Yes. He talked about blood tests. And—oh yes—this really got me. He told the jury how much the judge's brain weighed."

"How much did it weigh?"

"Exactly three pounds."

"Why was brain testimony admitted? Do you know?"

"I don't. But it was just about the only interesting thing in my whole trial. Will they weigh my brain after they kill me?"

"I'm not going to let that happen."

She ignores my words; she's worlds ahead of me.

"Will they autopsy me?"

"Not if I can help it."

"You can't. My friendly guard, Wanda, told me they always have to autopsy anyone who dies in prison. Is that true?"

"Probably. Why?"

"I just don't want them sawing off the top of my head. It isn't much, I'll give you that. But it's mine, and it belongs in one piece. Will you stop them from butchering me, Michael?"

"We'll talk about that if and when we get to that point."

"Michael, we reached that point a couple of days ago when the Supreme Court turned me down. We're there."

A guard sticks her head inside our room. "About done?"

I glare at her. "Why? Is there a time limit?"

"Are you angry, Mr. Gresham?"

"I'm not happy. My client hasn't been receiving her HIV drug. Why don't you toddle off to the warden and see if you can find out why? Can you do that?"

"Geesh!" She closes the door—slams it, actually. When I look back at Cache, she's smiling. She's a tweaker, a meth head. You can always see it in the teeth. But that's for another day, too.

She lets out a long sigh.

"Michael, aren't you just spinning your wheels here?"

I study her face. "Well, why did you write to me? You asked for my help. Here I am. And now you're asking me why?"

"That was before I knew you. You're real, now. And I don't want you to go down with a sinking ship. You're too nice for that."

"Let me worry about which ship I go down with. Believe me, there've been lots of them."

"I relate."

"I'm here because you're my child and I already love you. You just don't know that yet. But that's how I roll, to use your vernacular."

"Got it." Her eyes are glassy. A chord has been struck.

So I back out.

"But don't get all sentimental on me. It's a father's job to love his kids. I'm just doing my job."

"Yeah, yeah. I know, I know, that's for another day, too."

The guard again sticks her head inside our room. This time there are no words, but I understand the icy stare. She's about to have me thrown out.

"So does she get her medicine or not?" I demand of the guard. "Or am I going to have to take this shit-hole in front of a federal judge?"

She only continues staring at me with a nasty look. I've seen that look on women before. Evidently so has my daughter; she looks away if only to avoid a confrontation with a guard who could make her final days very miserable. She's right. I drop it and turn away.

Then I stand and hold out my arms to hug my new client, my daughter.

"No touching!" cries the guard.

"Oh, caught me! There I was, just about to pass your prisoner a square of Semtex. I was only going to hug my daughter."

"That will get you maced."

I don't turn to acknowledge her. Neither do I lower my arms. "Hugs," I whisper to Cache and thump my heart with my fist. She touches two fingers to her lips and points up and away through the ceiling, through the rooftop, through the clouds, all the way to heaven, as if she's just going to have a look around up there.

This is my thought. I'm her dad. We have nowhere else to turn but to each other.

"Right," says Cache. "Life is but a dream, dad."

I'm beguiled by this young woman. It overwhelms me, not knowing how to deliver the miracle she needs.

My shoulders sag, and I drop my arms.

"Later," she says and turns away.

"Tomorrow."

"Don't be a stranger."

"And the day after and the day after."

She leaves; the room is empty, and I feel like the father who has just sent his child off to bed with a fairy tale.

I sit down and wait for the guard to come and walk me out. Sure enough, not fifteen seconds later, a burly guard wearing a liver-colored deputy shirt with a wide brown tie and silver tie clasp strides confidently into the room. "You've gotta come with me, sir."

"Well, why don't you take me by the warden's office, then. Because I've gotta stop there, sir."

He moves aside to let me out of the room then turns me to the left. He follows on short, choppy steps like a goat. With a commanding voice, he directs me to the right, to the left, straight ahead, up these steps, until we come to the end of a long hall. The door is decorated with yellow geometries of glass probably installed before Cache was born.

"Go on in. I'll wait here."

"Thanks," I tell the guard. It's a good thing he's done for me; he certainly didn't have to bring me here.

The secretary inside—a doughty woman whose eyeglasses are perched halfway down her nose—looks me over and scowls. "Who brought you here? You have no appointment. The warden's calendar is empty."

"I'm a citizen, and I'm a lawyer. Depending on what her honor, the warden, tells me, I may or may not sue this prison tomorrow and every one of you in federal court. Is that enough bona fides to get me in to see her?"

She abruptly stands and turns away then opens and disappears through the oak door at her back. I strain to see inside but am only allowed a short glimpse. But my mind already knows. A broad, blemished desk from the Eighties, covered with files and books and papers scrawled with important notes, all held down by the woman sitting behind in an executive chair from the "Let's do ugly" section of the office furniture catalog.

Moments later, when I am led inside, my preconceived notions of the scene dissipate and fall away. Because sitting behind the desk is a youngish woman of maybe forty with a *Vogue* haircut, comfortably wearing a Dolce & Gabbana navy blazer. I'm certain—without even seeing—there are tailored gray slacks on her side of the desk.

She doesn't stand, but she does rock back in her no-nonsense chair. She lays aside her pen and grips both armrests.

"Can I help you, Mister--"

"My name is Michael Gresham. I'm the attorney for one of your prisoners."

"Who might that be?" She leans forward and places her hands on her keyboard. She is listening and will bring up Cache's record.

"Cache Evans. My client is HIV positive and tells me she isn't receiving the antiviral medication that is keeping her alive. I want to get that fixed."

Looking at her screen, "I see her here. There's nothing about HIV. Is she on the communicable cell block?"

"She's on death row."

"Okay, yes, I see that now. Goodness, we have a signed execution warrant and an execution already on the calendar. It also says that her appeal was rejected by the U.S. Supreme Court. So she's done all the appeals she gets. What new dances does this new lawyer have for my prisoner to try out?"

"Are you serious? Why new dances?"

She leans back and crosses her arms.

"I'm as serious as the armed security officers who are coming to throw you out for forcing your way into my office without an appointment!"

So much for the D&G suit and the uptown haircut. I'm being eighty-sixed.

"What about her medication?"

"I have no record of your appearance on her case, Mr. Gresham. I don't have to answer you. In fact, her health is confidential."

Which causes me to come unstrung. I haven't been asked to sit and so I'm still standing, and I lean halfway across her desk, placing my face maybe two feet from hers. "This prisoner also happens to be my daughter! How ugly do you want this to get, Miss Section-1983-Civil-Rights-Lawsuit?"

She recoils. "There's no need for lawsuits, Mr. Gresham. I've already decided to look into this and get her the medicine she needs."

"Good."

"If I think she needs it. God knows, with her execution a month away what difference does it make if it's become full-blown AIDS by then or not?"

"Goddam you!" I curse at her and just then the door to her office is slammed back against the wall as three armed guards storm the room.

They rush up to me and, after I lose the shoving match, they have me standing with my hands behind my back as they attach the handcuffs.

"There's no need for this, gentlemen," I say through clenched teeth. "I'm on my way out of here to sue this dump in federal court just as fast as I can. I'll go without resistance."

Ignored. One of them seizes the cuffs and begins shoving me along. Outside the office, I raise my voice, complaining there's no need. The procession stops beside Ms. Angry Secretary's desk. "I'm unlocking the cuffs," says the first guard through the door. "But I'll fucking Mace you to death if you give me any cause. Understand me?"

"I do. Keep the Mace in your pants. You won't be needing it."

With an escort on either side and the man with the Mace behind, we leave the warden's lair. Five minutes later I'm being shown the front door, and I am too happy to get out of that place and take a deep breath of clean, free air. The rain has quit. A figure stands from the bench on my right and turns around. Marcel. Calm, true, loyal Marcel. All this time.

"Ready, boss?"

"Yes. Sons of bitches."

"Their loss, boss. They should see you on a good day."

"That's right. Bastards."

"So let's go kick some bastard ass. You ready for that, boss?"

"Get me on a plane, Marcel. We're going to Spokane and read some files."

"I've already got us a flight on the four-forty-five. Snacks and drinks."

"I'll have coffee."

"I'll tell them, boss. Bad in there?"

"You have no idea."

"Yes, I do. It's written all over your face. I can see how bad."

"Coffee on the plane? I'm ready, then."

DAY 2/30

C ache shared her full history last night when I called
after Marcel and I checked into our rooms in
Spokane. Evidently, the prison switchboard had orders to
put me through regardless of the time. Threats of *Section
1983* lawsuits can have effects like that.

I absorbed Cache's telling of the middle school years, high
school, beauty school, and even a year at the community
college where she studied biology with the goal of becoming
a child cancer oncologist. She wants to treat little kids with
cancer. Well, she had my heart right there.

I will make that happen. I have no idea how, but it will
happen. Willpower is a beautiful thing in the face of government, courts, laws, and death machines. You can do this,
Michael. There, said and all but done.

After sunrise but before rush hour, Marcel and I meet
downstairs for breakfast. We divvy up the day. He will go
to the courthouse in Spokane and make complete copies
of all documents. Same with the Washington Court of

Appeals and Supreme Court. I, in the meantime, will hop online and chase down all federal cases filed on behalf of Cache, including all motions—especially the habeas motions—all appeals, and all rulings. I will then boil everything down to the ten key points I'm left to work with.

The first inquiry, has Cache been treated fairly? I'm about to find out. Setting up my laptop and a yellow pad of paper on my dining table in room 1611 of the Davenport Hotel, I ring down for a large carafe of coffee and lots of cream. It will be hours—a full day, maybe—before I surface again and I'll need all the legal meth coffee offers.

I go online and connect to Pacer. Pacer provides access to all federal courts.

In the District Court for the Eastern District of Washington, Cache's lawyer, the same Kelly Larsyn, filed for a writ of habeas corpus. A writ of habeas corpus is a court order to a prison official ordering that an inmate be brought to the court so it can be determined whether or not that person is imprisoned lawfully and whether or not he or she should be released from custody. It's that simple.

And habeas corpus has already been done in Cache's case. The process was drawn out, but in terms of what actually happened during that time, it was less than intense. A simple petition was filed, the government responded, a hearing was held with Cache present, testimony was taken, and the court ended the hearing with a hint it would try to expedite the ruling. It did anything but, actually. It was a full two months before the court made its ruling, holding that the conviction below was well supported by the facts and the law. Was Cache being imprisoned unlawfully? No, said the federal court; due process was followed. So there you were. Short but sweet.

Where did Attorney Larsyn go next? Where did he turn after losing the habeas case for his client?

I got Cache on the phone.

"Your dad here, Cache. I've looked at the District Court file, the habeas petition and hearing."

"What's that?"

"That's when you were taken to the federal courthouse in Spokane. Do you remember that?"

"I was high. It's all a blur."

"What do you mean, you were high?"

"A guard gave me some 'ludes. I took them and got wasted."

I know the answer, but I ask anyway. "And what did you have to do to get the Quaaludes?"

"You can't guess, Michael?"

"Okay."

"So what happened at my hearing?"

"Kelly Larsyn filed a petition for a writ of habeas corpus."

"Which is what?"

"Literally translated, a writ of habeas corpus is a court order to 'produce the body.' It's usually filed by people in prison."

"I still don't remember. Did it help me?"

"Only in theory. Unlike other countries where you can be

thrown in jail and held forever without a trial, in the U.S. the habeas petition is a check on the government against doing that. That's how it helped you. But only in theory."

"Like those guys at Guantanamo? Like fourteen years with no trial? George Bush had those guys arrested. Now he's down in Dallas doing watercolors while those poor assholes in Guantanamo are still playing soccer with a head of cabbage."

She is definitely my own flesh and blood.

"Your habeas petition had some interesting points, actually."

"Such as?"

"There was no proof beyond a reasonable doubt that it was your HIV that killed Judge Wilberforce. That's my opinion, not theirs."

"Why not?"

"There are hundreds of photographs in the court file. I haven't seen them yet, but according to what I've read Wilberforce threw lots of parties anytime his wife was away. Orgies, one neighbor said."

"He started with me when I was thirteen, Michael. It went on constantly because Mrs. Wilberforce had a sick father in Coeur d'Alene and she was going over there lots of weekends and staying with him."

"I'm sure, He appears to have been active sexually with a large pool of women."

"Pay to play," she said absently. "That's what they were."

"Pay to play. I haven't asked this but I should. How did you come to be HIV positive?"

"Remember I told you about the three boys who raped me?"

At just that moment, the light flashes on my room phone.

"Wait one second; I've got a call from the hotel. Be right back."

"Okay."

I set aside my cell phone and lift the room phone handset.

"Michael Gresham. How can I help?"

"Mr. Gresham, Robb Fordyce from hotel security. I've taken a man into custody who was trying to look in your room through the peephole."

"Really? How was that working for him?"

"I know."

"Why do I always get all the stupid voyeurs, anyway?"

"Are you all right, Mr. Gresham?"

"My daughter's in the clink at Purdy. Some guy trying to look in is the least of my problems."

"I hope so."

"Well, who is this guy?"

"He says he's your daughter's husband."

"My daughter, Cache?"

"I thought he was saying 'Cass'. Yes, Cache, your daughter."

"Describe him."

"Thirty years, average height, skinny as a rail, Indian as in India."

A thought occurs to me.

"What's he wearing?"

"Something that looks expensive. Suit, diamond earrings, pencil beard and mustache, ten diamonds on ten fingers, fur coat. It's real animal fur."

"You know that how?"

"His coat makes me sneeze. Animal dander always does that to me."

"What else?"

"He wants to call his lawyer. Big name criminal lawyer around town. They're always on TV yelling at the cameras. Kelly Larsyn's the lawyer."

"And he says he's Cache's husband?"

"Yep."

"He sounds like a pimp, Robb."

"He talks and dresses like one, too."

"What's his name?"

"He won't give me his name. He says the police have a warrant for him. Do I call them?"

"Not yet. Let me come down and talk to him first. What room are you?"

"Down the hall past the front desk. The sign says "Private Do Not Knock.""

"Be right there."

I return to Cache's call, but the line is dead. Doesn't surprise me; those calls are monitored, and I'm confident they cut her off after so many minutes of dead air. I'll call her back after I talk downstairs.

Into the bathroom, brush my teeth, comb my hair, step back and look. Not so great, especially the facial scarring where I was burned. The scars have been revised once by a plastic surgeon, but they're all white while my skin is dark. Two-tone Michael.

Downstairs I go. Then a short jaunt past the front desk and I'm standing outside the door with the sign saying, "Private Do Not Knock."

I push inside. It's a tiny office with a receptionist up front and two doors along the rear wall. The receptionist takes my name and tells me to go right in through door number two. I'm there in four steps and find myself in an office with a desk and two visitor chairs, all wood, all expensive, just like everything else in this incredibly beautiful hotel. Everything reeks of old established money.

"I'm Michael Gresham," I tell the robust-looking thirty-year-old behind the desk. "And you must be Mr. Fordyce. You're security."

"I am security. At your left is the man with no name."

Without turning to make eye contact with me, the young man on my left—wearing a very pricey Armani suit—says, "My name is Inder Singh."

"You're too light-skinned to be named Singh," Fordyce says in all sincerity, never-mind his racist profiling.

"That doesn't deserve a response," says Mr. Singh. "I'll be leaving now."

He stands, and I realize he's taller than me and much younger. He is powerfully built, though I can see why Fordyce called him skinny as he's not yet got the barrel chest and gut of an older man. I have little doubt he could take out both Fordyce and me. He turns and faces me. "You're Cache's father?"

"I am. So what?"

"She's my wife." He sits back down.

"Prove it," I say in a tight voice. "Prove you're married to Cache then we'll talk. Otherwise, I'm going to have Mr. Fordyce call the police."

"You're planning on keeping me here how?" asks Singh. He is smiling—more like a sneer.

At which point Fordyce pulls his desk drawer and lifts out a small Glock. He places it carefully on the desktop, so the muzzle is pointing directly at Singh's chest.

"I'll shoot you dead if you try to leave," says Fordyce.

I have no doubt he means it.

"A gun? Seriously, dude?" exclaims Singh.

"They said I needed a partner," says Fordyce, who jerks a thumb toward the front desk. "So I partnered up with Mr. Glock here."

"Back to my request," I say to Singh. "Please give me proof you're married to Cache Evans."

"I don't know what that means, man. Do you want to see our

marriage license? That would be in Las Vegas at the
Wishing Well Chapel on the Strip."

I ask, "How did you find me?"

"Cache told me where you were staying."

"What were you spying on Mr. Gresham for?" says Fordyce.
"There are laws against Peeping Toms in Washington."

"I was looking for Mr. Gresham's room, not spying. I wanted
to ask how I could help with Cache's situation."

"What did you have in mind?" I ask.

"I've got money if you need money to do the best job
possible for her. Do you need twenty thousand? Fifty thousand? Just say the word, Mr. Gresham."

I wave him off. "Put your wallet away. This isn't about
money."

"What's it about, then?" asks Singh.

"It's about luck. Remember the house odds in those casinos
in Vegas where you blew ten grand after your wedding?
Those odds were six or seven percent your favor. The odds
of walking Cache out of prison are half that. Or less. You a
praying man, Singh?"

"I'm a Sikh."

"So call up one of your gods and tell her we need a rabbit.
We don't want to pull empty air out of the hat now, do
we, Singh?"

"No. But I don't pray, either. I helped her other lawyers,
you know."

"How?"

"I paid them over a quarter million dollars. Are you going to lose?"

"Where did you come up with a quarter million dollars?"

"I earned it. My business earned it."

"That would be what business?"

"I'm into fornication management." He laughs at this. He's the only one who does.

"So you're a pimp. Are you my daughter's pimp?"

"Oh, hell no. That would amount to a conflict of interest. Bobby Z is Cache's pimp. When she's working, anyway. That's off and on lately. I'm her sole means of support."

I look at him levelly. "Not from now on, pal. You're talking to the lady's father. She's mine to look out for."

He flops back in his chair. "Whatever. She'll do what I say anyway. You're a day late, Mr. Gresham."

"So here's what I need you to do, Mr. Singh. I need you to fade into the background. Your face, your clothes, your gemstones—it's a huge loser in any courtroom. I don't want you around, don't want any judge or anyone else connecting you to Cache."

"No can do, sir. She needs me to keep an eye on you."

"You're very close to getting your ass kicked by a man twice your age," I say coolly. "You wouldn't want word of that to get out on the streets. Your girls might stop paying you off. Then you'd have to sell all those diamonds they've paid for."

He tosses his head back and laughs. He's ignoring me.

"And you thought I was kidding?" I jump up and slam my fist into the side of the pimp's head. It is my best punch. I'm not a little man. He flies to his left, and his head hits the wall. He's stunned. I have my chance to kick his ass.

But I don't.

"What the fuck is wrong with you, man?" he mutters through his shock. "I love Cache."

Fordyce has placed his hand on his Glock pistol. He caresses its barrel. Now I understand why Singh didn't stand up and kick the living hell out of me. Smart man, as I'm not so sure Fordyce wouldn't just shoot the son of a bitch if he decided he'd seen enough.

"As I said, you show up in one of my courtrooms, and I'll break your legs. Do you understand me?"

He's eyeing the gun. He doesn't respond right away.

Long silence. Singh rubs his jaw and examines his fingers for blood. There is no blood. I'm just a little upset with myself for losing it and striking the guy. That isn't like me. But Cache isn't like my typical client, either. She's my daughter; I'm surprised that I've developed such a strong protective streak almost overnight. That can't be all bad, considering the road that lies ahead.

"Do you understand me?"

Singh shakes his head. "You don't want me in a courtroom, fine. But I do want to help. She's my wife, and I love her. You wouldn't understand, but it's true."

"Help, how?"

"You need a witness turned up, Mr. Gresham? Just say the word. I know everyone on the street. Gimme a name, and you'll have them in your office like magic.

"I've already got an investigator."

"Who said anything about investigating? I'm talking unwilling witnesses, Jack. I'm talking other whores who screwed our dead Judge Hiram Wilberforce, for openers. That grab you?"

I stop. Now I'm facing him, and he turns to stare at me.

"It does grab me. Give me your phone number."

I hand him my phone, and he enters his number.

"I can give you a list as long as your arm of the ladies who ever fucked this judge. Guess what? There's beaucoup HIV there, too. Lots of cases. So how do they know it's Cache's HIV that killed the guy? How can they know that?"

I have no answer. I've been asking myself the same question. Maybe he can be of use.

"I'll call you when I get to that point, Mr. Singh."

"Mr. Gresham, I don't want to bust your bubble, but you're already at that point. If you don't realize it then Cache is royally fucked."

There's no response to that. None needed.

"Let him go, Fordyce," I tell the security officer. "He might be useful to me."

"You get the hell out of my hotel," Fordyce snarls at Singh.

Singh waves a hand at the security officer. "Forget it. I'm already gone."

"Then you can go. But if I catch you back here, I swear you'll wind up in a dumpster five blocks away. Count on it."

"Sure, sure," says Singh. "You can see my hands shaking, right?"

I stand, he stands, and we leave the tiny office. Without another word, when we reach the front desk he turns left, and I go straight toward the elevators.

I look down at my right hand. It's aching. It feels broken.

Suddenly I need a toilet. My bowels are threatening to cut loose all over the gray carpet favored by the Davenport's decorators.

Upstairs I fly, and I make it into my toilet just in time.

I know all about fear and how it attacks me.

My hands are shaking as I perch on the throne.

I finish up and wash my hands and lift cold water to my face. I don't know when I last hit someone. It's been so long that I don't even remember. Maybe never?

From the suite's couch along the window, I call Marcel.

"Where you been?" he asks. "I've been calling you."

"Hotel security caught someone standing outside my door. I went downstairs to talk to him. It's some guy claiming to be Cache's husband."

"Okay. What else?"

"He swears he can produce a roomful of women with HIV

who had sex with our dead judge."

"You get his number?"

"Yes."

"Give it to me."

I read him the number from my contacts.

"What are you going to do?" I ask.

"I'm going out to meet Mr. Singh. I'm going to test him and find out what he knows."

"You're going to test him? How?"

"I'm going to stick a gun in his ear and count to three."

"Easy, Marcel."

"You're running the legal case?"

"Yes."

"I'm running the street case. Are we straight about that?"

Marcel is someone I'd never want to cross. Or insult.

"We're straight."

"Good. Now jump into bed and get yourself some sleep. I'll be over in the morning."

We hang up. Chastised, I order a pot of coffee and turn back to the appellate cases on my computer. After a half hour, I'm tired and very sleepy. My hand still hurts. I think about Marcel. So eager to help. I slide into a deep sleep.

I'm glad he's on my side.

Marcel would be a terrible enemy to have.

DAY 3/30

As promised, Marcel is at my door pounding to be let in. I'm groggy—sleep was long and deep—so it takes me a minute to open up.

"Come in."

He's carrying two ventis from Starbucks. Extra cream in mine, which he hands to me. A large gulp; I all but inhale. The brew is dark and cool enough to swallow right down. Now I feel like I can talk.

"What happened last night?" I ask.

He takes a swallow of his untreated cup of coffee.

"Mr. Singh gave me the names of five prostitutes and where I can find their pimps. I'll be on the street today with my recorder."

"What are we looking for, exactly?" I want to make sure we're on the same page.

"We're looking for a whole clutch of women—plus one young man—who could have infected His Honor."

"A young man?"

Marcel smiles. "Seems the judge was a switch-hitter."

"Okay. So we can prove other women might have infected him. Women besides Cache. One question: can AIDS be tracked back to one person by DNA or something? Or is the source untraceable."

"That's a good question for Google," he says. "Grab your laptop."

My laptop is there on the table between us. I swing it around and make the entry into the search engine.

"Interesting," I remark to Marcel as I read. "It says here that complex scientific tests known as 'phylogenetic analysis' should always be done in HIV cases to compare the viruses of the complainant and the accused. If the two viruses are different, then this proves that there was no HIV transmission between the two people. If the viruses appear to be similar, it means that HIV transmission from the accused to the complainant could have taken place, but it does not prove it 'beyond a reasonable doubt.' It is still possible that it was the complainant who had transmitted HIV to the accused—or that both were infected by people sharing the same type of virus."

"Or by the same person," Marcel says.

"Exactly. So the test can rule out or rule in possible transmitters, but it isn't like DNA where the exact person can be pinpointed."

"It cuts both ways. While it might rule her out, it can't say it was or wasn't her if it's the same virus as the dead guy."

"That's how I read it. Tell you what; I'll find a medical expert and see if I can come up with something."

Marcel waves his hand dismissively. "You kidding? You think the other lawyers haven't already done this?"

"It doesn't show up in any appellate briefs."

"You've got to be kidding me! Any eighth grader would know to ask this."

"Maybe her lawyers knew but just didn't raise it," I say, always the conspiracy theorist.

He leans back. "You're saying maybe her lawyers were in bed with the prosecutors? Why would that happen?"

"Because the dead guy's a judge and the prosecution needed someone to pin it on. How's it look if the prosecution reveals he was a serial purchaser of sexual services?"

"Was he married?"

"He was. Plus, he had three daughters by a prior marriage."

Marcel grimaces and shakes his head. "Of course. But it had to come out at trial that he'd been with someone. How did that look?"

That one I already know. "His wife was threatening divorce. Cache knew about this."

"And he was claiming he was innocent, that she blackmailed him."

"Exactly. The fact he was using prostitutes, that can't look good to anyone in the prudish judicial world he inhabits. So they need someone to take the fall. That turns out to be Cache."

"Because she's a nobody and can't fight back."

"They sacrificed my daughter to protect the judge."

"Were viral samples taken from the judge?" Marcel asks.

"I'm sure they were."

"Of course Cache was sampled, too," he says. He already knows the answer.

"Of course."

"So were the comparisons made between the two samples?"

"We'll be finding that out this morning."

"How?"

"I'll be meeting with the gal who prosecuted Cache. I intend to pin that down."

"Good luck with it. Either way it falls, it's something they're not going to want to discuss with you."

"Meaning?"

"Meaning if the samples weren't taken and compared, someone dropped the ball big time, prosecution and defense. And if the samples were taken and weren't compared, then both the prosecution and defense were in on some cover-up."

"You're reading my mind, Marcel."

"Which isn't all that hard to do, boss, as well as I know you."

"I'm sure. There's also another angle I'll be asking all trial lawyers about."

"What's that?"

"It's something I need more information about. But it could set our girl free."

"Then what are we waiting for? Let's get to it."

"Let's."

Fifteen minutes later, just as I'm leaving the room, I get a call from the Purdy area code. It must be Cache.

"Hello, daughter."

"This is Warden McCann. I'm calling about your client, Cache Evans."

My pulse jumps. "I'm listening. How can I help."

"Your daughter has been taken to the hospital, where she's been placed on life support, Mr. Gresham. You need to come now."

"What hospital?"

"Saint Anthony Hospital. That's in Gig Harbor. Canterwood Boulevard, tell the cab driver."

"What happened?"

"We found Cache in her cell this morning hanging from the bars. She'd made a noose out of her mattress ticking and tied it around her neck. She was unconscious and wasn't breathing. Nurse Okijura performed CPR until the EMT's showed up. They got her intubated and rushed her to the hospital. She's under twenty-four-hour guard, of course."

"Of course. After all, she might suddenly jump up and run back to the effing prison where you negligently let her hang herself!"

It took me away like a wild river overrunning its banks. They had been negligent. Who wouldn't foresee a death row inmate trying to hang themselves just to get it over with? Certainly, this fool on the phone didn't see it. I catch myself in the middle of my rant. I'm going to need to apologize now that I've aired my grievance.

"Look, I'm sorry for that."

But I'm talking to myself. Every time I talk to this prison by telephone, they end up hanging up on me. This one I had coming.

"Marcel, trouble with Cache. She attempted suicide. We're going to split up. You stay here and work up the interviews. I'm off to her hospital."

"Roger that."

I throw a few things in my bag and head downstairs for a ride to the airport.

Four hours later, I'm in Gig Harbor roaring up Canterwood to St. Anthony Hospital.

I know what room she's in as I rush inside the hospital. I know because I called the warden back and apologized for what I'd said. We talked and agreed it was a difficult time and she gave me the room number—ICU, actually—where Cache could be found.

Up two floors and down two hallways and around. Then there it is. ICU.

At the desk, I give them her name, but they all look at each other and refuse to tell me where Cache is undergoing treatment. Then I get it: her location is confidential because it's the department of corrections policy not to divulge inmate identities. So I shake my head and plunge ahead, passing the glassed-in ICU suites, slowing to see if Cache is there. Then, at the far end, on the far right, I find her all alone in an ICU suite. All alone insofar as other patients. But there is a nurse with her, and she's standing with her back to me studying the vitals console. There's also an armed guard leaning back in a chair just outside her room. He gives me a sour look as I approach. He touches his gun.

"I'm her dad. And her lawyer."

"ID."

I flash my driver's license and D.C. bar card.

He nods. I'm surprised that's all it takes for me to be allowed to pass.

I approach the nurse from behind.

"Hello," I say just above a whisper. The nurse doesn't startle but turns her head to see me.

"You must be her dad. Warden McCann said she was going to break with policy and get you in to see her."

I realize that my call back to the Warden paved the way for admittance to Cache's ICU suite.

"Tell me the truth," is all I can say.

"She's been on the ventilator since she arrived. Her vitals aren't what we like, but she's moving blood. She hasn't been scanned yet for brain activity. That will happen in the next forty-eight hours."

"To see if she's worth keeping alive."

"To see if your daughter is brain-dead. If she is, they'll have me shut off the vent. If she isn't, then no one will be able to tell you how long she'll be here and in what condition she'll end up. I've seen hundreds of these cases."

At that exact moment, I'm pierced by a sudden thought, a sudden terrible thought. Which is this: what if the state decides to remove the ventilator that's keeping her alive as a way of carrying out the death sentence?

"Mr. Gresham? Did you hear me?"

My eyes come back into focus. A second nurse has come in. Except her name tag says she's an M.D.

"Yes, I'm Michael Gresham."

"I'm Rachel Cardoza, Cache's staff doctor."

"You've done many of these cases?" She's very young.

"Internal medicine. Johns-Hopkins, two-thousand-four."

"I'm Cache's father. We only met a couple of days ago, so can I hug her? I've never touched her."

"Sure. Hug away. She might even know it."

I approach the bed from the left side. My daughter's head is turned slightly to her right, enabling me to run my eyes along the breathing tube until it disappears inside her mouth. My lips pass over it as I lean across and kiss her lightly on her forehead. My hand passes over her and I clasp her left upper arm and give a squeeze, enough to let her know I'm here.

I feel like I've known her forever.

Then I straighten up and backhand the tears from my eyes. She's desperate, and I'm desperate with her.

Which Dr. Cardoza must sense. "Would you like some coffee? I'm heading back to the nurse's station, and I can have someone bring you a cup. Or soup? Maybe half of someone's sandwich? The refrigerator is always full of some pretty good stuff the nurses bring in."

"Coffee, please. That would be great."

"Well, listen, Cache is wired into the ICU's network. If she has any kind of event, someone will come running. So even though you're here alone with her after I leave, you're really not. Someone can be here almost instantly."

"I appreciate that, Dr. Cardoza. And I appreciate your generosity with other people's food."

I couldn't help it. I was once told I was a lot like my mother, that she had a slightly twisted sense of humor, too.

She's laughing as she strides out of the ICU and I follow her with my eyes along the glass wall to where she disappears behind many panes of glass. I think of alternate universes, for some reason, and it connects in my mind that Cache now exists in a new universe—a universe where she might have a spark of hope.

I hoof it back up to the nurse's station, and they turn a phone around. I use their yellow pages and make a call to the Apple Store. My credit card is good there: a new laptop is on the way to my daughter's room at St. Anthony Hospital. Now I can work while I wait with Cache.

I next call Verona and give her the update about her new stepchild. She's aghast at the whole thing. We discuss this, and then we commiserate about our physical separation while I deal with Cache. The other kids are at school, so there's no chance to speak with them. We have home-schooled Mikey and Dania the last two years, but they began demanding to attend public school because their friends went to public school and so Verona and I gave in. Despite the fact that there are people who would like to see us dead, we gave up the safety that came from keeping the kids home and schooling them where we could keep a close eye. Gave it up and sent them off to school entirely without protection. Talking to them every day is a must for me. I'm sorry they aren't around now. But they're not. Verona and I run out of small talk. We say we love each other; we say goodbye.

I return to Cache's suite and take the chair closest to her. The lights have been dimmed in the room now. The only sound is the whoosh of the ventilator. Cache doesn't move. She reminds me of an Italian sculpture of the Madonna.

Except this one needs my help.

DAY 4/30

I've spent the night in the bedside chair. There were even moments where I drifted into a fitful sleep, only to be jarred awake by staff cruising for patient vitals in the middle of the night.

I'm sitting there about to go begging for coffee when in walks a dwarf, a man I've never seen before.

"You looking for someone?" I ask.

"You Michael Gresham?"

"I am."

He hands me a dozen sheets of paper stapled together. I don't read but instead, address him.

"So, what's this?"

"You've been served."

"You're a process server?"

He shakes his head. He's wearing a blue suit, a heavily

starched white shirt, and a red and navy rep tie. Very Old School.

"I'm Kelly Larsyn. I'm Cache's lawyer. What I've just handed you is the lawsuit that was emailed to me early this morning. It's from the Washington State Department of Corrections."

"What's the gist of it?" I ask.

"The state is after a new death warrant. They're asking the court for an order directing this hospital to remove all life support from your daughter. They're trying to convince the court that removing life support would amount to executing the death warrant, that she would die just like the court has ordered."

"I was afraid this might happen."

He raises his right hand as a witness about to be sworn. "These buttholes are serious, Mr. Gresham."

I stand and pull my trousers out of my crack. Long night. Larsyn watches without comment but shakes his head just so.

I tell him, "This might actually be a maneuver I can use against them."

"Exactly my thinking. Get them involved in Eighth Amendment litigation and drag it out as long as possible. It keeps your daughter alive, Mr. Gresham."

"Mr. Gresham's long dead. I'm Michael."

"Okay, Michael. I'm Kelly."

"You represented my daughter through the trial and appeal.

I must have a million and one questions for you, sir."

"We'll get to that. But how about some logistics first. The lawsuit you're holding hasn't been filed yet. This is a courtesy copy from the Attorney General's office. But it will be filed today, I am told. Probably around noon. Do you plan on answering it?"

"I would, but I'm not a Washington-licensed lawyer."

"File for *pro hac vice*. Her lawyer just for this one case."

"I was getting to that. Will you act as my local counsel if I do?"

"Of course I will. I've gotten to know Cache very well over the past couple of years. She's like a daughter to me. I love this kid, and I'd do anything to help her."

"You would? How about joining me as co-counsel in the litigation that's bound to be created by her situation?"

"Really? You'd want me? I'm the lawyer who lost her trial and her appeals. You're saying you find my track record appealing?"

"Felony cases usually are lost at trial, has been my experience. I don't hold it against you. Although I do wonder why Cache wasn't allowed to testify about her rape by Judge Wilberforce."

"Because the judge who tried Cache's case is Judge Wilberforce's uncle. He's the chief judge and all but anointed his nephew to get him appointed to the bench. Any other questions?"

"Nope, you just answered the only one I had. So let's get to work."

"Fine." He extends his hand, and we shake. "I'll get myself back to the office and wait for this thing to get filed in court. Meanwhile, I'll prepare a motion for your admission *pro hac vice* and get that on file just as soon as the lawsuit is filed by the AG. You should be an attorney of record on the case by five o'clock."

"I couldn't ask for more. Thanks for every bit of it."

"You've got it. Now, let's kick some bureaucrat ass."

"Let's. Thanks for coming by."

"As I said, I love this kid, and I knew you'd be here."

"Hey, aren't you going to ask how she's doing?"

He smiles. "I stopped at the nurses' station. I'm up to speed."

"Wait. What's the state's basis for wanting to remove life support?"

I see a pained irony in his eyes. "The assistant attorney general handling the case called me. Off the record, the state doesn't want to pay to keep her on life support. It costs too much to keep her alive. That's their position."

"Oh, my God."

"Bean counters."

He turns and hurries out. I collapse against the wall and slap it over and over.

They don't want to pay for her! I'm fighting back the tears of a father who has just been told his daughter's life can be measured in dollars, and she's just spent them all. The callousness of the people behind this feels like someone's got their boot on my gut. It actually hurts. I want to swing at someone, reach out and dislodge eyeballs—this is one father who would kill for his kids to keep them safe. Cache is part of my protectorate. And I swear by God I will not let her down. Do they want to see too expensive for the state? Just wait until I cost them millions in court and watch as they try to hang onto their life support, those mean little government jobs that hurt rather than heal in this new age of crazy, out-of-control government.

I force myself to sit in my recliner and steady my breathing. Concentrate on my heart rate and coax it down from the ledge. Dear Jesus Christ Almighty, I am furious. And I am scared. I cannot watch this one die.

My phone's haptic thumps against my chest. Marcel's calling. I let it go and continue trying to calm myself. I've had my phone turned off overnight. I'm sure Marcel's floating on the ceiling since he's been unable to track me down. The restriction in my chest loosens a notch. Now I can return his call.

"About time you called, Gresham," he says in his most unfriendly voice. I know it's only temporary.

"Cache is in the hospital in Gig Harbor. I flew over."

"Hospital? What the hell for?"

"Attempted to kill herself. Choked off her oxygen for who knows how long? I'm with her in ICU. She's vented and unconscious, as you might expect."

"How'd she do it?"

"The usual: bedding torn into strips makes a noose. She's found dangling from the bars of her cell."

"Of course. Don't they always try to hang themselves?"

"Yes, unless they provoke another inmate in order to get shivved in the heart. That's been known to work every bit as well."

"Okay. Do I come over or do I stay in Spokane and keep running down witnesses?"

"How is that coming?" I ask.

"It's coming. So far I've got five women who'll testify about the judge's parties. 'Safaris', the girls called the parties; hunting trips."

"Hunting willing flesh."

"That's a nice way to put it. I would've called it whoring."

I let it slide. I know Marcel's heart. He's referring to the men.

"Okay, it appears there's another development, Marcel. The State of Washington DOC is going to file to remove all life support. They're going to ask the court to allow them to do this instead of the usual execution by lethal injection. They're going to argue that withdrawal of life support is even more humane than lethal injection."

"Holy Christ!"

"I know. I cannot begin to believe this."

"So you're ready to litigate this to hell and back?"

"Actually, the state is going to file before I have to sue them. I'll be filing an answer and Civil Rights counterclaim and move the case to federal court."

"I'm not sure I understand all that, but I know you do.

Okay, so I stay here, and you stay with your daughter. In the next day or two, I should finish up with the women. Then I want to come to Gig Harbor and have a look at Cache—I've never seen her. Plus, I want to check up on you, Michael."

"I'm fine. In fact, I met Kelly Larsyn today, and he's going to help me on the civil case. He represented Cache through the trial and appeal."

"Hell, Michael, he lost both cases. You're sure this is the guy you want?"

"I've seen enough to know I would most likely have done the same. A tough case to begin with. Plus, the trial judge was the dead judge's uncle. Figure that one out."

"Why didn't this Kelly Larsyn ask for a new judge? Why didn't he claim the new judge was prejudiced by the death of his nephew?"

"I've read the file like I said. It appears Kelly did, in fact, do that and Judge Maxim turned him down."

"Maxim? I thought the dead judge was named Wilberforce."

"Mother's married name. Judge Wilberforce's mother and trial judge Maxim were siblings."

"Got it. Complicated little case about judicial incest."

"I don't know about that. But it reeks of conflict of interest. That much I do know."

"But that was raised on appeal, right?"

"Yes, but the appeals court reject it as a reason for over-turning the trial court. They relied on the trial judge's freedom to do what he thought was right. Plus, they said the record reflects no judicial prejudice in favor of the state."

"And he thought it was best if he stayed on the murder case about his nephew. This stinks from here to Florida."

"Agree, but it's a dead issue. We have to move on."

"So what do you do next?"

"It's too soon to tell anything about Cache. So I'm going to stick around the hospital. There's a possibility they'll be doing brain scans today. I want to be here for that."

He whistles softly. "They're going to assess whether she's brain dead."

"Exactly. I can't leave her alone just now."

"No, no, you stay right there with your daughter. Don't worry about my side of the street; it's covered."

"I know that. But I need you here tomorrow."

"Done. I'll cab over from the airport."

"St. Anthony Hospital. Gig Harbor."

"See you there."

I hang up and am left with the feeling that I'm more alone that I've been in a long time. But then I stuff it down. I need to focus on my daughter and how she's alone except for me. And what of her mother? What about Millicent? I go online and locate the business where I think she works. I call them, but they've never heard of Millicent Evans. Not surprising; I have no idea what Millie's last name is now. She could've remarried after Evans or whatever. But I keep calling around, hoping "Millicent" triggers recognition in someone.

A half hour later I'm still dialing when it suddenly occurs to me that Kelly will have Millicent's number. I call his office, and his secretary gets clearance to give me Millicent's number. She also advises me that Kelly has already called the mother. She is said to be on her way up from San Francisco, where she now works in a different genetics lab. She's no longer in La Jolla.

I wonder how I'll react when she arrives. What do you say to the woman that hid your daughter from you for almost thirty years? Do I start screaming and jumping up and down and threatening her? Or do I listen to her and try to understand why she did it? Clearly, I need to know her thinking. I mean, my God. Cutting me out of the picture was a big flipping deal. There better be some major reason for it. But in the end, no reason she can come up with will excuse what she's done. I'm furious.

So I wait in my recliner alongside Cache's bed, sweeping my feet aside as the nurses come and go to take vitals and administer drugs. The more I know about all this, the less I know. Brain injuries are never pretty and more often than not are devastating where there has been a lengthy denial of oxygen. I say yet another silent prayer and continue to browse on my laptop for Civil Rights cases connected to end-of-lifesaving measures. There isn't a lot, but there's enough to keep me busy looking.

Around noon, I'm drowsy after a tuna sandwich preceded by an almost sleepless night last night. Just as I'm nodding off again, in walks Millicent looking like she did thirty years ago.

"Michael," she says, extending her hand, "I didn't know you would be here. How did—how did—"

"Kelly didn't tell you I was here?"

"It wasn't Kelly who called me. It was a secretary. How did you know about Cache?"

"Cache wrote to me. From death row. I dropped everything and came to help. But that's not the first order of business, Millie. Why didn't you tell me I had a daughter?" I'm just able to control my voice. I have no doubt she hears it quaver with rage.

She stands, hands on her hips, staring back at me.

"Well?"

"Let's not do this here in Cache's room. For all we know she can hear us." She pushes past me and goes to her daughter. Millie is wearing a white linen coat with a pink button-down shirt, a pair of pleated slacks with a brown belt and brown penny loafers. She's dressed but not overdressed. Her face still retains the youthful beauty that once lured me in and held me captive. I was in love with her all those years ago, and I cannot for the life of me remember what took me away from her. Then it comes to me: I was a ten-year-down-the-road lawyer following law school, with a law practice just on the verge of turning more profit than I'd ever thought possible. That was it: the money lure had taken me away. For the life of me, however, I can't remember what Millie had even wanted. Was I just a fling for her? Or was there something there? I know I'll never know now.

She bends low and plants a kiss on Cache's forehead. For the first time in her life, Cache has both parents there for her at one time. My heart falls: it's far too late in coming if she never knows. Far, far too late. A hot fist rises through my chest and threatens to choke off my throat. Her broken heart speaks to me and takes me away. How hurt she must have been. The whole moment swirls around me like a dream.

"How long has she been like this, Michael?"

"This is her second day. They found her slumped against the bars of her cell, a noose around her neck."

"A noose? Where did she get a noose?"

"She made one out of her mattress. It's very common."

"Why weren't they watching her more carefully?"

"I guess we both want to know that. Speaking of watching her carefully, what's been your part in the murder trial and the appeal, Millie? Have you been there for her?"

"Of course. Kelly Larsyn has become like a son to me. We speak every day."

"He's in Spokane, and you're in San Francisco?"

"I can be up here in just a few hours. I've always been just a phone call away. I've never missed a court appearance by Cache. Plus, I've attended almost all hearings when she wasn't there. Motions to suppress evidence, motions for a change of judge—that kind of stuff."

She turns away from Cache and takes the chair beside mine. It is a folding chair with a padded seat, the kind they use in church basements.

"Who's the guard outside?"

"Department of Corrections. Cache is still legally under their jurisdiction."

"Why guard her? She's comatose."

"It's the law, Millie. He's protecting the public from our daughter, and he's stopping her from escaping."

"Oh, sure."

"Again, why didn't you tell me about her?"

"Tell the truth, I was mad and hurt by you walking out."

"It was just a fling, Millie. You knew I'd only be in La Jolla for two weeks."

"It felt like we went past that."

"And that's your excuse?"

"I didn't want you to have the satisfaction of being involved in this lovely creature's life. I wanted her all to myself. There. I've rehearsed all of that in case I ever had to face you again. Now you know. I was angry and wanted to hurt you."

"Congratulations, Millie. You succeeded."

"But Cache lost. It was a huge mistake I made."

"Tell Cache that. I'm a big boy, but she's innocent. It was a terrible thing you did to her. I'm her father."

"How many kids do you have?" she asks trying to change the subject.

But I'm not going there. I've been screwed over, and I want to hurt her. I want to hurt her enough that it gets the time back that I missed with Cache.

Which is insane.

But it's where I am.

I have become a child in my anger and lostness.

"I've got a call to make," I tell Cache's mother. "Excuse me."

After two calls to information, I have the number for the Attorney General of the State of Washington.

It is time to confront the Assistant Attorney General who's out to kill my kid. His name is on the lawsuit Kelly gave me.

Time to let him know the awful truth: that he's in grave danger. From me.

But he's not in. So I leave a terse message: Cache's dad is waiting for you in her hospital room. You would be smart to get here and talk with me ASAP. If you fail to come, I will without notice sue the state, sue the attorney general, and sue you personally.

Her dad has arrived.

DAY 5/30

I've just passed another night in Cache's hospital room. Millie found a motel and cleared out around ten o'clock, leaving me alone with Cache and the night shift and hissing instruments with their blinking LEDs. It isn't that I wake up with the sunrise, it's just that I give up trying to go back to sleep since the four a.m. vitals and meds. Through it all, Cache hasn't stirred, not once. Or emitted any sign that she's alive inside the body we're all watching over.

I bend down to study her in the dim light. I am intent on memorizing her face. Her neck is mottled with bruises from the noose.

The night nurse sticks her head in to tell me she's going off. The soles of her running shoes squeak as she hurries inside and erases her name from the small green board. She then writes in white chalk the name of the day nurse. Amanda substituting for Regina. So be it. They're faces in the dark, coming and going, a constant swirl of activity in the face of a looming coma.

Three hours later, a plump, bald, man wearing thick eyeglasses and carrying a battered red briefcase strolls in. "I'm Franklin Lemongrass," he says without offering to shake my hand. "I'm the attorney general you threatened yesterday."

"It's a smart thing you did, Mr. Lemongrass, coming here. I was going to sue the shit out of you today."

He smiles and says in a ragged croak, "Where I come from we sue back. You'd do well never to forget that, Mr. Gresham. I assume you're Mr. Gresham?"

"I am," I say, and offer to shake, which he ignores. I quickly withdraw my hand, the turtle yanking his head back into his shell. I'll be damned if I ever offer to do that again.

To my utter astonishment, he backs up to Cache's bed and sits his plump ass down on the thin cover just this side of her feet.

"Hey, asshole," I cry, "off my daughter's bed! What the hell's wrong with you?"

He stands but isn't kidding when he says, "Actually we're paying for this bed. I'd hoped the prisoner wouldn't mind sharing."

"Listen, pal, in here she's the patient, not the prisoner."

He stands and turns. He lowers his briefcase back onto her bed. This time I don't object; it is somewhat limited in here insofar as furniture. And of course, there is no desk table, so I let it slide.

"What I've brought with me," he says, opening the accordion

top of the briefcase and searching inside with his fingers, "is a consent decree."

"Consent to what?" I ask. "What does the State of Washington wish me to consent to?"

"To withdrawal of life support."

"Are you frigging crazy? You actually think any father would sign that?"

He turns around, facing me. "Why not?"

I climb to my feet. I tower over him. He's trapped between the bed and me, and I'm not moving away.

"Because you assholes left my child unattended. You gave her the chance to hang herself. Your failure to supervise has resulted in injury to her brain. It might even be permanent."

He smiles. "Permanent is relative, Mr. Gresham."

"Meaning?"

"Meaning she's only got a few weeks until we execute her anyway. It makes good money sense to stop it now, to stop paying for all of this," he motions with his hand, indicating the life support hoses, tubes, wires, and light panels.

"So the state, in all its wisdom, wants to unplug my daughter and let her die?"

"Think about it, Mr. Gresham. It's more humane this way. She dies without anticipation. No final moments of terror as she's being strapped to a table to take the needle. No hysterical nights, days, weeks of waiting to die. Nice and easy and she's over," he emphasizes these last words with the snap of his fingers. "Gone, presto, gone!"

"You know, Mr. Lemongrass, I'm furious right now. I don't want to hurt you, but I'm afraid I'm going to. You should leave."

He turns away and contemplates the panel of lights monitoring my daughter.

"It's all too much. Too expensive."

At just that moment, Millie enters the room. She catches me looming behind Lemongrass just before I attack him.

"Michael? Who's this?"

"This is Franklin Lemongrass from the AG's office. He wants us to sign a consent decree allowing the state to withdraw life support from Cache."

"What did you say? Did I just hear correctly?"

I shake my head and motion to the human roach. "Ask him yourself."

After that, Millie takes it up with Lemongrass. He dodges, he feints, he throws a light jab, he throws another, then Millie hauls off and wallops him with a blue streak of cuss words I wasn't aware she even knew. Now Lemongrass is backing up to the room entrance, briefcase in hand, inserting his stack of papers inside the accordion maw as he retreats.

"One thing," he says, pausing at the door. "I'll be filing the motion today that will convince Cache's judge we should be allowed to proceed. By refusing to sign you're only prolonging the inevitable. We will execute your daughter, Mr. And Mrs. Gresham. Make no mistake."

"Asshole!" I shout.

"Bastard!" Millie shouts.

Then he's gone, and we're left shaking with anger. Neither of us can verbalize what we have just seen and heard in any form that makes it possible to discuss. It's an outrage, and we won't even speak what he wants.

We're sitting silently side-by-side in the two chairs. Millicent wonders aloud whether Kelly Larsyn has seen the consent decree Lemongrass was touting. She absently pulls her phone out of her purse. "I'm calling Kelly."

"Yes."

"Mr. Larsyn, please," she says, punching the speakerphone button.

"Yes, Mrs. Evans," says the receptionist, who evidently recognizes Millie's voice.

Then Kelly comes online. "Millicent. I was just thinking about you."

"How so?"

"Franklin Lemongrass has just filed a motion to withdraw Cache's life support. By the way, is Michael there with you?"

"He is."

"Michael, I have the *pro hac vice* motion on file. I signed your name electronically. Hope that's okay."

"It is. We discussed it."

"So the judge's office indicated we'll have a signed order by close of business today."

"Good enough. How do you want to work the Lemongrass motion?"

"I've been thinking about that. I think it would be good for you to field this first salvo. Nail them good. Go in with your anger and brilliance I've heard about. You'll cut this son-of-a-bitch wide open."

"Suits me perfectly. I need someplace to focus my rage right now."

"Good, good. And Millicent, how goes it with you?"

"I was here and talked to that little bastard. He wants to execute my daughter by unplugging her. I swear if he gets it done I will execute him right back with my brothers Smith and Wesson. You might remind him of that."

"That would be a crime to threaten his life. No can do. You don't really want me to anyway."

"Oh, but I do," she says. "I very much want him put on notice that I'm taking this personally. If he wins, he loses. Tell him that, Kelly. I'm directing you."

"You're not my client, Millicent, so I'm seriously not going to tell him any such thing. And don't you contact him, either. They'd love to throw your ass in jail. Be good for now. Promise me?"

"No, I don't promise you. I'm getting some coffee."

She leaves her phone on the bed, face-up, still connected to Larsyn.

"You know, Kelly, I want to argue this motion, but I really need you and your staff to go over my written response."

"Sure we'll do that."

"Are you being paid yet for this work?"

"No."

"What's your fee for processing a case like this?"

"Fifteen thousand."

"Do you have a credit card processor?"

"Eleanor does. She's our office manager."

"Have her call me. I'll drop my Amex on her and get you taken care of. I want the bit in your mouth every much as mine. I think we'll make a good team."

"As in you hit them high because you're tall and I hit them low because I'm a dwarf?"

We're laughing as we say our goodbyes and end the call.

Millicent returns a while later with two coffees. Mine has cream. Has she remembered after all these years how I take my coffee? Or is she just lucky today?

"I seem to remember you taking yours with half and half, Michael. Or has that changed?"

"Hasn't changed. Thanks for getting."

"No problem. I just needed to step away."

"I know."

She sips her coffee as she blows it cool.

"You haven't changed," I say. I immediately wish I hadn't gone there—too personal.

"Neither have you. Just as handsome and rugged as ever. Except what happened to your face?"

I involuntarily reach and touch the scarring on my face.

"I was burned. Tortured and burned. I didn't give the right answer when asked. Something like that."

"I can't imagine. You poor thing."

"Over and done, Millicent. We get older; we come down with scars and droopy skin. It's part of it."

"Droopy skin, I suppose. But third-degree burns, definitely not. Did you get the people back?"

I swallow and wipe a napkin across my mouth. "Not yet. But I'm not done, either."

"Good on you. Mess them up, Michael, whoever did it. Not that you're any less handsome. Here's one old lady who still finds you hot."

"Well—"

"In a good sense."

"Sure."

"And if you want to take me to dinner while you're here I certainly won't object."

There, said. That old doorknob just turned.

"I'm going to be pretty busy," I say. "Lots to do here."

"Sure enough. I wasn't being seductive. I just meant we use our time wisely by putting our heads together about Cache. When they release her, we're going to need a plan."

"You haven't had a plan?"

"Once she discovered her father was alive she wouldn't even speak to me again. There hasn't been a plan."

"How old was she when she found out?"

"Thirteen. Found out about you on the Internet. Of course."

"She didn't contact me."

"She wouldn't. That wouldn't be Cache—too shy to ever reach out like that."

"But she grew apart from you? Figures."

"How so?"

"You deprived her of a father, and she knew it. Knows it. If she hates you, it's well-deserved."

"Michael!"

"Hey, live with it, Millie. Truth is truth."

There, I've re-established the wall between us. I need it, and she needs it too, although she doesn't know it at the moment. A little Michael Gresham in her life right now would be ugly for us both. No thanks.

That door is closed and will remain closed.

DAY 6/30

The next morning, I swing by St. Anthony Hospital to check on Cache. Last night I finally gave in and checked into a hotel for a night's sleep.

I haven't seen her since about six yesterday evening. By then I had turned into a zombie and hardly recognized my own name when a nurse spoke to me. So I hurry up to her floor and trot down the hallway to her room. A respiratory therapist—who recognizes me—is checking the breathing tube and pump that is keeping Cache alive. She straightens and steps past me, allowing me to be with my daughter privately for a few moments. "There you are, Mr. Gresham."

This morning Cache looks the same, although her hands are arranged differently. The RT, when I ask, tells me this is because she's been turned in the bed. She is quick to explain to me that no, my daughter hasn't moved her hands and arms herself.

It saddens me again, seeing her like this.

It's a short visit. I'm off to see the governor this morning. I slowly retrace my steps back along the hallway and take the elevator down to the cafeteria, where I load up on a large coffee and three donuts. I'm munching on cake donut before I even pull out of the parking lot in my rental SUV.

Then on down to Tacoma where I wait in valet parking outside Millie's hotel. She's to meet me at eight o'clock. It's ten minutes before, so I switch on the radio and catch up on the baseball scores. I'm not ordinarily a baseball fan, but I'm not ordinarily waiting for an ex-flame in front of her hotel, either. In fact, the bright idea occurs to me to leave the radio turned on even after she climbs in so we can avoid any talk that might lead to anything like intimacy. I'm congratulating myself for thinking this little scheme into being when Millie comes hurrying through the rotating front door and looks around for me. I tap the horn. She spots me and waves.

She piles in, lugging along a huge purse and a laptop case that is jammed inside. She climbs in and sits back in the passenger's seat. She shrugs. "Don't ask," is all she says, meaning her overstuffed purse. I don't, pointing instead at the radio and its recounting of last night's baseball. I feign a serious interest in last night's scores. Millie gives me the space to do that. The radio host drones on while I follow the 705 Freeway to the 5 Freeway. Then onto the 5 south to Olympia. It's only about thirty minutes away by the time we've merged into traffic.

The radio drones on. Now we're into the St. Louis Cardinals and their hopes and problems as a ball club. Out of the corner of my eye, I can see Millie with her head slumped against her window eyeing the traffic coming at us. Leave well enough alone, I remind myself.

"Well," I say when the tension in the car is almost unbearable, what with her blankly staring ahead and me acting like it's a real job handling the SUV in the morning's very light traffic. I have no doubt: she gets it, and my plan is beginning to over-ripen. "Well. Let's hope the governor is in a good mood this morning."

"Do we have an appointment?"

"No such thing as an appointment with the governor. He doesn't make appointments with nobodies. I was told by his staff to show up and present some compelling reason why I just have to see him one-on-one. He may or may not make time for us."

"Sounds like a busy man."

"Yes. But he's about to have his day interrupted because I'm not leaving until he sees us. Cache deserves no less."

"Then that makes two of us."

"Team!" I say and hold up my hand to high-five. She misinterprets my intention and grasps my hand and squeezes it.

"You're a good guy, Michael Gresham," she says still holding my hand. At last, I wrest it away without seeming to wrest it away—two-hands on the wheel kind of wresting.

"Thanks, Millicent. You're not so bad yourself."

"How about some AC?" she asks. "It's stifling in here with the seaside humidity."

"Sure enough."

When I can't locate the AC controls when feeling around the dashboard without taking my eyes from the freeway, she reaches over and lifts my hand out of the way and places it on my thigh. Seconds later, the AC spins up, and cool air relieves the anxiety that's causing me to form sweat droplets on my forehead and around my lips.

"It is stifling," I add as if the humidity is causing me to sweat so profusely.

But it isn't the humidity or the inside air, and she knows it, for she looks away with a wry smile and says something that sounds like, "That's my Michael, always dodging and feinting."

I ignore the comment.

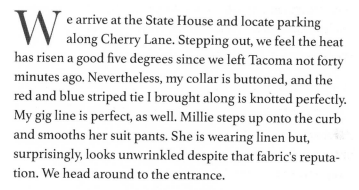

We arrive at the State House and locate parking along Cherry Lane. Stepping out, we feel the heat has risen a good five degrees since we left Tacoma not forty minutes ago. Nevertheless, my collar is buttoned, and the red and blue striped tie I brought along is knotted perfectly. My gig line is perfect, as well. Millie steps up onto the curb and smooths her suit pants. She is wearing linen but, surprisingly, looks unwrinkled despite that fabric's reputation. We head around to the entrance.

The receptionist has no idea who we are, of course. So we explain in great detail the story surrounding Cache, including the attempted suicide, the possible brain damage, and the steps taken by the Washington Attorney General to euthanize our daughter. At this point, Millie is crying into a wad of tissue, and I'm wiping my eyes as I recount the past seventy-two hours. No doubt, this is the person we have to convince in order to see the governor.

She picks up her phone, taps in a call to the inner sanctum, then whispers and listens. She hangs up. They'll be breaking for mid-morning coffee and photos in about an hour; we should have a seat. She's sorry to keep us waiting. "He wants to see you," she concludes.

We take facing chairs in the waiting area. I immediately grab up the business section of an abandoned newspaper and begin reading about the Yen on the Japanese market. I read where Bitcoin has surpassed one million yen. I know just enough about international economics to know that Bitcoin isn't my retirement vehicle.

Every time I look up, I spy Millie sitting with her right knee caught in her clasped hands, her dangling foot tapping out the time to some inner rhythm while her eyes pass back and forth across my face. I ignore her smile and keep reading.

Forty-five minutes later, the governor's office doors fly open and several men and women—all carrying briefcases—come hurrying out. Two uniformed state police follow them partway out and then step back inside, closing the door behind them.

"That's your cue," says the receptionist. "Let me buzz."

Which she does, nodding while she talks.

"Wait three minutes and then go on inside. He's peeing right now."

I do my best not to crack a smile and instead nod like I hear this kind of toilette talk about governors all the time.

At last the doors come open. Millie precedes me into the governor's office. His name is Jackson L. D'Nunzio, and his face means nothing to me because I don't live here in Washington State. Without looking up until the very last second he continues writing at his desk and finally stands, extending a well-calloused shaking hand. We pump hands too long. He moves away and waves us to sit down.

"I've heard about your daughter, Mr. and Mrs. Evans. Terrible stuff."

"Actually, I'm Michael Gresham, and this is Millicent Evans. Yes, we're the parents of Cache Evans, and yes, we're distraught and terrified."

"How about bringing me up to speed. Jimmy Accardo is my administrative assistant but he's run up to Seattle, so I'm not getting my usual thirty-second briefing. How about you supply that?" he asks, directing the request to me.

"Our daughter was arrested, tried, and convicted of aggravated murder of Judge Wilberforce over in Spokane."

"I remember hearing about that. Nasty business."

"Yes, well, what you probably didn't hear is how the so-called victim raped our daughter when she was just into her teens while she was living in his house as the nanny for his kids. He then used her essentially as a sex object for the next several years, which included him passing her around like a toy for his friends to rape. This went on four years until our little girl broke away from CPS altogether and hid out on the streets of Seattle. She supported herself as a prostitute. At some point, the judge learned he was infected with HIV, and that turned into full-blown AIDS. As he was going through the medical process, he blamed our daughter for infecting him. He was all innocence. The prosecuting attorney of Spokane County bought it. They prosecuted Cache, and now she sits on death row in Purdy. She was waiting to die in thirty days when the guards failed to keep an eye on her, and she attempted suicide. Thank God, it failed. But she now is hospitalized in St. Anthony's in Gig Harbor with no indication whether her condition is permanent. As if this weren't enough, the attorney general of Washington has now filed in court to withdraw our daughter's life support."

"Really? How can that be?"

"Exactly my point. That would be cruel and unusual punishment under the Eighth Amendment to the Constitu—"

"No, I mean why would the AG file it? Why not the office of the prosecuting attorney? Wouldn't they have jurisdiction? I'm not a lawyer, so I'm just shooting from the hip, Mr. Gresham."

"Who did or didn't file it isn't the issue, Governor D'Nunzio. The point is, your state is attempting to euthanize our little girl while she's very, very sick."

He leans back from his desk and peers to the left. Two aides are standing by, one of whom is taking notes without looking up. The other bends down and whispers to the governor. The governor shrugs and takes a deep breath, nodding all the while. "I'll tell them," I think I hear him say to his aide.

"Now, Mr. Gresham and Ms. Evans, here's what I propose. Let me call the Spokane Prosecuting Attorney and see if I can find out why the AG is in on this. Maybe then we can get to the bottom—"

"Please, governor," Millie wails. "Our daughter is unconscious, and your people are trying to kill her. Do something, for the love of God."

The governor places both hands together on his desk. I've seen powerful men assume this pose before. It always comes right before they do a hatchet job on someone less powerful.

"Ms. Evans, your daughter is a convicted murderer. Please try to remember where that leaves me. And please try to remember that I'm the state officer who has been asked to pardon her and refused. If she is put to death while unconscious, it's my wish for that to happen. Now, is there anything else you can tell me?"

I sputter and stop and start, but finally manage, "Yes, I want to tell you that I'm going to sue everything in this state—including you, sir—if this is allowed to proceed. I'm—"

"Well, Mr. Gresham, sue away if you please. It won't stop the execution of your daughter. But sue as much and as often as you feel you need to. Our Attorney General will represent the defendants and give you a run for your money."

"It's not about money," Millie says in a small voice that sounds very far away.

"I misspoke, no it's not about money. It's about the orderly administration of justice in my state. Okay, time's up. I need to get back to my meeting."

"Roads and bridges?" I ask.

"Education. Now, excuse me."

The uniformed cops step forward and take a position on either side of us. We step out in lockstep and continue through the doors and on outside to the stairs we scaled two hours ago.

We are exhausted. Millie is crying. Maybe I am too. I'm having trouble seeing and my eyes sting.

But it's the last bite they'll get of me.

It's on, brother. It's on.

~

No sooner are we belted into the SUV and rolling north on the 5 Freeway when Kelly Larsyn calls. He's Face-Timing, and my phone has the same ability. So we connect and look each other over.

"You've been to see Governor D'Nunzio, right?"

"Yes. Waste of time. Roads and bridges, bridges and roads."

"Well, here's an eye-opener for you. Judge Lakin just called me about coming to court next Monday. Wanna guess why?"

"No. Tell me."

"The frigging AG has now filed to move the execution date up by two weeks. That would leave us just one week to file appeals and make our case to the feds."

I'm surprised but not shocked. "What's their rationale?"

"Same as before. That it costs a hundred thousand dollars every day she's kept alive on life support. By moving it up two weeks, the state saves one-point-four-million dollars. We've gotta take drastic action to stop these assholes, Michael."

"Totally agree. Any chance you can come by my hotel tonight?"

"Are you forgetting? I'm in Spokane. You're in Gig Harbor."

"I know that. But I need you to fly over and plan on staying a few days while we put together our response."

"I don't get it. Why can't we do that online?"

"Because you and I are going to set up a demonstration here in the hospital and I need your expertise on Washington state evidence and procedure."

"So you need me to cross the T's and dot the I's?"

"Exactly. Are you packing?"

"No, but I will be. See you in the a.m."

"You know where to find me. Just come on up to the room. I'll be up early."

"Later."

We end the call, and my screen goes blank.

"He's an interesting fellow," says Millie, who has been viewing Larsyn over my shoulder."

"What do you know about him?" I ask.

"He's the most aggressive lawyer I've ever seen in court. It's a miracle for the state they managed to convict Cache in the first place."

"What stands out most in your mind about the trial?"

"That Mr. Larsyn didn't let Cache testify. The jury needed to hear about Wilberforce raping her and then passing her around to his cronies. It would've turned out much differently."

"Why do you think he didn't let Cache testify?"

"You want the truth?"

"Absolutely, Millie. I want the truth."

"He didn't let her testify because he wanted to be appointed to Judge Wilberforce's court. He wanted to be the judge to replace the dying Wilberforce. You can't ever tell him I said this."

"You have any proof of this?"

"Two times the clerk of the court nudged me aside and told me to make Larsyn let Cache testify. She said for me to be careful, that Larsyn wanted Wilberforce's seat on the bench."

"Anything else?"

"I caught Judge Maxim and Larsyn in the judge's office during one break in the trial. I was lost, looking for the ladies' room. I came up the hall and heard two men laughing their heads off. I recognized one of the voices as Kelly Larsyn. I'd heard him laugh before."

"What did you do?"

"What any mother would do. I stopped to listen."

"Could you make out what was said?"

"I did. I heard Larsyn say she wasn't going to testify."

"What else?"

"I heard Maxim say he was fast-tracking Mr. Larsyn's appointment to take over Judge Wilberforce's court. Those were his exact words, 'I'm fast-tracking your appointment so you can take over as soon as we're done with this trial.'"

"What did Larsyn say?"

"Nothing. Nothing I could hear, anyway."

"Have you ever told any of this to anyone?"

"I filed a complaint with the prosecuting attorney's office. I wanted the whole case investigated for fraud."

"What happened?"

"What do you think?"

"Nothing."

"Nothing, that's right. And before you ask me why I haven't told you this before, let me explain something. Ever since I walked into Cache's room, you've been trying to keep distance between us, Michael. To tell the truth, I didn't know I could even trust you."

"You serious?"

She nods. "Until today, when I heard you tell the governor how many ways you were going to sue him. Then I knew whose side you were on."

I'm beside myself. How could she—"How could you even think I might be holding out on my own daughter?"

"I'm scared, Michael. I'm really scared. I don't know who to trust."

It is all I can do not to take her by the hand and reassure her. Or pat her knee and tell her I'm on her side.

But I don't. I love my wife, Verona, and nothing's going to

come between us. Especially not the estranged mother of my daughter.

I make a mental note to call Verona just as soon as I'm alone.

"Well, it obviously didn't happen, Millie. Judge Wilberforce is very dead, and Kelly Larsyn hasn't taken his seat on the bench."

"That's because they took all of Judge Wilberforce's cases and distributed them to the other judges."

"What, they closed his court?"

"Larsyn is running for judge in the next election. He's already got signs up, so I'm told."

Something about this sounds shaky. Ordinarily, when a judge dies or steps down the chief judge or the supreme court or the governor appoints somebody to fill in until the next election. That hasn't happened with Judge Wilber-force's seat on the bench. Something to find out about.

We lapse into silence the rest of the way back to Millie's hotel.

As soon as she's inside, I whip out my phone and make a call to Verona. I miss my wife, and I'm relieved I didn't get impulsive and entangled with Millie. She's beautiful and charming and smart as hell, but she's also out of bounds.

Until I got to be this age, I didn't even know there were bounds.

DAY 7/30

At half-past-seven there's a knock on my hotel room door. I answer, and there stands Kelly Larsyn, dressed to the nines in Ito Benellini shoes, a perfectly fitted Verleta suit, and a silk shirt and tie. He's holding an orange and two Starbucks coffees. He thrusts the larger of the two coffees at me.

"Take and drink. Do this in remembrance of me."

"Really, Larsyn? Must you?"

He smiles. "It's all I had on a moment's notice. Next time I'll have something more contemporary."

"How about, 'I just jumped out of the clown car to come up here.' That work?"

"It works. And so do we. That table there?"

He's indicating the dining table/desk that occupies the far wall in my suite, just below a second window filled with morning sun.

"Yes, that table. What's in your briefcase?"

"Yellow legal tablets and a laptop. Plus my pills."

"What pills?"

"Anxiety meds. This case is wearing on me. It's been almost two years, Michael."

"Which reminds me. There's something I've meant to ask you."

"Shoot."

"Who ended up filling Judge Wilberforce's seat on the bench? Who got the judgeship?"

Larsyn tosses his bag onto the table and hops up on a dining chair. He places one foot under the other leg as he prepares to work. But my question bothers him. I can see it in his eyes and his stony face. He's doing his best to register no response.

"I don't think they've filled his seat, although I don't follow the politics all that closely."

"Would you be interested in serving?"

"Can't. This case is still pending, and now you've roped me in for another four or five months, it looks like. I'm guessing they'll have someone appointed any day now."

"And they didn't come talk to you?"

"Someone might've called me. I truly don't remember. Now, what's our strategy, Michael? You've hired me, and I'm ready to get it on."

We're finished with the topic, as far as Larsyn's concerned.

But his answer has been vague. Lawyers like Larsyn know precisely what's going on with judgeships and vacancies where they appear in court. It's as natural as breathing, to an attorney. Larsyn will need to be watched. And I'll put Marcel on the judgeship issue the next time I speak with him. If Larsyn is withholding something, Marcel will snoop it out. I smile inside. Larsyn just doesn't know who he's dealing with, when it comes to keeping a secret from the likes of Marcel. We're only getting warmed up here.

"I want to head off in a new direction today," I tell him. "I want to establish that Cache is still alive even though unconscious and unresponsive. I want to establish that she's not brain dead. Once we can do that, we can avoid the state trying to use brain death against her."

"How would they use it against her?"

"By proceeding as if it doesn't matter what they do. They'll try to argue she was dead anyway, that they were just cleaning up her room."

"That's interesting."

"It would be an interesting argument for the state to make. And could very likely be made. I just don't want to be blind-sided by some genius at the AG's office suddenly hitting on the idea that my daughter is already dead and it's just a matter of unplugging the life support and letting her body go."

"Had not thought of that. Michael. You're already impressing me."

"I'm not here to impress you, Kelly. But just think how we'd look if we weren't ready for some bright assistant AG to make that case. So, we make ready for that."

"By establishing that medically she's still alive."

"Yes and that legally she's still alive, too. The two aren't the same."

"No, I think I knew that."

"The issue is in flux. In many medical circles, no brain stem activity means she's medically dead. Which usually means legally dead—but not always."

"Sure."

"So, this morning we're meeting with Cache's patient care team. They're going to decide in the next twenty-four hours whether Cache is alive. The team consists of a neurologist, a neurosurgeon, and a priest—don't forget, we're talking St. Anthony Hospital."

"Got it. The logic in a team like that is obvious."

"We want the scientists to be very careful about all this. Both for legal and medical reasons but also for spiritual reasons, at least in my universe."

"Don't want to be spanked by the Big Guy?" says Larsyn.

I ignore it. "Let's talk about the doctors involved."

A half hour later, we're headed for the hospital and a meeting that I've arranged with the patient care team. We hurry through the hospital's main doors and take the elevator to the neuro floor. Larsyn stares at the elevator's floor lights as we ascend. I admit I'm perplexed about the whole judgeship thing. And whether Millie heard what she thought she heard about Judge Maxim telling Larsyn that he was going to fast-track the dwarf's appointment to the Wilberforce court. Or was she wrong about that? Knowing Millie and her patient, scientist's way of understanding the world, my money's on her having heard right. Larsyn has become my target. And even now, Marcel has begun nibbling around the edges of the issue, thanks to a text I sent him before leaving the hotel. Larsyn couldn't be more at risk than he is today. Why would I say that? Because if I find he purposely kept Cache from testifying in order to secure a judgeship for himself, there will be blood. That's a promise.

The elevator doors whoosh apart, and I smile at Larsyn and let him go first. He has no clue.

We find the chief neurologist's office and take-over the small waiting room. Larsyn picks up a copy of Neurology. I find the People and start thumbing and quickly realize I haven't heard of most of the people inside.

At nine o'clock an Asian woman peers through the inside door and asks us to follow her. We're led down a narrow hallway with maybe a half-dozen offices, all with closed doors, along either side. At the end is a door with a glass pane on either side. She pushes it open and stands aside. "Dr. Collingsworth," she says with a smile.

Dr. Collingsworth rises from his desk and shakes our hands after saying his name. He is a clear-skinned, white-haired physician wearing a sparkling white lab coat. He smiles and asks us to sit down. Now that we're introduced we can get right to it.

"You're not only the patient's lawyer, but you're also her father," he says to me.

"Yes. And Mr. Larsyn here is the attorney who's been there for her up to this point."

"Why haven't you been on her case? Don't lawyers help family members, like doctors don't treat their own family?"

"I didn't know she even existed until recently. It seems her mother was keeping her existence hidden from me. Now, I've spoken with you by phone, Dr. Collingsworth—"

"Matt. Please call me Matt."

"—Matt. You're at a point where you can do some necessary testing, as I understand."

"Yes; if you like, I can give you the twenty thousand-foot view of what I have planned for Cache."

"Please do."

He leans back in his chair and shuts his eyes for a moment. Then he comes forward in his chair.

"Our first inquiry has to be whether Cache's brain-stem is alive. There are various steps we follow. The first step is to establish whether a competent cause of brain-stem death exists. In other words, just because someone is unconscious, we don't suspect they are whole-brain or brain-stem dead. There has to be a significant injury. So give me the particulars that you have."

He looks at me.

"Well, it appears Cache was lying on the mattress in her cell at lights-out. Exactly at ten o'clock, which is when the last roll-call of the night was taken. Alive and well. She is said to have even told the guard goodnight."

"Okay, that's what I've been told."

"At four a.m. There's another round by the night guards. This time she's found slumped against the bars of her cell, her body facing inward. There's a makeshift noose of mattress ticking that has been looped up and over the topmost horizontal bar of her cell. Then it runs down to the noose, and that's where she's found, dangling with her legs crumpled up beneath her."

"So maybe as many as four hours have passed with her in this death pose."

"Death pose?"

"That's what we'll call it. Meaning she's not moving and maybe there's no pulse, no breathing."

"That's what the hospital medics said. They worked on her twenty minutes with the shock paddles and breathing bag and finally got her heart started and her breathing restored. 'Diminished breath sounds' is how I think they put it."

"Yes."

"She was then rushed here, to St. Anthony. You know more about her than I do since then."

"A four-hour passage of time would definitely establish the first criteria: a significant injury. In this case, a compromised airway. We've made extensive inquiries and done tests to prove or disprove. We have also had to rule out other causes of deep coma, such as hypothermia, hypotension, drug overdose, and a small group of neurologic conditions. CT scans

and an MRI have done this work already. We can confidently say it was the self-imposed strangulation that brings
her to us."

"What comes next?" asks Larsyn. He's been furiously
tapping our conversation thus far into his laptop. I like him
just a little bit more for it.

"Next came the physical exam. Or exams, I should say. We
have determined that she's in a very deep coma state, unresponsive to any stimulation and not breathing on her own.
If there is any response, the patient isn't brain-stem dead. So
far there's been no response."

"I think I've seen some of that testing going on," I say.
"Maybe a nurse or two have tried a few things with her with
me there."

"Sure. We've also established by step three there are no func-
tions by the brain-stem. This means looking for reflexes
whose pathways run through the brain-stem. If any of those
reflexes are present, it means those pathways still work and
at least part of the brain-stem is alive."

"These reflexes are what?"

"Well, there are six of them. Eye reaction; eye movement
doll's eyes; eye movement cold caloric; and eye movement
blink or corneal reflex; number five is gag reflex; and the
sixth is the apnea test,"

"I expect these have all been performed?"

He moves his computer mouse and clicks through a few
screens. "Yes, several times now. A bright light has been
shone into her eyes on ten different occasions the first full

twenty-four hours. The pupils are so far fixed and dilated. No neurological response."

"And 'doll's eyes'?"

"If the head is moved rapidly from side-to-side the eyes will move in their sockets and remain fixed as if staring at a spot straight ahead. This is the result of a neurological reflex. If, on the other hand, the eyes move side-to-side with the rolling head, then this indicates no neurological function. This demonstrates that the brain-stem is not working."

"How did she do?"

"Let me just gloss over them first and then we can get down to the specifics, okay?"

"Okay," I agree, although the waiting is painful. There must be something positive about all of this, otherwise, why haven't they indicated that removal of life-support is indicated?

"The next is eye movement, cold caloric. When ice-cold water is injected into the ear of a normal person, it cools down the balancing movements in the inner ear and triggers eye movement. If there is no eye movement, then this tells us the brain-stem isn't working."

"Good heavens," says Larsyn. "That sounds terrible."

Ignoring him, Dr. Collingsworth continues. "Number four is the eye reflex by the blink or corneal reflex. When the brain-stem is working, the eyes blink when the cornea is touched. When the brain-stem is not working, no blinking occurs, no matter what the stimulation to the cornea. Gag reflex, number five, works much the same. We use an instrument to touch the back of the throat. If there is no gagging that tells us the brain-stem isn't working."

"Good God," I mutter.

"I know," he says with a shake of his head. "Some of this is pretty primitive and off-putting. Ordinarily, I don't do details like this with family because most people don't want to hear specifics. That's most people; some do. And of course in legal cases such as this one we always give up everything we know."

I just want to finish the preliminaries. "What about the apnea test, number six?"

"Apnea testing is the most important test used to confirm brain-stem death. The short description is that the ventilator is shut off and if the patient is not breathing then this shows that the brain stem has no function."

"Sounds pretty cruel," Larsyn mutters.

The doctor turns to him. "Not if you're dead, Mr. Larsyn. And if you're alive you're usually unaware."

"Can we back up to the machine testing?" I ask. "So that I can make my list of what's been done insofar as imaging and machine testing?"

"Confirmatory testing is done by my orders after the functional testing we've been talking about. This consists of repeating the CT and MRI scans. Then I order an electroencephalogram. I also use brain blood flow studies. These are of three types. I use the nuclear blood flow method."

"That's it?"

"Pretty much. It's very thorough, and I'm in the highest

ninety-nine percentile of certainty when I'm finished, if not one-hundred percent."

"The confirmatory studies are mostly about blood flow to the brain?" I ask.

"Exactly."

"And when will the final pronouncement be made in my daughter's case?" This is the one I've hesitated to ask. This is the one I've dreaded asking.

"Well, before we do anything final, there's something I want you to see. Let me buzz up an RT, and we'll meet in your daughter's room. You can run along now, and I'll be there in about thirty minutes."

Larsyn and I back out of the room. He suggests we drop by the cafeteria for coffee. I tell him to go ahead, that I'll meet him in Cache's room.

We separate and I walk through a short maze until I find Cache's nurses' station and then head directly down the hallway to her room. She's inside, under the watchful eye of Millie. Millie hardly acknowledges me when I enter. But then I see why: she's been crying and doesn't want me to know. Her hand clutches a wad of tissue that she uses to blot her eyes. Then she turns to me and smiles. "Here's our daughter. Just like we left her. And isn't that tragic?"

"I just finished with Dr. Collingsworth. He's going to show us something when he gets down here in about thirty minutes."

"Show us what?"

"He didn't say. But I've got a feeling we're just around the corner from learning whether Cache's brain-stem is dead. Do your praying, if you pray."

"I pray to the thing that makes it rain. That's my higher power."

"Whatever," I say, and scootch beyond Millie, up beside Cache's head. I bend down and kiss her forehead. I'm sure I'm not the first to do that today. She doesn't move, and her eyelids don't flutter, unlike movies where a kiss awakens a patient from a deep sleep. Not this time. So I squeeze her hand and take the chair on the other side of Millie.

Nothing is said. We listen to the sounds the life-support makes, the sounds the monitor makes, and our own breathing. Twenty minutes tick past. Then Larsyn appears in the doorway, a 20 oz. Styrofoam cup in hand. He nods at Millie and fastens his eyes on Cache. I try not to think about him colluding to prevent her testimony about the rape by Wilberforce. But a wild, animal feeling drives up through my chest, and I want to attack the dwarf, to crush him into the tile beneath our feet. It passes; I remind myself that nothing is certain about Larsyn and Judge Maxim; Millie could've just heard wrong. But still, there is the fact Cache didn't testify. The absence of her testimony has his fingerprints all over it, of that I am sure. Bastard, anyway. Then I'm angry again, and that's how I feel when Dr. Collingsworth and two other people stroll into the room.

"Everyone, this is Dr. Munoz, a staff neurosurgeon, and this is Father Monsini, a Franciscan priest on the staff of St. Anthony."

"Hello."

"I understand you practice in Washington, D.C.," Dr. Munoz

says to me. "I went to med school at Johns Hopkins, just down the road. Have they changed presidents since I left?"

"Have they changed presidents?" Then I realize he's making a joke at probably the worst moment for me. "Yes, they've changed. So what are we doing, doctors?"

"We're waiting for a respiratory therapist."

She hurries into the room at that moment. She's wearing navy slacks and a white coat with a large nameplate and her photo hanging from one of those self-retracting gadgets. She is quite pale, but her lips are glossy red. I don't catch her name; I'm scared to death of what's about to happen because I think I've just figured it out.

"Just to recap, one of our most reliable tests is the apnea test where we remove the patient's breathing tube. Actually, we don't remove it; we just disconnect it. Maria? Would you?"

The newcomer in the white coat steps around us and slides along the bed to the respirator. Her body blocks us as she lingers there, arms moving, bent to her machine and our daughter.

Dr. Collingsworth narrates. "The apnea test will test for the absence of autonomous breathing. This is breathing by the patient without the machine. This is the most important test used to confirm brain-stem death."

The respiratory therapist turns her head to us. "The short description is that the ventilator is shut off and if the patient is not breathing then this shows that the brain stem has no function. Are you ready, Dr. Collingsworth?"

"Go ahead, Maria."

"The tubing attached to the ventilator is being removed from the patient. Notice that the tube going into the patient's trachea is left in place. Oxygen is now blown into the lungs. I'll now monitor her for eight minutes or until her carbon dioxide reaches a specific level that tells me to stop. It would do that because there's no transfer of CO_2 for oxygen."

Dr. Munoz speaks up. "Any movement of the chest during the test is considered a sign of breathing. Also, our monitors can measure even the most minute movements of respiratory muscles. If the brain-stem is totally destroyed, no sign of breathing or attempted breathing will be seen. If not, we will catch even the slightest movement."

I sit silently but aghast that my daughter has now had her breath of life removed. I'm certain she is now dying.

Suddenly, Millie jumps up and runs from the room.

"I understand," Dr. Collingsworth whispers.

We're all focused on Cache's chest. The respiratory therapist is poised over her, watching for the slightest sign of movement. Every few seconds she looks up to the monitors beyond Cache's head.

Then, not fifteen seconds after being disconnected from the respirator's airflow, Cache's chest abruptly raises and lowers.

"Oh!" Dr. Collingsworth exclaims.

We continue watching and praying. Then, there it is again. And again.

"Your daughter is breathing, Mr. Gresham," Dr.

Collingsworth sings out to me. "Mrs. Gresham," he calls out into the hallway, "your girl's alive!"

Millie returns, skirts around Cache's bed, and approaches from the far side. She watches as our daughter gasps for air again and then again.

It continues in this manner.

"Disturbed and shallow," says Dr. Collingsworth, "but by God, she's alive."

"Praise the Lord," exclaims Father Monsini. He touches the cross on his chest.

I am weeping now, openly and without shame. "Oh, my God, thank you, I tell everyone present. Thank you all!"

Larsyn edges over and squeezes my shoulder. "Congratulations, partner. You've got your daughter back."

"Enough, Maria," Dr. Collingsworth orders the RT. "Restore the machine function."

Maria turns back to her machine and reattaches all tubing. Now the machine is breathing for Cache again.

"Why the tubes if she's breathing on her own?" Larsyn asks."

"In due course, counsel. We'll work our way into self-sustained breathing. One step at a time."

"Yes, but in the movies—"

"Look around, Mr. Larsyn. This isn't a movie," Dr. Munoz says in a detached voice. "This is someone's life."

"Sorry," says Larsyn. He moves apart from me.

I think we've just witnessed nothing less than a miracle. But that's the old Catholic rattling around inside of me, the man whose peers spot the Savior's blood on statues and see Mary's silhouette in their English muffins. It can be confusing when the real thing comes along.

"So?" I say to Dr. Collingsworth. "Is the team prepared to sign affidavits stating Cache Evans is alive?"

"We are," says Dr. Munoz without consulting the others. Dr. Collingsworth nods.

"Good. I'm also going to want to video Dr. Collingsworth. I'll need you to go over the things you described to us this morning, meaning the tests and what they reveal, and then recount what we've seen in here today."

"Spare me from court stuff, please," says Dr. Munoz.

"Consider yourself spared, Doc. I just need one video for my court filing."

"I'm happy to oblige if it will help my patient," Dr. Collingsworth says to me.

"Thank you, Doctor," Millie says and turns to hug him. He obliges her.

I cannot stop the tears seeping from my eyes.

My daughter is back.

DAY 8/30

We're all relieved, all of us in Cache's corner, but the reality still is there: this is day eight of the thirty-day countdown to her execution. Regardless of what we've established so far, the execution date is still approaching. I am determined to see it rescinded.

My mind is spinning every day and my nights are full of night sweats and moments of clamoring awake, grasping at the dark images swirling over my head in my hotel room. These images are old acquaintances. They always come over me during times of high stress from the practice of law. Many lawyers would know exactly what I'm talking about.

While we were at the hospital yesterday watching Cache breathe on her own, Marcel was in Spokane, where he somehow acquired the complete dependency file on Cache. This is the file maintained by CPS, the confidential file. It is a crime to obtain it. But...we have it now, and I'm reading. The chief caseworker, while Cache was a minor, is a woman named June DeWitt. Her notes and memos swell the file to where, in paper form, it's a good three inches thick.

The entire file has come to rest on the table in my hotel room. I will take this day to review it. I need to absorb it, not just review it, because I'm confident it will contain incidents and occurrences that could be very helpful in saving Cache's life. Or even—best of all worlds—setting her free. When I'm finished with the file, I'll be ready to begin writing my response to the AG's motion to accelerate the date of execution. Larsyn is scheduled to take Dr. Collingsworth's video deposition this afternoon, so the entire day belongs to me.

First up, a carafe of coffee from room service, plus a pineapple Danish and a blueberry muffin. Enough caffeine and carbs to lift me way up before body-slamming me into the mat. At least that's how Verona describes my dietary habits. She might be right, but it still works for me.

I read through the notes quite quickly. It appears there are two stories contained in them. One is Cache's story. The other is Judge Wilberforce's story. They totally disagree with one another. I begin reading again, this time much slower.

I make my notes. Cache ran away from home when she had just turned eleven. When the caseworker approached her on the street, the reason given for leaving home was that the girl had just learned her father wasn't dead, that he was living in Chicago. Upon finding this out on the Internet, she became enraged at her mother for keeping her father secret and fled. She took with her only the clothes on her back and two-hundred dollars in savings bonds her grandparents had given her before they passed. The caseworker had Cache declared dependent and placed her in foster care at Serenity House. Problems developed. Less than a year later Cache was placed with newly-licensed foster parents Hiram and Dot Wilberforce, who couldn't have children of their own.

Which isn't entirely true: Hiram had offspring from a prior marriage, but they were with their mother. Dot couldn't conceive but wanted to parent a child. Her religious beliefs compelled her to do so. When Cache moved into their house, Hiram Wilberforce was a judge sitting in the trial court. They lived in Spokane and kept a time-share in San Diego. Dot was active in her church and a street ministry. She planned on raising Cache with those time-honored religious values. In short, she meant to save Cache's soul. Her calling was a youth ministry.

When Cache turned thirteen, living with Judge and Mrs. Wilberforce, Dot became pregnant—miracle of miracles.

A few weeks in, Dot became increasingly moody and distant —according to her best friend Frieda M____(last name redacted for privacy). That was when—we can only guess— she refused sex with the judge. Perhaps this explains why she never became HIV positive. At any rate, Cache says the judge began catching Cache alone around the house and "crowding her." This consisted of him placing himself between the young girl and a wall or a bookcase or a closet —pinning her in and smiling at her. Then he would say inappropriate things, such as asking what she felt like when she was raped and did she enjoy it. Cache responded by retreating to her room. She later says she didn't tell the social worker this was going on because she feared she would be taken out and placed somewhere even worse. So far, the judge had only leered at her and said "nasty things"—the girl's words. She knew from experience and the rape by three boys at Serenity House the world could get much worse than what Judge and Dot Wilberforce offered her.

When Dot's baby was born, Cache began part-timing as the child's nanny. The judge paid her for this. Her employment was never reported to the caseworker. Then one night, after the judge was up late at his Friday night poker game, and after the whiskey bottles were emptied, he entered her room and raped her. Holding his hand over her mouth and flattening her into the mattress with his ape body, there was no way she could resist. The raping turned into a daily thing. Then he began paying her for sex when Cache said she was going to run away. She stayed and no longer resisted.

The caseworker goes on to say Cache became "Like an hors-d'oeuvre, passed around at stag parties for everyone's pleasure." In other words, the judge had become magnanimous, offering his foster-daughter to his guests because that's what good guests with sexually abused dependents did—at least in his sick mind.

The story then turns to the judge's version of what happened. Caseworker June DeWitt recounts the judge's yearly physical where a standard blood test came back positive for HIV. He was infected. His condition worsened. Dot hounded him about the source of the virus, angry that he had been sexual outside the marriage as there had been no blood transfusions or any of the other mechanisms by which the disease could infect him. Then she was threatening divorce. The judge countered by breaking down early one Saturday morning in their bedroom. The nanny, he blubbered, one day told him she was going to report him for rape if he didn't give her money. He was horrified; even an accusation would see him tossed off the bench. He might even be prosecuted for sexual assault on a minor. That meant he would never work again. He gave in and began paying her. Then she insisted he have sex with her so that she could get pregnant and start receiving WIC benefits. He had done as she said. She now owned him. This was the story he told June DeWitt when Cache turned up HIV positive herself. June's file notes indicate she was skeptical, but she had no proof positive that either one of them was telling the truth.

"How did it happen?" Dot asked her husband.

The judge began shaking all over. "I was in the shower, and the door suddenly opened, and she stepped under the water with me, totally nude. I was stunned yet found myself with an involuntary erection anyway. After that, my resistance faded, and she accomplished what she had come to do. It was over in less than three minutes, and then she was gone.

"Why didn't you come tell me?"

"I felt like I had done something wrong. I was also scared because she was a minor."

"So that's how you came down with HIV? That little tramp! You're going to go straight to the prosecuting attorney and swear out a complaint against her. And we're having her removed from our home."

"That's not a good idea. She's going to report me if we make her leave."

"Absurd! Nobody would believe a runaway, a dependent. Besides, what proof does she have?"

"She told me she kept my sperm in a safe place."

"Meaning?"

Now he was full-on weeping. "She transferred a sample of my sperm to a handkerchief you gave her last Christmas.

She threatens me with turning it over and ruining me. It's evidence that could send me to prison!"

"We're going to the police. They'll believe you before they believe her."

"I don't think telling the police about this is a good idea. If there was any sex at all, I'm guilty because I'm the adult and she's a minor. Besides, what would the police prosecute her for, Dot? Think about it. Calm down."

"They would arrest her for giving you HIV! That's a crime!"

He stalled her off. His doctor administered virus-suppressing drugs. During all this time Dot, to her great good fortune, was even then refusing all sexual advances from her husband.

The anti-virals worked for two years until one day he woke up and could hardly stand. He was weak and very sick. He went straight to his doctor, who told him evidently the suppressants had quit working. Dot gave him two options: the police or divorce. He went to the prosecuting attorney, and a criminal complaint was filed against Cache. They decided she would be tried as an adult. Before it could come to trial, his virus had turned into full-blown AIDS, and he was on his deathbed. After he died, the state added another count to the complaint, this one for aggravated murder. Cache was convicted at trial after she wasn't allowed by Larsyn to testify and tell the jury about the sexual assaults.

~

It's mid-afternoon by the time I finish up with the juvenile file. My heart is aching for my daughter. No matter which side you believe, the fact always remains that Cache was a minor. The judge was guilty whether he was forced or it was him raping her. She was a minor, and the law had to look no further.

But it didn't stop there, the ruination of my daughter. Millicent had refused to tell her about her dad. Seriously, that's the entire genesis of her undoing. Judge Wilberforce deserved to die. If he weren't already dead, he would be. Cache's dad would see to that.

Why the same HIV hasn't killed Cache, I don't know. Partly, I'm sure, because she got on the anti-viral medications that have kept her HIV from destroying her altogether. Why the judge died, and she didn't—I've read about this for hours. There doesn't appear to be a clear-cut explanation for how this happens.

But one thing I do know: right now, as she's lying unconscious at St. Anthony Hospital, I have made doubly sure she's receiving her full anti-viral dosing.

~

Larsyn finishes up with the video session and comes to my hotel room just after five o'clock. He's headed back to Spokane on the seven o'clock redeye, but I've asked him to debrief me first.

"I've sent you the video of today's session by email. It should already be on your computer," he tells me. "It was amazing, Michael. Dr. Collingsworth was very forceful and one-hundred-percent the advocate for Cache. To hear him talk, she was hours away from climbing out of bed and making coffee."

"Please."

"You get my meaning."

"Yes. Tell you what. You go ahead and write the response to the motion to accelerate the execution date. I'll research the issues and be prepared to argue the motion on Monday. Does that square with you?"

"Hell, yes. You've paid me to do the entire job. Now you're going to do the oral argument? How could I complain?"

How can I tell him I'm only doing it because I no longer trust him? Knowing Cache's full story as I do now, and knowing that Larsyn had access to the same CPS reports, I don't trust him out of my sight since he didn't let her testify. Coupled with Millicent's comments that she heard him conspiring with Judge Maxim to take over Judge Wilberforce's court, Larsyn is way down on my list of trustworthy helpers. In fact, the more I watch the guy drink the iced tea room service brought up, the more I want to drive my fist into his face.

But I don't. The last thing Cache needs right now is to have her best advocate thrown in jail for assault.

So I keep my mouth shut. I've cut Larsyn off from arguing the motion, which I'm sure wouldn't go Cache's way if I allowed him to speak for her. No, this time her father will do her talking. And I will keep my enemy close by.

They will execute this innocent child only over my dead body.

Marcel flies to Gig Harbor and hands me this notice, dug up from the general files of the Spokane Chief Judge's Office:

 Spokane, WA

Notice of Judicial Vacancy Spokane County *Hon. Hiram Wilberforce has passed away. In the interim, the Chief Judge of the Superior Court has assigned cases to sitting judges, but it's now become apparent that a full-time judge is needed to replace Judge Wilberforce. Governor Jackson L. D'Nunzio is now seeking interested and qualified members of the Washington State Bar Association to submit applications to fill this position. The Governor's application for judicial appointment, the Uniform Judicial Evaluation Questionnaire, is accepted by the Spokane County Bar Association and several minority bar associations for evaluation purposes. To be considered for this*

vacancy, applicants are strongly encouraged to promptly submit complete applications, along with a short resume and the Waiver and Authorization to Release Information, and schedule judicial evaluations with the county bar association and the statewide minority bar associations. All applications must be completed and submitted to the Governor's Office, with all judicial evaluation ratings submitted to the Governor's Office of General Counsel as soon as possible.

"So here's your smoking gun, Boss," Marcel says when I've finished reading and re-reading.

"Larsyn. He's going to be appointed now. Probably about the time we finish up with the State's motion to accelerate. Bastard!"

"What do you want to do with him?" Marcel's look is one I've seen before. He gets it. His face and eyes are nothing less than murderous.

"For now, nothing. For later, we'll talk. This is personal. Whatever we decide about Larsyn works for me."

"No, I say he has an accident now. A terrible accident in his little yellow Porsche."

"Yellow? Really?"

"It fits him. Coward!"

"He took fifteen-thousand from me, and he's ready to see Cache die. He deserves a terrible accident, you're right. Just not quite yet, okay?"

"Okay."

"Promise me."

"Promise."

"Now let's talk about Cache. It'll help clear my head."

We spend the next ninety-minutes reviewing my notes from her file. When we're finished, Marcel is fit to be tied. He's back on Larsyn and the terrible accident. I need to calm him down, so I suggest we go out to dinner. I call Millie; she's up for it. In fact, she sounds pleased to hear from me. I figure with Marcel along it will be a nice dinner, drop her off, then head back to my hotel with Marcel. No harm, no foul, right?

We're driving south on Angeles Road when I suddenly slam on the brakes. The car ahead of us just hit a dog. Now the dog is lying on its side in the road, trying to get up. After switching on my hazard lights, I'm up and out of the car. Marcel beats me there and scoops the whimpering animal up in his arms.

"Hit the GPS. We need it to find an animal hospital."

I run back to the SUV and manipulate the GPS. It instantly locates an animal hospital. Marcel climbs in beside me, cradling the dog on his lap. The animal's eyes are open. It's trying hard to wag its tail.

"What is it?" I ask.

"As in, breed?"

"Yes."

"English Setter, I'd say. Maybe a Springer Spaniel. Hard to say with all the blood."

"Where's it bleeding?"

"Looks like the upper hind leg. He almost made it across, but the car nailed his back end."

"Is he going to live?"

"He's going to live. Just step on it!"

We locate the hospital and rush in with the dog. The vet tech at the front desk is immediately up and rushing the dog back through a swinging door. We're told to wait in the lobby after we give the admitting clerk the particulars.

"Whose dog is it?" she asks, looking from Marcel to me then back to Marcel.

Marcel nudges me. "It's his. Michael Gresham."

"Wait," I interrupt, "it's not my dog. We found it in the road."

The admitting clerk is very serious. Her white face and black-rimmed glasses give her a ghostly glow under the fluorescent lights. "We'll have to euthanize him if you don't claim him."

Euthanize? That is too similar to Cache's predicament, at least in my exhausted mind.

"I own him," I tell her. "You want a credit card?"

"Yes."

"American Express work?"

"Yes."

I pass her the card and shut my eyes while she fills out several forms and then runs my card. She hands it back to me. Marcel and I finally sit down. It's been a long day.

Marcel looks down and sees all the blood on his arms. He's up and strides back to the admitting clerk. I can hear him ask for a wet towel. He gets much of the blood off his hands. Then he heads to the restroom for the rest of the cleanup.

Now I'm worried about the dog. What am I going to do with a dog in Gig Harbor, Washington?

Two hours later, the same vet tech materializes before me. I've been dozing off.

"Good news," she says to my sleepy face. "He's going to pull through. Dr. Knight repaired his leg, he's splinted and has a plastic collar on so he can't get his mouth around to the wound. What's his name? Just for our records."

"His name's Lucky," Marcel says when it appears I have zero idea about a dog's name.

"Lucky it is," says the tech and off she goes to the clerk to add the name to my new dog's records.

Then she returns. "Dr. Knight will be out to talk to you. We're going to need to keep Lucky overnight. You can pick him up around noon tomorrow. That work for you?"

"It works just fine," Marcel says, again answering for me.

"Wait," I say to Marcel, "where am I going to keep a dog? The hotel won't let me have a dog in my room."

"You'll have to get a place. Something furnished that allows pets."

"I can't; I have a family waiting—"

"Michael, you won't be leaving here anytime soon. After you save Cache's life, you're going to have to help with her rehab or her placement. Trust me; rent a studio and buy your dog one bowl for water and one for food."

"This can't be happening," I mutter. "Not in the middle of the rest of this mess."

"Hey, look at the bright side. You have a dog now. Two hours ago you were dog-less. Sounds almost miraculous to me."

It hits me then. Millie. We haven't called her. I ask Marcel to give her a call and explain our situation. He gives me a sour look, but he does it anyway.

As Marcel is calling Millie, Dr. Knight introduces herself to me. She's wearing a white smock and a frazzled look. We talk, and she explains the procedure Lucky underwent and what will happen next. Long story short, I'm to pick up my dog at noon tomorrow. The entire vet bill will be around fifteen-hundred bucks. I tell her that's fine and ask her if she knows of any short-term studio apartment rentals. She gives me a tired look, shaking her head. She retreats through the swinging door.

"She isn't happy," Marcel reports about Millie.

"Tough darts. If it weren't for her, none of this would have happened. She can jump in the lake, isn't happy. Bite me."

"Michael, that sounds nothing like you. What say we go back to your room, order up a porterhouse with mashed potatoes and green beans, and get you tucked into bed?"

"Bite me. You're the reason I now own a dog and need a studio. Why did I ever bring you out here?"

"Why? Because Lucky wouldn't have been lucky if not for

me. And oh yes: Larsyn would have seen his next birthday if not for me."

Terrible accident.

My self-restraint has melted away.

I'm all in.

DAY 10/30

S aturday morning rolls around. Time to find a studio apartment. Also, I haven't seen Cache in thirty hours. So I crawl out of bed and my bath and dressing and light breakfast I decide that first I'll check in on Cache. It's a short visit I have planned and then find the apartment. I'm picking up Lucky this afternoon and need a place to go with him. I've called the animal hospital twice, and he's improving every time.

Cache, however, isn't improving. There's just no change. Plus, she has developed bed sores on her pelvic girdle. The sores have Dr. Collingsworth worried, according to the day nurse. So I take my usual chair beside her bed and reach over and pat her ankle. I have my eyes shut and am praying. Good thoughts for her, anyway.

Which is when I feel her leg twitch. The leg attached to the ankle I've been patting. I wait to see if it happens again. Almost imperceptibly, the leg twitches a second time.

I lean back to study her face. No change there. As I'm

watching her face, I see her mouth move as if she's trying to speak. The tube, of course, prevents this. As fast as I can get my hands on it, I hit the call button for the nurse. She comes running.

"Watch," I tell her.

Then I reach and touch Cache's ankle ever so lightly. Her leg elevates off the bed an entire inch! The nurse chuckles and says something about calling Dr. Collingsworth, but I'm no longer listening. Cache is again trying to speak— I'm sure that's what the movement of her mouth means. Or maybe it says she feels the tube and it's making her gag.

The day nurse returns with the respiratory therapist. She watches Cache's face while she tickles her ankle. Again, the face moves as if in pain.

"She's awake," says the RT. "The tube is gagging her. Get the doctor," she orders the nurse, who presses the call button on the lavaliere microphone all the staff here wear. She connects with a male voice and explains the situation. He sharply says to do nothing, that he's on his way.

And he is. Minutes later he rushes in and performs several tests with his penlight.

"There's not only pupillary reaction, but she's also even opening and closing her eyes," he announces to the group.

"Angelina," he tells the RT, "let's disconnect the tube and see what we have."

The RT unscrews the hose from the tube, disconnecting the life support system.

It's undeniable: Cache's chest is raising and lowering, raising and lowering.

"Pull the tube," the doctor orders the RT.

"Cough, honey," the RT says to Cache. There's no response; now the RT expertly works the tube up and out while Cache thrashes her head from side to side. Apparently, she's gagging on the tube and doesn't stop until it's withdrawn. Now it's out, and she tries to say something.

"What is it?" the RT asks her. "Do you want something?"

She nods—or appears to. Then we hear her whisper, clear as a bell.

"I want my dad."

I am shocked, and tears flood my eyes. Now I'm openly crying. My shoulders shake. The nurse passes me a clutch of tissues, and I blow and wipe.

My daughter's first words were to ask for me. I can't stand up and hug her fast enough as I whisper in her ear, "Your dad is right here. And I'll be here with you as long as you need."

"Water." Her second request.

"Astonishing," I say to Dr. Collingsworth. He turns to me and nods from her bedside.

"It is," says the doctor. "Her words are a huge hope for complete recovery. I couldn't be happier."

Angelina lowers a plastic cup of water to Cache's lips. Cache tries to lift her head and manages an inch or two. So the RT reaches for another cup, this one with a straw, and tries that. Contact. Cache takes a long drink, chokes, and starts again.

We all watch, amazed. I want to jump and shout but manage to control myself.

Millie walks in and stops. Her eyes widen, and her mouth moves soundlessly. Then she rushes to our daughter and takes her hand. Lowering her head, she puts her face beside Cache's and whispers to her. By now, even the guard outside the door leans in to inquire.

"She woke up," I tell him. "We're witnessing a miracle here." He obviously isn't impressed and disappears back to his hallway watch. My guess is that he's calling the prison on his shoulder microphone about now.

Millie turns and faces me. Her shoulders are shaking as she comes to me and hugs me. "Thank you for being here," she says.

I'm resolute in how I feel about this. "I'd have been here from the start, Millie, if only I'd known."

"I've made a mess of it, haven't I? You're right to be angry with me. I'm so sorry, Michael. I had no right to keep her from you. Damn me!"

"Easy. You're forgiven, and now you can forgive yourself, too. It's all good now, Millie," I finish, ignoring the fact that the original fight for Cache's life has now reared up to challenge us again. But this time I know even more what I'm fighting for. I'm fighting for the life my daughter has reclaimed here today. I'm fighting not just for Cache, although that's ninety percent of it. But I'm also fighting for Millie and me to heal. We've both cried over our daughter.

Now it's my turn to perform. My thoughts immediately

focus on Larsyn. How different might the jury verdict have been if they'd heard Cache's story? We'll likely never know.

Suddenly, I feel the full weight of this awesome responsibility settle down on my shoulders again. And I am dumbstruck. There couldn't be more at stake than this.

B ack in my room, all things are new. I see the flocked wallpaper at the head of my bed. As I sit to change into my hiking shorts and sandals, I notice the mattress is a pillow top. Room service arrives with a blueberry bagel and plain cream cheese. I see my food again. Darkness has lifted from me, and everything is new. It's a welcome experience.

I've still got time to pick up Lucky. I call the hospital and tell them I should be there in two hours.

I open my laptop and begin typing. An hour later, I access the court file online and see I've been added as counsel on the case with the right to file pleadings. I've prepared a counter-motion to the state's motion to accelerate the execution. I'm asking for the court to order the guards on shift at the prison when Cache hung herself to cooperate with me in a recorded interview.

My plan is twofold: first I'm going after the state on the theory that its negligence in failing to supervise Cache has resulted in cruel and unusual punishment in that her attempt to kill herself was easily anticipated had they only been acting reasonably. Then I prepare a second motion, this one asking that the case be re-opened for new evidence based on the negligence of her attorney, Kelly Larsyn, who didn't allow her to testify. I go into details here, including an affidavit to be signed by Millie recounting the conversation between Judge Maxim and Larsyn where Larsyn's ascension to the bench is discussed. With this, I also include a prayer for relief that we be given access to the state bar association's file on the appointment to fill Judge Wilberforce's judgeship. My logic tells me that I'm going to turn up a letter written by Judge Maxim encouraging the appointment of Larsyn to fill the opening. After all, Maxim is the chief judge, and his recommendation carries a ton of weight. Accessing that recommendation only serves to add fuel to our position that Larsyn purposely kept Cache from testifying to please Judge Maxim, the uncle of Judge Wilberforce. The uncle with the ax to grind. The uncle out for payback.

I read a third time then expand the motion to include another argument, this one proposing that the trial court's verdict be vacated for the reason that Larsyn colluded with the trial judge to see Cache convicted. This prong of the counter-motion will cause some people to squirm and will open eyes to possibilities as yet unseen.

Finally, I request a change of judge from Judge Maxim to an unbiased judge, someone who hasn't encouraged her conviction by colluding with Larsyn. It's a straightforward motion and will be supported by Millie's affidavit and the letter of recommendation in the state bar association's file that I'm sure we're going to turn up. I believe it's enough to hound Maxim into recusing himself and appointing a new judge. We'll have to see.

Millie is called, and I request she drop by the front desk to sign the affidavit I've prepared. The office has a notary available so she can sign under oath. I don't invite her to my room because I don't want to be alone with her, true enough. But even more important: I have a dog to pick up from the animal hospital. He's there waiting to go to his new home.

Now I'm off to collect him up and find a small apartment that extends a welcome to us both. There's also dog food to consider, bowls, and the rest of what Lucky will need. Mental note to self: rawhide bone. Don't forget a rawhide bone.

～

The hotel concierge has located a small publication that lists all the rentals available in the area. I circle the dog-welcoming ones and begin to make calls. Three appointments are made.

Beside me in my rented SUV sits Lucky, who, I've been told, is probably a purebred Springer Spaniel. I don't know much about dogs, so I assume that's a good thing. The animal hospital advises me the humane society is running an ad to try to locate Lucky's real owner. The ads are rarely successful, I'm told.

Lucky and I don't strike paydirt until we try the third apartment complex. They are friendly to dogs and have a furnished studio I can move into today. I pay first and last month's rent, sign a six-month lease and give them a security deposit and a pet deposit as well.

Now the place belongs to me. And Lucky.

The Petco out on Borgen Boulevard lets me bring Lucky inside the store. We grab a cart and head down the aisles. A clerk helps us locate a favorite pellet dog food and loads a fifty-pound bag of the good stuff into my cart. Other necessaries are located after walking the aisles for ten or fifteen minutes, and now Lucky's needs can be met. We go through checkout and, just inside, just beside the exit doors, is a machine that makes a name tag for your dog. You can also include your telephone number on the reverse side. I loop Lucky's leash around my wrist and begin typing the particulars into the machine. The tag pops out. It easily attached to Lucky's new collar. So does his vaccination tag from the animal hospital.

Now we're all set, so back to the new apartment.

We unload and head inside. The utilities are included; everything is ready for this new tenant plus one. An hour later, Lucky has eaten, and I've ordered a pizza and quart of root beer. A grocery delivery service comes at seven p.m. with several bags of necessary—and some unnecessary—groceries. The kitchen is fully outfitted, including coffee maker, so now I have fresh coffee in the supplied navy mug, and I'm settled in front of the TV with my new companion on the couch beside me, licking his balls.

Great. It probably says something about my taste in dogs, but I don't even begin to go there. I do have some pride remaining.

∾

It's probably two hours later when I get a call from a cell phone with a private number. Probably a burner, a throwaway phone. Knowing I might very well regret it, I answer. I have to play the message through twice before I realize what it is I'm hearing. Someone has dictated into their computer and what I'm hearing played back is the computer's artificial voice delivering me a message. It includes the words "yellow" and "terrible accident."

I know what I know. Marcel has just tipped me off.

It's coming.

MARCEL

Marcel dials the number Inder Singh has given him. He speaks with the girl, a sophomore at the local university. Yes, she tells him, she has been with Mr. Larsyn on many occasions. Marcel has confirmed the setup and the process.

Her name is Iris Cambell. She's twenty-years-old and majoring in cello. She's at university on a full-ride music scholarship, but it isn't enough to live on and enjoy some of the things she enjoys that cost money.

Like cocaine. She's addicted—thanks to Singh and the others who field calls from her clientele, deliver her to her appointments and take her pay. She's addicted because they want her addicted. All of the girls are addicted to something —Marcel knows this to be a fact. He knows it's how street-world operates. Without chemicals, the system would come unglued.

He decides she's just what he needs.

Marcel meets Iris at the girls' softball field near her university. It's nighttime and the field lights are off, and there's no one around.

They join up at second base. She goes to light up a Salem, and he snatches it from her before her lighter can flare and give them away.

"Please, Iris. If anyone sees us together, it's off."

"I need something before I do this. Just a taste to get me through."

"After."

"Will he be there?"

"He will. But he'll be asleep after you give him this."

He passes her a small baggie.

"What is it?"

"A barb. A little something to give him a good night's sleep. A very deep night's sleep."

"What else do I have to do?"

"I just need you to drop in on him. Play like he called for you. He'll take advantage of it because he's mad about you. It should go without a hitch."

"Okay. I give him the stuff in the baggie, then what?"

"Take the pictures with his camera. Post them on his *Instagram* page. Then leave. Just walk out the door and don't speak to anyone. Keep this hat low on your face. There're video surveillance cameras everywhere. Remember how I showed you."

"Wait. He doesn't have an *Instagram* page."

Marcel smiles. "Which is why we get to make one for him."

"With--"

"Yes."

She looks up at the stars. They are wheeling—from her view—across the night sky in a dizzying dance. She loves it and almost falls, but he catches her, steadies her, brings her back upright.

Then her face clouds.

"Are you going to give me more money for this?"

"How much are we talking?"

He knows he's being gentle, an alternate universe beyond the pimps. He's letting her control the terms of the deal. This way she won't later have regrets and think she was cheated. This way, she sets the terms, and she knows they're good for her because she chose them.

"I don't know," she says, choosing her words as carefully as she's able. "Another thousand?"

"How about two-thousand?"

"You're kidding me, right?"

"I'm not kidding at all. Check your mailbox at the student union. The money will be there waiting for you tomorrow."

She looks at him, studying his face. But the face—with much of the night—is a blur. She's had too much of something, and she knows it. Then she forgets why she was attempting to memorize his face, to begin with.

She cannot remember.

The chemical wave laps at her feet.

She no longer cares why.

DAY 11/30

The next morning, I awaken in my new apartment. Lucky has slept beside me all night long.

I call the front desk of my hotel.

"Yes, Mr. Gresham. I was on duty when Millicent came into the hotel. She signed your document and our office staff notarized her signature."

"Hold it right there. I'm on my way."

"Certainly, Mr. Gresham. It's safe with us."

Now what to do with Lucky? Give him the run of the apartment? Or lock him in the bathroom. I decide to lock him instead in the laundry room, as it's on the outside wall just in case Lucky starts howling. Closing the door to the laundry room behind me, I feel like he's safe yet far enough away from any neighbor that his yowling won't be noticed. At least not all that much.

As I'm driving the SUV back to the hotel, a snippet of something Millie told me in the early days of this journey comes

to mind. During the trial court phase of Cache's case, a
court clerk asked to speak to her about something she'd
seen in Judge Maxim's office. What that was, I can't
remember—if she even said.

The front desk turns over to me the signed affidavit from
Millie. Next, I locate the business room and take a scan of
her statement, attach it to my counter-motion, and file it
electronically with the court in Spokane. So far so good.
Then it's back to my SUV to see how Cache is doing today.

Driving along toward St. Anthony—I can see it in the
distance—my cell phone alerts me to an incoming call.

"Hello?"

"Michael Gresham?"

"Speaking."

"This is Nancy Lloyd. I'm a clerk of the court in Spokane. There's
something you need to know about your daughter's case."

"How did you know to call me?"

"You just filed a counter-motion in the case. It's my job to
check it for official filing."

"Okay, go ahead."

"Well, I was the courtroom clerk at your daughter's trial.
One afternoon, two weeks ago, while I was working another
case, I took a new paper filing to the judge's office. He wasn't
in so I left it on his desk. This is standard procedure. But
this time I happened to notice a letter on his desk, and it
contained the name of Kelly Larsyn, so I stopped, snuck a
look around, and read it."

"You were suspicious of something? Why?"

"All the clerks, including me, felt Cache should have been allowed to testify. We had all heard the rumors about Wilberforce and his wild parties and his young girls. But we've been afraid to come forward. We're afraid of Maxim and Larsyn and afraid of losing our jobs if Larsyn gets appointed to the bench."

"And the letter was addressed to the state bar association?"

"No, it wasn't. In fact, it was addressed to a local bank and instructed the bank to open a new account in the name of Committee to Appoint Kelly Larsyn. It also said it contained a check for ten-thousand-dollars from Judge Maxim himself."

"Did you tell anyone about this?"

"There was no one to tell. Judge Maxim was the judge on your daughter's case, and Larsyn was the defense attorney. I'm scared of both of them. But they used her. They trapped her. So, Dot Wilberforce gets to keep her husband's state pension. It's over ten-thousand a month. And she gets to shine at the garden club and the country club and the women's club. A scandal was avoided, thanks to Maxim and Larsyn."

"And all it cost them was my daughter's life."

"Yes."

"I could use a copy of that letter. I don't suppose there is one."

"We have one."

I swerve over to the curb; my hands are shaking so hard I have serious difficulty steering.

"We have one?"

"I took a picture with my camera. Do you want me to email it to you?"

She takes down my email and seconds later I hear my phone's tone alerting that a new email has arrived.

I thank the clerk and end the call. Now I do access the email on my phone. I am trembling as I read the attachment.

It's exactly as the clerk just told me. The letter is from Judge Maxim and indeed references a ten-thousand-dollar check for Larsyn's appointment campaign.

Except that's not what it is, not at all.

It's really a payoff. A payoff for Larsyn allowing Cache to be convicted.

I pull up around the corner, into a CVS lot. With the aid of my laptop, I'm online with the court in a blink. Thirty minutes later, I've supplemented my earlier counter-motion with the next evidence: the shot of Judge Maxim's letter.

Now we have newly-discovered evidence that wasn't in existence at the time of her trial.

Now we get a new trial. And we get a new judge. Plus, a judicial complaint will be filed by me.

For the first time, I'm feeling hopeful. For the first time, I have something solid to work with.

Now on to see Cache.

∾

The guard outside her room has been doubled. Now that she's conscious she's twice as likely to make a run for it? I shrug at them as I round the corner. "Don't worry, gents; you won't have to guard her once when I finish up." They smile and give a thumbs-up. They seem to treat her pretty well. They seem to like her. It makes me proud.

She's sitting up in bed talking to the nurse when I walk in. Without hesitation she lifts her arms a few inches as if to hug me. I don't hesitate; we hug and exchange a long look. This one is definitely mine, and I'm loving this kid.

"How are you doing?" I ask.

"Much better. I actually ate some ice and some Jell-O. Throat." She points at her neck.

"Still sore, eh?"

"Yeah. How are you enjoying Gig Harbor?"

"It's a pretty neat place. I got a dog."

"You got a dog? I didn't know you were looking."

"He was run over. We rescued him."

"We?"

"Marcel and I. Marcel is my investigator. We're making lots of headway on your case."

She looks to the nurse and then back to me.

"What case?"

My heart falls. "Your case you were in prison over?"

She smiles then laughs. "I know. I'm only being funny. It just feels so good to be out of prison. This is my first time in over two years. Except for court a couple of times."

It's an opening, so I jump in. "Speaking of court, is there any reason you didn't testify at your trial?"

"I wanted to. Mr. Larsyn said I would convict myself if I did. It turns out I also convicted myself by not. Can't win."

"Tell me exactly what he told you, Cache."

"Exactly, huh? Let's see. He was very touchy when I brought it up. Like he was angry about something. When I first brought it up, he said something like, 'Don't even go there, Cache!'"

"Don't even go there? Asking about testifying set him off?"

"It did. So we talked another minute, and it was clear he didn't want me on the witness stand. I didn't bring it up again."

"Did you ever hear him say anything to anybody else about you testifying?"

"Not really, no. He might've talked about it with my mom, but I wasn't listening. They talked about everything and by then I was just tuning them out because I knew I was a goner anyway."

"Why a goner?"

She smiles. "Who is the jury going to believe, the Honorable Hiram Wilberforce or me? They had all the statements he made to June DeWitt. He looked totally innocent in it all—according to him."

"Tell me about your initial placement with Judge Wilberforce."

"Not much to say. After my problems at Serenity House, I was glad to go anyplace else."

"You mean the rape at Serenity House?"

"I do. That's when I thought I got HIV. One of the boys was a heroin addict. Dirty needles equal poor me."

"When did you find out about the HIV?"

"Much later. They examined me at the hospital after the rape. That's when they tested my blood the first time. I was clean then; no HIV."

"When did the HIV first show up?"

"It was later. I was living at the judge's house by now. At one point it was time for another blood test. I figured no big deal. But they called me in with June DeWitt. She's my case-worker. They tried not to scare me, but it didn't work. I heard the news, and then I started bawling. I couldn't stop for two days. It wasn't fair. I knew I was hosed."

"So what about when Judge Wilberforce had sex with you the first time? What happened there?"

"Not much. But it was before the HIV test where they found me positive. Anyway, it was a Friday night. I won't ever forget. He just held me down and put it in. He had his hand over my mouth, and I couldn't breathe. So I didn't struggle. Then he rolled over and didn't say anything. He caught his breath, stood up, and said, 'Nice. Thanks." Then he walked out. It happened every day after Dot got pregnant. She wouldn't let him near her. In fact, she was mad at him for getting her pregnant. She was very protective of her figure. But she was very snooty about everything. Her nails, her hair, her smile lines. I know she had work done on her eyes after the baby came. She said the pregnancy gave her crow's feet. Whatever. Give me a break."

"So he began raping you before the positive test?"

"It was before."

"Did you ever tell Judge Wilberforce about the test?"

"I didn't. I wanted him to catch it from me."

"You were in a rage?"

"Wouldn't you be, Michael? I was also naive. I didn't even know it was rape, what he was doing. I just thought it was legal because I wasn't fighting him off now. Besides, there was no one to tell. I knew if I told June I might go back to Serenity House and get hurt again. At least he wasn't violent. Not after that first time."

"So you were forced to settle for mild rape. The alternative was violent rape."

"It sounds sick when you put it that way."

"Cache, I'm only telling the truth. You had nowhere to turn. I'm sorry I wasn't there for you."

"That's what made me so mad, Michael. I just knew you would have helped me. I hate her."

"Millie?"

"Millie. She really screwed me over."

I don't know how to respond to that. I agree with Cache.

Millie's choices were destructive. That's the mild way of putting it.

"I suspect she knows and she's very sorry."

"Then why won't she apologize? Look at me. I'm on death row; I have HIV, I've been used by men and cast aside as soon as the sperm swim off. It isn't all Millie's fault; I'm responsible for my choices. But there were also many times when the thing wasn't my choice. I didn't choose to be raped all those times. But I was in that environment, that exact time and place for it to happen because Millie lied to me about you. I hated her after that. I still do hate. I've forgiven her, but I hate her. Can you forgive someone even if you still hate them?"

She has me there.

"I don't know."

"Well, how do you feel about Millie? She screwed you over too."

"She did do that. I don't know if I'd phrase it exactly like you have it there, but I do understand why you're saying what you're saying. It's a bad deal all around. One person started it; three people have suffered over it. What happened was counterproductive all around."

"That's how you'd say it? Counterproductive?"

"No, I'd rather say she really screwed me over, because she did."

"Well please stop what you're doing, Michael."

"What's that?"

"Saying things you think a parent should say to their kid. Just be yourself for shit's sake."

"Well—"

"I can't have a liar holding my hand when my heart stops, and my breath floats off. So just say the truth to me from here on. I've only got nineteen days left."

"You're counting?"

"Of course. Just like you and everyone else who knows me. Whatever."

She slumps down on the bed and pulls the blanket and sheet all the way up to her chin. "Damn, I'm scared of dying."

"I'm scared for you."

"Stop it!"

"All right, I'm scared of dying too. Everyone is."

"Hold my hand, please!"

I reach and take her hand. Very gently I apply pressure so that she feels I'm warm and alive and I'm with her. One-hundred percent I'm with her. I pull her hand to my cheek and touch it there. Come with me, I'm saying. Become part of my life, and I'll walk you out of here. I'll give you life a second time.

But she abruptly pulls her hand away.

"How long since you've shaved?

Enough of the internal drama, I tell myself. It's time to do what you do best.

Trounce them in court.

∾

I come home and am greeted at the front door by Lucky; Lucky, who should have been shut up in the laundry. Without stopping I head to the laundry room. Lucky ate my apartment. The laundry room door was still closed, but where before there had been drywall, now there was a hole that had been chewed out of the drywall through which Lucky slipped, setting himself free.

I call the front office of my apartment complex and tell them my dog damaged the wall, and I am prepared to pay for its repair. They're kind and sound like it isn't the first time this has happened. Or least something like that. They advise me they will have maintenance repair the damage and present me with an invoice for the cost. The invoice will be due with next month's rent. They couldn't be any fairer than that, so I thank them and end the call.

"Lucky, what am I going to do with you?" I've plopped down on my purple couch, and Lucky has joined me, sitting at my side, his head in my lap.

"So you got lonely? Is that it?"

My phone chimes and I answer.

"Michael, Verona here. You haven't called me in almost a day. How's she doing?"

"We've had a miracle. She's sitting up in bed talking and telling me I'll have to be more honest with her if I want to hold her hand at her death."

"Oh, my God!"

"I know. She's something else. I wish I'd met her long, long ago."

"But you didn't."

"I know. It just makes me sad."

"I am so glad for you. And her."

"Yes, but we're not out of the woods yet."

"Are you ready to kick some ass, as you put it."

"I'm ready; it starts tomorrow in court. I'll be arguing against the state. We have a pretty strong argument seeking a new judge. I'm also requesting denial of the motion to accelerate her execution. That part is moot now anyway, now that she's conscious."

"Good."

"Well, how are you? Kids okay?"

"Kids are fine. They hardly notice you're gone, far as I can tell. Which tells me we're doing a good job with them, so far."

"They're independent of us?"

"They're confident in us. They know we'll always come back to them."

"How about you? You're confident about me?"

"Speaking of, is Millicent around?"

"Yes, she's here."

"You haven't lapsed back into old patterns with her, right?"

It takes me a second or two to get it.

"Have I slept with her? Is that what you're asking? The answer is No."

"I just worry. I know I don't need to. That's a lie; you have a penchant for bedding women whenever my head is turned."

"Is this why you called me? To ream me out over something I haven't done."

"Maybe not done, but maybe considered. Is that possible?"

I have no answer for that. We both know my spotted history.

"Michael, I think I'm going to fly out and join you for a few days."

"What about the kids?"

"I've already called Danny's parents. They would love to come here and visit their grandkids for a few days."

"Come on, then. Lucky and I will be happy to see you."

"Lucky?"

"My dog. I got a dog."

"We already have a dog, Michael."

"But this one was a bargain I couldn't pass up. Sometimes we have to spend to save."

"Meaning you got Lucky free?"

"He got hit by a car. Marcel and I took him to the animal hospital. There's a rule that says if you pay to patch them up then you own them."

"Okay, I'm on my way. No, not tomorrow. The next day."

"Why the delay?"

"Mikey has a soccer game that I promised him I'd attend. I won't disappoint him. Day after tomorrow I'll be with you."

"Let me know your flight and time. I'll be waiting."

We say our goodbyes and end our call.

I reach down and scratch Lucky's ears. He rolls his eyeballs up at me.

"Hello. No more walls, okay?"

His eyeballs don't move. Online I locate a dog boarding service. It's only twenty minutes away, so I load Lucky into my SUV and drop him off. I'm reassured he's in good hands, but then I renege. I can't leave him there alone. It's too soon to do that. Screw it, I tell myself, I'm going to drive to Spokane and take Lucky with me tonight.

I take a shower and change into cutoffs and my Joe Walsh T-shirt. The rest of the daylight is spent developing and making notes of my argument for tomorrow's court hearing. It seems to be making a whole lot of sense. At least to me.

At dusk, I pack and load and put Lucky in the front passenger seat beside me. I stop at Petco and buy a dog safety harness for my vehicle. Now Lucky's ready to roll so off we go.

Six hours later we're checking into a dog-friendly hotel with just enough time left for me to review for tomorrow's court action. Court is at eleven. I've asked Larsyn to stay away. At first, he was miffed, but then he saw I was serious and agreed. I will go it alone tomorrow.

As Cache told me earlier today, "It's how I roll."

DAY 12/30

I've just learned that Franklin Lemongrass, the Assistant Attorney General who visited me in Cache's hospital room, will be representing the State today. We will argue against each other in Judge Maxim's court and learn whether Cache will die now or a week or two later. It's almost moot at this point, true. But what isn't moot is that I get a change of judge ordered by Maxim and that he gives us a new trial.

Cache isn't well enough to be here, of course. I've let the court know she officially waives her presence. No problem there.

Marcel has come across the street from his hotel room here in Spokane. He is seated at my left.

There's a rustle at the courtroom door on my far left. Judge Maxim files into court dressed in his black robe and white shirt beneath and black necktie. He wears clear-frame glasses, and he reflects a yellowish hue as if maybe he's jaundiced. He takes his place up above us all and nervously shuffles the files on his desk. He looks at the clerk and gives a slight nod. The clerk calls the court to order.

"Mr. Lemongrass!" the judge booms down in a voice that bounces off the walls and would rattle the windows if there were any. "It's your motion, please proceed with any argument you wish to make."

Lemongrass hops to his feet; he's holding a yellow tablet with his finger marking his place as he begins speaking.

"Your Honor, this is a simple enough case. The defendant tried to take her life in the lockup at Purdy. She ripped up a mattress and tied a long rope of ticking around her neck. Then she looped it over the bars of her cell and slumped almost to her knees, shutting off her oxygen supply. She was found much later and rushed to St. Anthony Hospital in Gig Harbor. She remains there today.

"Now, at the time I filed this motion to accelerate her execution date, defendant Evans was in a deep coma. The doctors didn't know whether she would ever regain consciousness. The cost to the State of keeping this prisoner alive in the hospital was just over one-hundred-thousand dollars per day, a ridiculous cost for someone who would be dead in two weeks anyway. The motion made sense then, from a dollar standpoint and it still makes sense now. Accounts Receivable at the hospital tells me the State is now incurring costs of sixty-thousand per day to keep the prisoner in intensive care, even now that she's awake. In just under two week's time at sixty-grand per day, she'll run up costs over eight-hundred-thousand dollars. Nearly a million dollars wasted just so a dead-woman-walking can remain hospitalized another fourteen days.

That just doesn't add up, both financially and legally. So, the State makes its motion to accelerate and asks that it be granted. Additionally, the State has moved to withdraw the defendant's life support, which is now moot. But in the event she lapses into unconsciousness again we'll be right back here, renewing that motion and asking for an accelerated hearing."

"Very well, counsel. Please be seated. Mr. Gresham, are you ready to respond?"

I jump to my feet. "I am, Your Honor."

"Proceed, then."

"I'd first like to address the counter-motion I've filed for a change of judge."

"No, I'd like you to argue the motion to accelerate, counsel."

"But Your Honor," I protest, "if you grant my motion for a new judge then there won't be a need to argue the acceleration motion. It will have to be decided by your replacement."

He narrows his eyes at me. The lens in his eyeglasses shoots a glint of morning light directly at my face. I blink hard. "Counsel, your motion for a change of judge is denied without comment. Please proceed to respond to the acceleration motion or do you want me just to go ahead and grant it without argument?"

"You're denying my motion for a change of judge?" I cry. "Has it escaped the court's notice that I've attached a letter from you, Your Honor, to a Seattle bank with a ten-thousand-dollar contribution to Kelly Larsyn's judicial appointment committee? Is the court seriously asking my client to believe that your contribution is anything other than a payoff to Mr.

Larsyn for his refusal to let my client testify so your deceased nephew, Hiram Wilberforce, could be avenged?"

"Counsel, keep going with this, and you're headed to jail on a contempt charge. If there's anything your client doesn't need right now, it's to have her lawyer in jail for contempt. Your choice."

"Just so you know, I'll be appealing the court's denial of my motion for a change of judge."

"Understand, counsel. Appeal away. Now, your response sir. This is your last chance."

"Your Honor, while there might have been many facts about this case in dispute at trial, the key element of all elements is that your nephew, Judge Wilberforce, had sexual intercourse with my client. Not only did he have sex with a minor, but that also makes her a victim incapable of consenting to the act regardless of his ludicrous claim in the CPS notes that she had blackmailed him."

"Careful, counsel, it was I who instructed the jury on aggravated homicide by killing of a judge. That was all taken into account by me in formulating the instruction I gave and in ruling certain key facts proven at trial. Facts needed to justify the giving of the motion."

"Which I can only understand is your rationale for totally ignoring that his sexual assault victim was a minor. Isn't that what's happened here?"

"Counsel, I'm not a witness in this case. Asking me questions won't be countenanced. Do it again, and you're off to jail."

"Is that how the court avoids these compelling facts? By

putting the advocates of these compelling facts in jail? Then jail away, judge. It won't be the first time for me."

He knows I know I have him. There's no way in hell he can put the lawyer of a death row inmate in jail this close in time to the execution date. It would be automatic grounds for overruling the execution warrant by showing evil intent or a conspiracy against the inmate. I can virtually say anything I want without exposure.

"Counsel, last call. You can finish your response or I will grant the State's motion and won't put you in jail. But your daughter—client—will die just that much sooner. Stall at your own risk, sir."

Slick: he turned the tables on me without any effort at all. Nicely done, Judge.

"As I was saying, Your Honor, the State's rationale, based as it is totally on irrelevant financial concerns, should be summarily denied. It deserves no comment. We in the United States don't execute people because it's cheaper to do so. The notion itself shocks me, and it shows a total disregard for the humanity of this prisoner at least and violates her constitutional right to be spared cruel and unusual punishment. And here's another thing for the court to consider. Send my daughter off to die at an early date because it's financially justified and I will file a lawsuit against you personally, Judge Maxim, that will drain your resources every month when you pay your legal bills for the rest of your life. That's the sentence I will pass on you. Grant this motion by the State at your own risk, sir!"

Back at you. He fumes, he turns seriously colorful, running

from a yellow jaundice to a purple rage to a blazing white that only wants to strike back with all its power.

But he can't. For the reasons I've given. Mainly that I'm the lawyer for a death row inmate. That's a Get-Out-of-Jail-Free-Card anywhere in the U.S.

"Counsel, the motion will be granted. The date of execution will be moved from August 4 to July 25. For members of the media in attendance here today, this order by the court will save the State about a half-million dollars in hospital costs. Is there anything else, gentlemen?"

"Yes, what's your address where I can have you served with my lawsuit, judge?"

"You are found to be in contempt of this court, Mr. Gresham. You are sentenced to jail for seven days. You will report to the jail within twelve hours of your client's execution. Is that all, sir?"

He has me after all.

But seven days is nothing compared to eternity. I can do seven days standing on my head.

Now if I could only step in and be the life sacrificed for this state's notions of right and wrong instead of my client, my daughter, Cache Evans.

It's time to appeal.

Lemongrass tugs at my arm as we're filing up the aisle, leaving the courtroom.

"Got a minute?"

"Yes. What's up?"

"I'm going to get her."

"Say again?"

"I'm going to get your daughter off the State's food trough. She's cost us enough already."

I'm so angered by this, so enraged, that I draw back my fist and am bringing it forward when I suddenly feel a strong hand arrest my swing from behind. I turn to see. Marcel. Marcel has stopped me from getting myself thrown in jail on an aggravated assault charge.

Lemongrass laughs, baring big yellow teeth at me. His voice and mouth and teeth remind me of a braying jackass. How could I not have noticed this before?

"Jackass," I snap at him.

"Hey, asshole. I'm turning off the spigot. Now what's the big brave man going to do, hit someone smaller?"

"Yes, I am. Except you aren't going to see it coming next time. And Marcel won't be around to stop me next time. And it won't be a fist. It will be something that sounds like a gun. Oh, that's right, you've never heard a gun just behind your ear before, have you? Guess what? You won't hear this one, either. But I will say your name. Then you'll know it was me just before the lights go out forever."

Lemongrass's blood drains from his jaundiced face. He jerks his head this way and that. "Anyone? Did anyone hear the threat Mr. Gresham just made at me?"

A blue-shirted sheriff's deputy following us up the aisle, nods.

"I heard him, Lemongrass. And I heard you, too. Even if he

does shoot you no one's going to try very hard to track him down. Not after what you said first."

We continue our slow single-file to the courtroom door where, at last, Marcel and I are free of Lemongrass.

I'm thinking only of destroying him on appeal.

And maybe just a little bit about procuring a gun.

~

It turns out Larsyn was in the courtroom when we made our arguments. Within the hour, he files his motion to withdraw as attorney of record and Judge Maxim signs off on the motion. No hearing, no argument, nothing; just grants the motion.

I'm upset with this development because I'm concerned it might affect my tenuous ability to appear on Cache's case because I'm not a Washington-licensed attorney and because Larsyn was, if you will, vouching for me. Now he's gone, and now that patina of legitimacy by association with a Washington lawyer is gone, too.

However, no one raises the issue, especially Judge Maxim. Evidently, it's the same thinking: you don't throw a death row inmate's lawyer off the case in the two weeks before her execution. If you do, there's going to be a huge appeal and a huge delay while the Court of Appeals calendars and countenances all argument. Maxim doesn't want that, so, the upshot is, I remain on the case without the association of local counsel.

So be it.

Just before the courthouse closes for the day, I file my emergency appeal and petition for post-conviction relief. Rules of Appellate Procedure 17.4 require certain pre-conditions for an emergency appeal, and I take all steps to meet those. I've already made the telephone calls and copies of filing to Lemongrass and the court of appeals.

The Chief Judge acts immediately and grants my motion to expedite. The Court of Appeals will hear my post-conviction petition tomorrow, right here in Spokane in the Division III Court of Appeals.

Washington State post-conviction appeals allow me to raise the claim of ineffective assistance of counsel in the trial court. We're talking Kelly Larsyn here, who advised Cache she shouldn't testify. In my petition, I reference the evidence that Larsyn should have used at trial, in the form of Cache's affidavit and the evidence that arose when Judge Maxim tipped his hand by paying off Larsyn for withholding the testimony about his nephew's rape of Cache. This is the letter Maxim wrote along with his bank deposit.

I'm off to my hotel here in Spokane.

Back at the hotel, I find Lucky all wagging tail and happy to see me. Lucky has been visited several times by the concierge service. He's been watered and walked and peed on all the planters on the front side of the hotel. I tip them a hundred dollars.

Marcel comes by. We talk for an hour or more. I unload on him—I'm not angry with him, just with the system, just with being home-towned by the good old boys. He presses me for alternatives. What if the court refuses to help her tomorrow? What then? I don't have any answers. He says he may have an answer, that we'll talk again tomorrow. What's he up to? He's closed-mouthed, and I know better than to press him to find out what he's planning. He does say he's going over to Gig Harbor tonight and I can only shake my head. Does this guy never tire out? We shake hands, and he's off, finally.

Now to get some sleep and wake up refreshed and ready for war, day two.

MARCEL

Marcel parks his second rental—a gray Corolla—two blocks away from hospital parking. He removes a black locker bag to take along. He is wearing black pants, black turtleneck, and black watch cap, so the night swallows him up. Ever so swiftly he makes his way to the hospital. Downstairs, just off the St. Anthony Hospital lobby, he steps into the restroom when no one is watching and makes his way to the far stall. Closing the door behind him, he undresses.

From the black bag, he withdraws green scrubs, tops, and bottoms. He puts these on, easing the trouser legs over his black running shoes. Then he wraps an expensive stethoscope around his neck and loops an ID badge and security key card on a chain around his neck. He drops the car keys in a pocket of his scrubs. The black bag accepts his black clothes. He folds the bag and crosses to the bathroom's used-paper-towels receptacle. Scooping an armful of its contents out, he stuffs the black bag below and then replaces the upper contents on top of the bag. Hidden away as the clothes are, Marcel is betting the maintenance people won't empty the receptacle before he returns. If they do, nothing of value is lost.

The elevator up to Cache's floor, bottom to top, takes less than two minutes. He commits the time to memory.

Stepping off the elevator, he passes by the nurses' station, averting his eyes as he goes. Then he stops. Secrecy won't help. So he returns to the nurses' station and introduces himself as a first-year resident on rotation to neuro. He's given very little notice by the nurses. Residents rank lower than whale shit, they've been known to say.

Then he resumes his hurried watch to Cache's room. Outside her door, he checks the sweep hand on his watch. Thirty seconds, nurses' station to guards sitting half-asleep outside the door. He adds in another fifteen seconds for taking out the guards. Forty-five seconds from the elevator on into her room.

The guards don't even look up as he passes by. Just another guy in scrubs going inside to take vitals and yammer and yaw about the patient like they all do.

He reaches her bed and finds her sleeping. Good, no need to play like he's a real doctor with her. He spends five minutes at her bedside, watching the sweep hand on his watch tick off the seconds. Then he steps up to the keyboard mounted below the flickering monitor panel. He acts as if he's inputting data into her chart, but is really just acting. Nothing gets entered. He turns to leave.

One of the guards is staring him right in the face. The guard reaches for Marcel's ID badge and photo and studies it. His lips move as he reads, looking from badge to face, badge to face, satisfying himself that the guy is who he is pretending to be.

"Just checking," the smiling guard reassures Marcel. "This patient is on death row. So no need to take perfect care of her." This time he smirks—a shared confidence weighted in humor. Then he backs out the way he came. Marcel makes a note: this one is the guard he'll take down first when he returns. Leave him with a permanent scar, maybe a blade down his cheek.

"Perfect care, your ass," he mutters to himself.

Back at the elevator, he's now almost seven minutes into his visit from the time he stepped off the elevator. Add in another thirty seconds to dress Cache in something loose and long, plus the flip-flops. Maybe eight minutes on the floor, two minutes up and down—approximately twelve minutes in and out. Maybe much less. It depends on variables he knows he can't control. But it will need to be timed so there's enough of an edge to make the bus that will be coming downstairs at the time Cache emerges from the hospital.

It can be done. One of the secrets that will give him an edge will be to call the guards into the patient's room as if they're needed there when he first arrives. Then he can dump them where he falls, out of the line of view of anyone in the hallway coming or going when he's done and out.

In the beginning, Marcel himself will be dropped off fully clothed in the scrubs with his ID and stethoscope, no need to change and hide clothes when he goes inside. Coming back outside with Cache, a bus runs until one a.m., stopping every twenty minutes just next to the visitors' lot. She will ride alone on the bus down two stops, where he'll be waiting with a car. This way there will be no memory of Cache with another person boarding the bus.

Will his plan give him enough time to execute from start to finish before a nurse making rounds comes into Cache's room? That's an unknown that must be planned for. Marcel doesn't want to hurt a caregiver, only take her out of the picture. He'll work on how that should be done in case he is interrupted, or the nurses look up and notice him leaving with the patient. If the latter were to happen he'd merely smile and say they were heading to radiology, so he'd wait and have her change clothes once they were on the elevator rather than back in her room.

It is coming together.

One last thing. Some of the guards are kind to Cache. Marcel wants to leave them uninjured. Of course, if it turned out to be tonight's clown guarding when it was no longer an exercise but the real breakout, Marcel would do whatever was needed to take him out. Nothing lost there.

At the lobby, he circles back to the men's room. Sure enough, his black clothes bag awaits him deep inside the silver receptacle.

He changes clothes and disappears out the main entrance.

The doctor is no longer in the hospital.

DAY 13/30

As I walk into the Court of Appeals courtroom 1, Cache's execution has been officially re-set by order of Judge Maxim for July 25. Today is the 16th, so we're only looking at nine days before they put the needle in her arm. Now I see why the Court of Appeals agreed to hear my appeal as an emergency matter and expedited hearing.

My pulse is pounding, and my eyes are playing tricks. So much depends on what I do in the next sixty minutes that I'm terrified. In these cases, the State has at stake only a number on a spreadsheet. In comparison, flesh-and-blood people have real lives at stake: children and relatives, loved ones, and husbands and wives. Who's undergoing the blood pressure/heart-rate spike? Me or Lemongrass? But I've done this many, many times. My discomfort is short-lived.

The dais where the judges sit is vacant. There are three chairs up there waiting for the men and women who are, I hope, Washington's best and brightest. The three-judge divisional panel is routine. The Court of Appeals never sits *en banc*. I take my seat at the wide table on the left, all alone.

Cache isn't able to attend—not yet—and Marcel is off interviewing potential witnesses. Ordinarily, my local counsel would be sitting right next to me, but Larsyn is no longer an attorney of record. So that leaves just me, and that's fine. Oh, yes, Millie has arrived, and she took a pew near the back of the courtroom. I see her as I turn to smile at the press. Always smile at the press.

At the table to the right of me sits Lemongrass and an older, reserved-acting gentleman who, I am going to guess, is the Attorney General himself. It's a case of first impression in Washington. He attends today because he wants the notoriety, the scent of a good murder case rightly handled where justice gets done in the name of the people of the State of Washington.

Horseshit. These two hacks want to execute my daughter because this is the age of the dollar in politics and they aim to present the AG's best case for re-election: if he wins today, he gets to boast how he saved the State $500,000 by the accelerated execution of a convicted felon who murdered a judge.

As these thoughts scrabble through my mind, I get angrier. Which is good: I want the anger to bubble up right now, a rich vein of it; anger will lend energy to my words.

As I'm revving up, the door on the far left side of the courtroom springs open and in file three robed and bespectacled jurists ready to do their best for the cause of justice almighty. Pious, smug-looking bunch of yahoos. Two men and a woman who resembles a young Shirley MacLaine with thick eyeglasses perched halfway down her nose. One of the men is quite short and Asian; the other is quite tall and African-American. The tall one reminds me of an NBA power forward on the Bucks; the short one can barely repress a smile, and I'm wondering what in God's world could seem humorous to him on this morning with a state-sponsored murder waiting on his plate. One never knows.

They take their places; the court is called to order; they pause and whisper among themselves, passing along a sheaf of papers and finally look up, one-by-one, awaiting the Chief Judge to start the show with the magic words judges get to say, "Counsel, it's your motion. You may be heard."

No sooner are the words spoken than Lemongrass is on his feet. He winds up, sucks down a lungful of air, and he immediately begins flailing the air with his arms. Spittle flies from his lips while he curries the judges with his words and economics. He tells them the July 25 execution date should hold if for no other reason than proper money management. It's the era of low-light government rooms and uncut freeway grass, and he drones on. A government can no longer afford what it once paid without hesitation.

He's quite brief in his presentation. Two of the three judges appear disinterested even after all that—a pulse-slowing observation for me. They look down, look at me, and exhale heavy sighs as if they'd prefer the first tee to this courtroom on such a pretty summer day.

Then I hear my name, and I snap to attention. I'm quickly on my feet waiting for absolute quiet in the room. Thanks to Marcel's well-placed phone calls early this morning, the courtroom—which is quite small, to begin with—is packed with press. Many of them are networks, I'm sure.

"May it please this Honorable Court," I lie, because I see nothing honorable about it so far, "let me begin by thanking you for agreeing to hear my response and counter-motion on such short notice."

The three judges seem to nod at me. Reserved, decorous nods not unlike how a library patron might react if a gnat were to settle on her nose.

"We are here today because the Attorney General of this state wants to trade dollars for death. That's right; he wants to accelerate by several days the execution of a twenty-eight-year-old female prisoner hospitalized at Gig Harbor. He is seeking to do this just because she costs the state money. If the State of Washington has its way, we will have moved, in the United States, from an ethic where human life is price-less to where the continuance of human life is a financial calculation. A financial calculation that terminates human life, not because of humanitarian ends, and calls it 'execu-tions' in pursuit of justice. The new standard assimilated into the attorney general's weaponry is murder for financial savings. Is this the kind of landmark case Your Honors wish to be remembered for? It's not, but that's not even the point. The point is it's medieval. It sets civilization back five-hundred years if allowed to proceed. It's up to you to stop it.

"I could stop right here because the picture of such a sicken-ing, cruel, horrifying future for the citizens of this state is so compelling that I'm guessing you would vote this minute to deny accelerated death. But I won't stop there. Let me get into the law as applied to our facts."

Now I present a compilation of state and federal cases that I've drawn together to demonstrate how far over the line of human decency the AG's motion has gone. The judges inter-rupt me twice—which is always welcomed by appellate attorneys. One judge asks why I came from out of state to represent the defendant. "I 'fess up: I'm her father, our knowledge of each other's existence is very recent, and I would do it anyway, anywhere, for anyone if the same case were called to my attention and if I were asked to represent the man or woman on death row. That is my truth in all of this."

The woman judge stops me by holding up her hand; she wants to know how else the state could "cut its losses" in such cases. I am shocked at the congruity between her question and the AG's wish. She appears to be already on-board with the notion of the state saving money in death cases. The only question for her appears to be just how far the state should go to protect its coffers.

"Cut your losses?" I reply. Here's what I want to say: "Other ideas might include cutting back meals to one every other day, no toilet paper, no clean bedding, and, of course, the waste of energy and water in providing hot showers. Probably these should be employed as well as pushing up the date of death."

But I don't say that. Instead, I say, "Where is the law or administrative rule that says the state should consider cutting its losses in death row cases? It seems that the humanitarian ethic of steering clear of accelerated death dates is enough to recommend that losses shouldn't be cut. At least not by an early murder."

"Murder! Counsel," says the Asian judge, "when the state takes a life it isn't murder. When the state takes a life, it's the administration of justice."

I don't hesitate. "You may be right, judge. But what about those cases where, like this one, the defense attorney counsels the defendant not to testify because, unbeknownst to the defendant, the defense attorney is coaxing the trial judge to recommend him to the judgeship recently vacated by the victim. By the way, the victim had raped the defendant when she was in her early teens. That juicy little tidbit would've come out had defense counsel allowed his client to testify. Now, sir, you may call it the administration of justice but I see it as state-sponsored murder carried out by a team of bush league bureaucrats who wouldn't know justice if it bit them in the ass!"

"Counsel!" cries the taller, older judge. "You are very close to being held in contempt of this court. I know the client is also your daughter and that demands a certain leeway as you're bound to be emotional. But please let's try to keep the lid on."

He's right—as far as he's concerned. I can already hear the whispers among the media poised behind me, whispers that will hit the papers and TV screens with some of what's been said here today. Hopefully, they've learned something about the state. Early executions done to save money won't please most citizens. More importantly, maybe some citizens will take the time to register their support of the defendant. The squeaky wheel and all that.

Now it's time to argue my motion for a new trial based on ineffective assistance of counsel in the trial court. I go into the payment by Judge Maxim of the ten thousand dollars to the Committee to Appoint Larsyn to Judge Wilberforce's seat on the bench. I wave around the image of the letter supplied to me by the assistant clerk of the court. There is also the new issue of judicial prejudice previously unaddressed by

Larsyn: the blood-kin relationship of the trial judge Maxim with the so-called victim Wilberforce. Judge and nephew. A few eyebrows are raised at this, and I can hear a stirring behind me from the spectators. Then I go into the rest of it, taking my time, presenting the miscarriage of justice my daughter has suffered, a pebble at a time. As I'm rolling along, I am sure they will grant a new trial with a new judge.

In another ten minutes, I've finished my oral argument and take my seat. Now Lemongrass gets to replay his original argument. That takes less than ten minutes. I swear the guy sounds somewhat deflated and less full of himself, probably attributable to the fact this charade might very well be broadcast to the entire nation at five o'clock and he doesn't want to come across as a hitman for the state.

We wrap up, the room goes silent, the three judges turn in their chairs and consult, and, astonishingly, they turn back, and the taller one announces the verdict.

"The State's motion to accelerate the administration of the death penalty is denied. The defendant's petition for post-conviction relief—including the counter-motion for a change of judge and a new trial—is denied. We are in recess."

Just like that. We are now looking at the original execution date of August 3. Nothing has changed, in the end.

I plod outside, into the bright sunshine, that I pray Cache gets to see and gets to feel on her shoulders some day.

Millie joins me at the flagpole. It flies the U.S. flag and the green, Washington State flag. Back to our left is a thatch of red bushes and off to our right is the roadside sign identifying the court to passing cars. It's a rather unpretentious little building, and that pleases me.

Millie is a mess. Tears stream down her dark skin. She shudders and spreads her arms wide to be embraced. I accommodate her and pull her close. "Thank you," she says through her wracking sobs. "Thank you for keeping our daughter alive nine more days, Michael."

I don't know if she's being sarcastic or means it, but I decide the latter. Millie, ever the scientist, doesn't do sarcasm all that much and maybe not at all. It's been a long time since I've just talked to her and much of her personality is forgotten by me. Verona, who is coming in today, would be happy to know that.

Suddenly the dam inside of me breaks.

"The sons-of-bitches denied my motion for a change of judge even in the face of a ten thousand dollar payoff and even in the face of a close blood relationship between the judge and the so-called victim."

"Something stinks to high heavens."

"Tell me about it."

"Where do we go from here, Michael?"

"State Supreme Court. I've already got the notice of appeal drawn up, printed out, and Marcel is on his way to deliver it because he didn't hear otherwise from me by noon. It's now 12:07 and time's up. I've also attached the identical motion for emergency hearing and crossed the T's and dotted the I's."

"Good on you, Michael. Thanks for that."

I stop looking around at the beautiful day and focus down on her. "Thank me? I'm her father, for godssakes. There's no thanking me! It's my duty, goddamit! And if you had recognized this twenty-five years ago and allowed me access to my daughter and her life we probably wouldn't be here today. Damn you, Millicent!"

She turns away, weeping again. And I feel like a total butthole.

"Come here," I say, turning her with my hand on her shoulder. "That shouldn't have been said. I'm sorry. Look at me. I'm sorry. Do you forgive me?"

She's weeping but manages to jerk a layer of tissues from her purse and removes her sunglasses. She wipes her eyes and then blows her nose.

"No need to ask. You were forgiven before you even said it. I deserved to be talked to like that, Michael. It's a terrible thing I've done. I can't and won't argue with that. It was, and is, terrible."

I pull my sunglasses out and hide behind them. "You know what? I feel like hitting Mickey D's and polishing off a Big Mac with fries. You ready to have a heart-stopping experience with me, Millie?"

"Sure I am. I came here in a taxi."

"Then we'll take my SUV. I think I saw the golden arches a few blocks back. Follow me."

While we head for the SUV, strolling under a cerulean sky that looks as if it hasn't seen clouds in years, Millie does the unthinkable. She reaches over, takes my hand in hers, and squeezes. Just as quickly, she disengages, dropping my hand back down to swing with my stride.

I appear not to notice.

But I have noticed. And I am grateful Verona is hitting town today.

It's just the kind of restraint I need while I'm increasingly unable to rein in my feelings. There's great comfort in a shared catastrophe. We are sharing this morning's right now, and we are very close.

I once loved this woman. Short, sweet, all true.

But there it is.

DAY 14/30

It's a new day—the fourteenth of thirty days.

I got Lucky the dog, and I got really lucky last night.

How did my life go from catastrophe at the court of appeals to an abundance of luck in my life?

It's all happened in my heart, where I really live.

Yesterday, Verona got in late, found my hotel, and rapped on the door while Lucky barked. It was good to see how Lucky's already become territorial. This is his place, he announced with his barks. Verona entered and did a slow look around. Like wives can be, she is territorial, too. It all looked acceptable and singular, so she relaxed. We hadn't seen each other for awhile, so we talked, drank ice tea, and talked some more. Then we snuggled up and made love until two a.m. It was very gentle, and we felt like one person.

Marcel calls and wants to see me this afternoon. He has something to run by me. I ask him to call later, maybe around two or three.

This morning, I am rested, relaxed, and ready to storm the
Washington Supreme Court. Marcel has arranged a ten a.m.
teleconference with one of the justices. He—or she, N.T.
McKinney—will decide whether the court should take up
the matter of the emergency appeal or just deny it out of
hand. I've got my foot in the door, in other words.

But first comes breakfast from the Escoffier kitchen of this
hotel. This morning's dining reminds me that Verona once
attended a month-long Paris culinary school, mastering
everything Le Guide Escoffier had to offer. This was while
she was living in Moscow with her first husband and their
children were young. Verona was very happy then. I know it
more than I hear it, however. I try to get her to speak more of
that incredible time in her life when there was youth, love,
and young children, but it's almost like she's afraid to
go there.

"It hurts to go back over those things," she says whenever I
try to bring it up. "The stars were aligned just so. Then
Mikhail died in that boat in Colombia, and the entire world
changed color. The leaves were no longer green and gold,
but gray; the sky was no longer blue, but an ashen wash; my
children's voices were no longer poetry to a mother but
became as honking geese. His death changed it all, and it
still is all changed. Thank God, there's you, Michael. The
colorless world is slowly recovering."

I can only look at her. But she turns back to the plate of food
before her. She won't look at me. I know how desperately
hurt she is, how much she still loves her dead husband. I
would give her back to him in a second should he reappear,
though it would break my heart because I love her more

than I have ever loved. But if it made her happier to return to him, I would step aside.

But it's not in the cards.

We eat, slowly and quietly, then we pour another cup and retreat to the loveseat in my suite. It is a houndstooth fabric, where we sit, black against white so that it, too, becomes gray. My poor wife, I am thinking.

"Hey," I shout, "why don't we do something terrifically fun today? Like drive over to Coeur d'Alene and have a late lunch or picnic by the lake. With a bottle of wine of your choosing?"

She places her feet side-by-side on the floor and stares down at the symmetry. She lifts her eyes to me to speak.

"No, I didn't come all this way to drink wine and look at a lake. I need to first go and meet our new daughter."

Did I just hear myself correctly? Our?

I love her for the way she takes on my life issue and joins me in it, making it our issue. That's when people no longer feel lonely.

"I thought you might say that," I reply, "let me call the Supreme Court at 9:59, put my petition on the record, and we'll head out to Gig Harbor. Lucky loves to travel."

"Good. You can try one more time to explain to me why we have a new dog. I'm all ears, Michael."

Good, she's back to her usual self.

At 9:59 I dial and find myself on hold while Lemongrass joins the conference call. At 10:02 a voice announces that Lemon-grass is on the line, then I am on the line, and Justice N.T. McKinney comes online. A new voice speaks up. "Gentlemen, this is Justice McKinney. I've read the petition for post-convic-tion relief that was denied yesterday by the Court of Appeals, Division Three, and the response. Mr. Gresham, it's your petition. Please present your case for an accelerated hearing in this court. I'll rule on that before the court takes up the post-conviction relief and its substantive complaints of error."

I clear my throat and begin. Mainly I make the same argu-ment that I made yesterday to the Court of Appeals except this time it's the Supreme Court I'm talking to, and that challenge is not lost on me. It takes all of fifteen minutes, and I'm done. Lemongrass sounds like a recording from yesterday's oral argument; nothing new there.

Justice McKinney cuts right to the point. "Gentlemen, it is my recommendation to the full court that this matter not be taken up by the Washington Supreme Court. We have been over these issues in the previous petition for post-conviction relief filed by Attorney Larsyn—although not all were presented then—and I see no need to rehash. Anything further?"

I make a last stab at showing how my motion for an emer-gency hearing is different than what was presented here by Larsyn over a year ago, but Justice McKinney is dismissive. I'm dead in the water. We thank her and hang up. Lemon-grass' voice is bouncy and glad when we say goodbye to the judge and thank you. I hate him now more than ever.

"Now what?" asks Verona, who was listening on my speak-erphone.

"Now? The federal judiciary is what's now. I'll put together a habeas corpus motion and ask for a writ. That's all that's left."

"You must be horrified, dear Michael."

I shake my head. "That's not desperate enough. I'm way beyond horrified, Verona. I'm desperate and dying inside."

"Desperate times call for desperate measures."

"Meaning?"

"Meaning it's time to act outside the box. It's time to do what no one is expecting."

"Such as?"

"Such as helping our daughter escape. Run away. Flee to South America while she's still in the hospital. There won't be a better time to escape from her guard."

"Guards, plural."

"Whatever. You know what I mean."

"You're not serious about running. Are you?"

"I'd much rather be on the run with Cache than watch her die for something that isn't her fault. No parent would disagree with me."

"True. How would it be done?"

"That, I don't know. That's Marcel's area of expertise."

"Let me think about it. In the meantime, let's hit the road. I'd like to see her before dark."

"How far is it?"

"Something like three-hundred miles. Maybe five or six hours."

"Then let's get moving. Daylight's a-burning."

"John Wayne?"

"John Wayne."

~

On the drive to Gig Harbor, we discuss Mikey and Dania—the younger kids—and Annie, our savant, as well as Danny's parents—presently watching the kids while we're gone. We also discuss my job in Washington, D.C. at the U.S. Attorney's Office. I've run out of vacation days, so there is much to share. We stop for coffee and pie at a Cracker Barrel. It's been years since I've been inside one and I see nothing much has changed. But we have excellent service thanks to a waitress who's premed at UW.

We load back into the SUV. We give Lucky a bowl of water and a piece of the plain hamburger we've purchased. Then we're off again.

Marcel calls. He wants to see me in person. He says he has an issue that can only be discussed in person. This must be what he was up to the other night when he left for Gig Harbor after sundown. We'll talk tomorrow.

Two hours later, we hit the city limits of Gig Harbor and follow the GPS to St. Anthony Hospital. The elevator takes us up to Cache's floor.

Except there is no Cache. We retreat to the nurse's station, only to learn she's been returned to the prison infirmary at

Purdy. We're stunned. I know Lemongrass is behind the sudden transfer back to prison. He's outfoxed me again.

We rush to Dr. Collingsworth's office. He's not available, but his nurse explains that he was in total disagreement with the State's demand that Cache be discharged into prison custody. In fact, the doctor called the governor himself and was told the governor was in complete agreement, that he'd already been advised of the discharge. There was nothing Dr. Collingsworth could do, the nurse finishes. She looks up at us helplessly.

For the first time in a long time, I am without words and direction.

Verona puts her hand on my arm as we ride the elevator back downstairs.

"Maybe it's time to take our case to Big Boy court."

"Federal court, yes."

"It's our only hope, Michael. You've said this same thing many times before."

"True."

"Our only hope, yes. It's Cache's only hope, too.

DAY 15/30

Verona and I decide to head south to Purdy and visit Cache early tomorrow. It's gotten late, and I'm probably best kept away from people right now with my exhausted attitude. I sleep until seven.

My mind hits the floor running at exactly 7:05.

I am in turmoil.

What can I do today that might save Cache? What is my best angle? My mind is moving at high speed now. I'm frantic and don't know where to turn. Then I remember Verona is with me in bed. I snuggle up against her, stealing a few last moments before the fight begins again.

Up and out. Make coffee, take Lucky out to pee and sniff, and back inside.

This is much better now. Dog—coffee—Verona; not necessarily in that order. I sit down at my laptop and take my first sip of Starbucks.

Federal habeas corpus appeals are notoriously difficult to

get. That's the first thing I have to remind myself. But if we are lucky enough to get one then we'll get a new trial out of it.

I begin preparing the petition for filing in the U.S. District Court. I have the option of filing either in Spokane or Tacoma, and I choose the latter. I want to remove it from the good old boys of Spokane as much as possible.

Two hours later, Verona awakens from her deep sleep. I'm quite a way down the road on my petition, and I'm ready for a break. We decided to visit Cache. Verona hits the shower, and I take a last look around the apartment.

While we were away, the apartment complex's maintenance people have replaced the missing drywall Lucky chewed away. I've picked up a wire kennel from Petco. I coax him into it when I hear the hairdryer erupt in its sonic whine. I slide the lock behind him. He's good for a couple of hours now, which is all we need.

Then we set out, me driving, Verona in the passenger's seat. We haven't driven one city block when she asks, "Will I be able to visit with her? Will they let me in?"

"Just remember, you're my paralegal/investigator. You're a member of my staff. That should get you right in."

"I'll tell them."

At the visitors' window, we are successful without blowback. They agree to let Verona in with me. (How could they not? Our client is facing execution in fifteen days.) We're led to a conference room that's new to me. It consists of a desk, two visitors' chairs, and a grated window looking out on a desolate landscape of dead grass and coiled razor wire running

around the top of a ten-foot chainlink fence. A mix of claus-
trophobia and disgust settles over me. Verona, across the
desk, nods solemnly. Something is up with her, too.

Cache is led into the room by a stout woman wearing the
liver-colored uniform of the guards in this place. The
woman is incommunicative and seems to disapprove of our
meeting with her inmate, which I couldn't care less about.

Cache waits until the door closes behind her and then shuffles to me—she's ankle-chained and waist-chained. She lays
her head on my shoulder and shudders. I pull her close and
just hold her without speaking. There are no words that can
make this moment right; no words can lift the oppressive air
in this place. Now she draws back and, without a word,
turns to Verona.

Verona hugs her, too, without hesitation. When she releases
Cache, the girl is crying soundlessly. All hope is gone, the
slope of her shoulders and downcast face tell us. She has
given up.

"I'm sorry I've been unsuccessful so far, Cache. I need you to
know that I'm doing everything I can."

"I know. This is your wife?"

"I am. My name is Verona, Cache. I'm the mother you never
knew you had just like Michael is the dad you never knew
you had. And like your dad, I'm one-hundred-percent
behind you. We're ready to give up everything we have to
save you."

"Okay. What's next?" she asks, and absently cups a hand in
front of her mouth and sniffs her breath. She pulls away
from her own air and scowls. "I don't even get a toothbrush.

I'm on suicide watch; nothing allowed that I might kill myself with. I'm sorry for my smell."

"I love you no matter your smell, no matter what you've done or haven't done in your life," I tell her. "If you had taken a gun and killed this judge I'd love you just the same. You're my kid."

This last part elicits more tears—the last thing I mean to do.

"I wish I'd met you twenty years ago. We would've been great friends."

"That's true. But it's not too late to start. I'm not going to lose you."

Verona shoots me a look of admonishment meant to say I shouldn't promise a result I might not deliver. But I disagree. I'm going to win this thing.

"I've started today writing a petition for a writ of habeas corpus. That's a fancy lawyer way of saying I'm going to the federal court and get you a new trial."

"I don't care what they call it. I just want to tell the jury my story."

"I know you do, Cache. And you will."

"I hope so."

Tears again, and this time Verona joins her, snuffling and dabbing with a monogrammed handkerchief from her purse. I can only sit here and watch, my heart breaking for both of them. So many bygone opportunities to love and be loved.

But I can't allow myself to wallow in it. I have to do this.

"So I need you to tell me the names of other women who you know had sexual intercourse with Judge Wilberforce. Can you give me some names?"

"Sure. There's Blistex, who always had cold sores; there's Wendy; there's Charlotte the Starlet from the porn vids; and Queen Reina, a tranny. I could remember more if you need."

"Do you have full names of these women?"

"What do you mean? I just gave you their names."

"I mean their full names. And where we might find them."

"The streets of Spokane, Michael. East Sprague is the street you want."

"Names?"

She shrugs. "You know all I know. Are they going to be in trouble? None of them have any money, just like me."

"The money goes to their pimps?"

"Yes. Like Inder Singh. He's my pimp. He told me he met you."

"When was this?"

"Sunday visiting hours a few weeks ago."

"He also told me he's your husband."

"Oh, no! He took care of me when it was cold and kept me from getting beat-up or murdered. But he's nobody's husband. He wouldn't ever get tied down."

"How can I get hold of Inder?"

She gives me his phone number from memory. "But don't

call before noon. He stays up late and sleeps in. He'll hate you if you wake him up."

"There's a worry for you," Verona says. She knows her way around sarcasm.

"What do you want with him?" Cache asks.

She has a right to know, and it's no secret.

"I want to get affidavits from the other women who had sex with the judge. Some of them will be HIV positive. We'll get their test results from the county and compare the viruses from all of them to the virus Judge Wilberforce had."

"What do you mean?"

"People with HIV who're taking antiviral drugs and who have suppressed the virus with those drugs cannot give the virus to someone else. I plan to show that was your profile. I also want to show your virus wasn't the same as his virus. That's point number two. If your virus is different from his, then you couldn't have given him HIV."

She looks steadily at me. "None of this was mentioned in my trial."

"I know. I've read all your transcripts."

"Why didn't my lawyer bring it up?"

"We'll get to that down the road. Now tell me, who is your HIV doctor?"

"Eleanor Riddell. She's in Spokane a block off Sprague downtown."

"How long did she treat you for HIV?"

"Ever since I got it."

"How old were you when you got it?"

"Didn't you ask me this already?"

"Maybe. I'd like you to tell me again."

"I was maybe thirteen. Maybe as old as fourteen."

"Just a little kid."

"Tell them that."

I look at her. "You know what? I just might do that very thing. Do you remember any of their names? Probably not, but I want to ask."

"Randy Rosenthaler, Brent Massingill, Dean Driney. That close enough for you?"

I'm not surprised. I would remember names too if I'd been through that horror.

Verona is giving me the evil eye, but I ask anyway. "Do you know where they might be found all these years later?"

"I heard Randy's Humvee hit an IED in Iraq. He's dead."

"What about Brent?"

"He became a counselor at Serenity House. Can you believe that shit?"

"No, I can't. Who runs the place?"

"Some state agency. It's a hellhole. It's outside the city limits of Spokane on the east side. No playground, no gym, just an empty field that freezes over in the winter. If you must know,

Brent was the main guy. He humiliated me when they were done."

"Tell me about that."

"He took pictures of me and posted them online. They got taken down, but everyone at SH saw them first."

I can hardly control my hand as I'm writing these things on a yellow pad. My anger has all but frozen my writing hand.

"What about Dean Driney?"

"Dean is not a bad kid. I think the other guys made him fuck me."

"That's no excuse. Tell me where he is?"

"He's an insurance agent in Seattle. That's the last I heard. He went to U-Dub on a track scholarship."

"Good enough."

"What are you going to do?"

"I need to think about that."

"Meaning you don't want to tell me?"

"Meaning you're on a need-to-know basis about it. Right now there's no need."

Verona stands and moves to the window. She braces herself with an arm across the glass and leans forward, pressing her forehead to the glass. "This place doesn't deserve someone like you," she says to Cache. "You're far too good for the likes of this. You're not even guilty of anything, so why are you even here?"

"Because my lawyer sold me out," Cache replies.

"That's true. Now we just have to make the court see what happened and how the jury verdict might have differed if your lawyer had actually defended you."

We then lapse into small talk for another half-hour until the same guard opens the door and sticks her head in. "Time's up," she says in her command voice.

"No time limit," I tell her sharply. "Attorney visit."

"You've got five minutes then I'm coming in and escorting my prisoner back to her cell. Attorney visit or not."

"How would you like to end up on the wrong end of a Civil Rights lawsuit?" I ask.

"Scare you, scare me. Sue away, white boy. I'll sue you right back for Civil Rights."

"Just leave, please," I ask her. No need to fight the little battles that go nowhere. I realize I'm jumpy, ready to take a swing at anything that looks like a target. So I turn away from her. The door closes as the guard retreats.

"Tell me about your other kids, Michael."

"Well, there's Mikey and Dania. The youngest is Mikey. Then there's Annie, our older daughter. She's working part-time at the U.S. Attorney's Office."

"Lucky girl. I'll bet she likes being around her dad all day."

"We're not around each other all that much. She works two floors down from me in a private office now."

"But she's free. That's what I meant."

"So will you be. Then you can come work with me, too, Cache. If you want."

Her eyes drop to the desktop. "There's something I haven't told you, Michael and Verona."

"Such as?"

"I have a four-year-old son. He's with Inder. That's his father, at least I think he is. He swears he's not, but I think he's wrong about that. My son is dark-complected, and so is Inder. But so am I."

My mind is instantly racing. A grandson? Are you only just now telling me this? Verona looks at me. I try to appear unruffled.

I keep my cool. "I'd like to meet him. Is that possible?"

"Sure. Just tell Inder next time you see him."

"What's your son's name?"

"Leon Russell Evans. Named after my favorite musician. I call him Leo."

"Leo. He's four, you say?"

"Turns four on July twentieth. A great day in my life."

"I'm sure that's true. What is Inder's address? Spokane?"

"Yes, Spokane. 2424 Margot Street. It's not a good neighborhood. We hang in a condo with two other pimps and some girls. It's a huge place that used to be a loft. There's only one window."

"Who's watching Leo now, with you incarcerated?"

"Inder."

"But when Inder's not around?"

"Anyone who happens to be there. We keep an eye out for everyone's kids. It's like a commune."

I'm getting the picture, and I don't like what I'm seeing. Not one damn bit. It's time to pay a visit on Inder. But first comes the federal court paperwork. It has to be filed today. So we don't argue this time when the guard reappears. We hug goodbye and make promises. Cache is led away, and another officer appears to walk us out.

Back in the parking lot, Verona speaks for the first time since we walked outside.

"A grandson? Are you kidding me?"

"I know. Jump in. We've got lots of miles ahead of us."

We pick up Lucky from my apartment and head back to the Davenport Hotel in Spokane. Lots of driving today; Verona is in the back seat lying down; Lucky is sitting in the passenger seat, his snout pressed up by the window, eyeballing the traffic we pass. He's a good dog, easy maintenance, doesn't feel the need to pee on every vertical object he comes across, doesn't bark when he hears a noise outside. A really good guy. I think Verona is getting attached to Lucky as I have.

Once we're in Spokane, the GPS delivers us to 2424 Margot Street. It's an old, industrial-looking building three stories high with a weatherbeaten front door. On the right side sprawls an automobile used parts-store with a junkyard out back filled with the rusted and crushed hulks of motor vehicles that have seen better days. On the left side of the building is a corner grocery with a massive sign advertising lotto and Bud. Everything a local man needs: car parts, games of chance, alcohol, willing women upstairs, and even babysitters. What could go wrong?

We park across the street, make a mad dash ahead of oncoming traffic, and pull open the front door. We're greeted by a gray staircase straight ahead and a white-washed door with no glass and no sign on our right. We take the stairs, me leading the way.

A locked door at the top brings us to a halt. A bare bulb is the only illumination. Cobwebs glisten overhead. Verona looks at me; I turn and rap my knuckles on the whitewashed wood. Voices can be heard inside, plus the wails of a crying child, maybe two crying children. No answer, so I pound on the door. An adult voice goes silent. Then it shouts out, "Who you looking for, fool?"

I guess I'm the fool. "This is Cache's dad. I need to talk to Inder."

We wait, and just as I'm about to knock again, the door opens a crack. A huge man, bare from the waist up, peers out at me. "Wassup, fool?"

"I'm Cache's dad. I need to talk to Inder Singh."

"He ain't here."

"When will he be back?"

"Dude, if I knew that I'ma be the po-lice. And I ain't the po-lice."

"Can we see our grandson?" Verona asks from off to the side.

"You his grams?"

"I am. I really need to hold my grandson."

"Thas all right. Get on up in here."

He stands aside, pulling the door open, and we are hit full-on in the face by a dope haze. I've been around, and I've been where my criminal clients hang, and I know the smell of vaporized rock and burnt weed. You never forget that toxic scent.

"Amy!" our host shouts at a woman reclined on the only piece of furniture in the room, half of a sectional couch. "Get Leon Russell out here."

"He's in back. You get him."

"Bitch, I ain't goan tell you twice. Little Leo, front and center."

The woman drags herself up off the couch, glaring all the time at our host, then lumbers out of the room through a door that appears to be a dark hallway. She returns moments later holding the hand of a small boy. He sees us and turns away. She jerks his arm and all but drags him to us.

"Easy," I say, dropping down to one knee. "What's your name?"

He looks away. I don't blame him.

"Your mama told me to come see you, Leo. I'm your grandpa."

Now he turns his head slightly toward me. Then he jerks away and it's only by leaping after him that the woman can grab his arm and drag him back around to us.

"Would you like to get some ice cream?" I ask. "It's hot in here." It is hot. It's July in Spokane, and muggy in here where there's obviously no air conditioning and the windows are all shut.

He nods without looking at me. "Ice cream."

I look at the black man, who has taken up a position on the divorced sectional couch.

"Can he come with us?"

"Hell no, man. I doan know you."

"I'm Cache's father."

"Cache ain't got no father. Leastways thas what she told me."

"I didn't know I had a daughter until she called me from prison. Right now she wants me to get to know Leo here."

"How we know you gonna bring 'em back?"

"You'll have to trust me. I have no reason not to return him."

"Hell no, dude. Ain't nobody leavin'."

"How about I leave a cash deposit here until I bring him back?"

"Like payin' bail to the judge?"

"Like that, yeah."

"How much we talkin'?"

"I've got five-hundred cash."

"Done. Lessee the Benjamin's."

I pull the money clip from my pocket and peel off five-hundred-dollar bills. I hand them over to the man, who by now has taken up a position between my grandson and me. He's staring at my money clip. It's still got green bills.

"How much more you got?"

"Another five-hundred. I stopped at my ATM last night and today."

"You pay up another five bills and you doan even gotta bring him back."

"Pay him, Michael," Verona exclaims from beside me. "Pay the damn money,"

"You're honestly selling me my grandson?"

"Thas right. One thousand dollars."

"Here we go." I unclip the remaining bills and pass them to my grandson's seller. He riffles the bills and nods. He reaches down and takes Leo's hand and places it on my own.

"Go on, now, Leo. This here's your grandpa."

Leo doesn't make any response. With his hand in mine, I move toward the front door.

"Don't you come back up in here, fool," we're told. "His old man gonna be pissed."

"Let him be. I can handle Mr. Singh."

"Mr. Singh? Who dat?" the man cries and then lapses into a long, knee-slapping laugh. "Get on now. Outta here."

We make the front door and head down the stairs. Leo resists the stairs, so I pick him up under one arm and double-time down to the street door. Across to my SUV we gallop and, once we're inside, Verona buckles Leo into the seat beside her in back. Now it's Lucky, Leo, and Verona.

It's done. We have our grandson, and no one knows where we're headed.

"Ice cream," Leo reminds us. I find a Dairy Queen on my phone and head that way. We eat and then Verona runs into a Target store. Fifteen minutes later, she emerges with a child's car seat. She expertly installs it—she should know how after raising Dania and Mikey through their early car seat days. We plunk Leo into his seat, and away we go. Traffic is light, but I don't hurry. I've got my grandson with me.

Thirty minutes later, we're headed upstairs—me, Verona, Leo, and Lucky—in the elevator just down from the Davenport's main desk. Once we're inside our room, Leo takes the measure of Lucky.

"Is he yours?"

"He is. And I can tell he likes you already."

"I like him, too."

"He needs some essentials," says Verona. "He needs clothes, underthings, toys, coloring books—stuff like that. I'm taking him to the mall."

"Sounds good. How about a suit, too. Something in blue he can wear with a white shirt and bright tie."

"You're thinking court appearance?"

"I am. It never hurts to have them there."

"Done. Okay, Leo, let's go the mall. We need some clothes and toys for you."

"Where's my daddy?"

"We think daddy's at work. But for now, let's have some fun. A shopping spree sound good to you?"

"Can I get a truck?"

"Sure, one truck coming up."

"Up the stairs?"

"No. Well, let's go get one."

"Okay."

After they've trundled off, I set up my laptop on the desk beneath the window and phone down for coffee and pumpkin pie. As I'm waiting, I'm thinking about the habeas corpus petition I'm putting together. In it I'm going to list Larsyn keeping Cache from testifying; Judge Maxim paying off Larsyn; virus differentials—though I haven't spoken to Dr. Riddell yet I think I'm going to strike paydirt on this one; and the other girls' affidavits who had sex with Judge Wilberforce. There will be more as I go along, but all in all it looks like the state had no proof beyond a reasonable doubt at trial because Cache wasn't the only girl with Judge Wilberforce. There were lots of others, maybe the same viruses, maybe not, but we'll never know. So why wasn't this raised at trial by the defense? My argument will be made that Cache was chosen as the fall guy because she had no family in the area, was homeless, had no money/power, and no one cared about her.

Her long history of arrest for prostitution beginning as a

juvenile will break hearts, as will her affidavit recounting Judge Wilberforce's serial rapes when she was thirteen.

With all this in mind, I'm sure she gets a new trial if—and it's a big if—I can get the federal court to even look at the petition. They might refuse on jurisdictional grounds since the case has already been before them once. My ace-in-the-hole with that is my own affidavit of Larsyn's fraud on the court when he appealed and petitioned the first time through. More than anyone, he knew Cache had been screwed, and he knew he was the one who did it. Of course, he brought up none of those things on appeal. That would have cooked his goose and ruined the overall plan. I am ready to make war by the time my coffee and pie make it upstairs to my desk.

Now I can dig in. Lucky wanders in from the bedroom and lies down beside my shoeless feet. He settles his head across my toes and sighs. Sleep comes over him in minutes, and I'm careful not to move my feet after. I like him there on me. I like Leo here, too. And of course, Verona.

My family is enlarging.

Now if I can just count Cache as one more among us.

Marcel and I show up for our appointment with Dr. Eleanor Riddell at seven-thirty the next morning, which is just after she has completed her hospital rounds. We meet in the cafeteria, as arranged. I'm wearing my Cincinnati Reds T-shirt for her to find me. No, I'm not a Reds fan; I found it in the Davenport Gift Shop though no one there could explain why it was on the shelf.

We're waiting at a table along the far windows of the cafeteria, both of us with our chairs turned, surveilling the entrance.

Sacred Heart Children's Hospital is where Cache was taken in, diagnosed, and treated for HIV when she was a young girl. Last night I spoke with Dr. Riddell, and she remembered the case without stopping to think, remembered Cache, and told me she had information about Cache's trial. She also told me that Cache was fourteen when she first began treating her.

Our wait is rewarded in just five minutes. She said her hair was orange and, indeed, it is, as we see when she enters the eatery. She walks with a heaving limp, and I wonder how she can still get around the hospital like that as it must be painful. She reaches our table and smiles at us.

"The hair is a rinse," she announces, "unlike the hair, the limp is real. Osteosarcoma, long bones, right leg."

"I—I—" I have no idea what to say.

"Bone cancer," she says, slapping the diseased leg as she speaks. "You, grab another chair," she directs Marcel, who's already on his feet doing just that.

"And you must be Mr. Gresham."

"Michael, please."

"Eleanor, please. Thank you for the chair, Mr.—"

"Call me Marcel. I'm the investigator."

"Of course you are, dear. You even look like a cop. Were you?"

"Oh yes. Scotland Yard, Interpol—many of them you would know about."

"Be a dear and fetch a coffee, lots of half-and-half, none of that powder crap. Now, Mr. Gresham, you want to talk about Cache Evans? Is that it? Don't worry about HIPPA. HIPPA can eat my shorts when it's like this. Anyway, I've followed her case in the newspapers. Do you know why they never called me to testify?"

"What do you mean?"

"I was all set to testify in her trial, but no one ever called me."

"Who was supposed to call you?"

"The dwarf. Landon?"

"Larsyn?"

"That's the one. Little bastard never called me and never called to apologize for the afternoon I waited around in the hallway outside the court."

"You were actually there?"

"Of course. I wanted to see it for myself. But they said I couldn't come in because I was a witness and witnesses were excluded from the trial testimony part."

"I understand. That's commonplace."

"Why didn't he call me, though?"

"Would you sign an affidavit about what you just told me?:"

"Of course, Michael. What all will it say?"

"That depends on you. What medical testimony did you have that would've helped Cache?"

"Well, your daughter contracted HIV at a young age. It was thought, by me and others, that it was those goddam boys gave it to her. I thought her life was going to get better because CPS placed her with Judge Wilberforce. It turns out that rotten no-good started in on her."

"Started in on her?"

"Rape, Michael. Good old-fashioned rape of a minor. He should've had his nuts cut off."

"Can't argue with your treatment plan, Doc," I tell her with a smile. "Now what medical testimony were you waiting to offer?"

"One thing. The state was proving that it was Cache who gave Wilberforce HIV. But what if he gave it to her? What if she was negative when she went to work for him? Or what if she was positive when she went there but I started her on the HIV cocktail before he raped her? Her virus would've been suppressed by the drugs I was giving her. She couldn't have given him anything. Except maybe the clap. The bastard deserved AIDS, and he got it. Good riddance. But there's a chance it didn't come from Cache. Do you follow me? Why wasn't that introduced at her trial?"

"We can get to that. Right now, it sounds like you're dealing in possibilities, not facts. Am I right?"

Marcel returns with her coffee; she gives him a gracious smile and mouths, "Thank you."

"Take some notes, Michael."

I place my recorder between us.

"That's fine; you may record me."

"Thank you."

"Oh, first of all. I saw on the TV she's on death row. That still true?"

"It is. August third."

"We can't let that happen."

"We won't. That's why your testimony is so critical, Dr. Riddell. Now suppose you school me again. I'm turning on the recorder."

She sits back, stretches out her arms, and yawns. Then she begins.

"Well, when HIV is successfully suppressed by medication, people with HIV can't transmit the virus to others. This is my observation over hundreds of these cases. It's also based on a study by a coalition of community health and HIV/AIDS organizations."

"How does that work?"

"Modern drugs for HIV can often achieve viral suppression, meaning levels of the virus have been reduced to undetectable levels in the blood."

"Okay, I follow that."

"But here was the testimony I was going to give that would've walked her out of the courtroom a free woman."

"Okay."

"Over one million people in the U.S. are currently living with HIV, according to the CDC. Of those, 86 percent are aware of their diagnosis, 37 percent are on treatment to stop the virus from replicating, and 30 percent are virally suppressed. A study published last year in the Journal of the American Medical Association examined the risk of transmission between a person living with well-controlled HIV and their HIV-negative partner. Among 548 opposite-sex and 340 same-sex couples having unprotected sex, only 11 of the HIV-negative partners became positive over about a year and a half of follow up. Would this testimony have helped, Michael?"

"So there was a chance that Judge Wilberforce could've

given HIV to Cache even if he was taking virus suppressant drugs?"

"There's a chance. Also, she could've given it to him. The trouble in all this is that no one can say one way or the other."

"So it can't be beyond a reasonable doubt that she gave him HIV?"

"No more than it can be beyond a reasonable doubt that he gave her HIV. It's medically unknowable who gave HIV if they share the same virus."

"You'll sign an affidavit saying this?"

"Of course. It's the truth, isn't it?"

"You're the expert. But I can tell you this testimony at trial would have ended the prosecution right there."

"Why didn't the little guy let me testify?" She gives me a wide-eyed look as if I might know something secret. And I do.

"I'm working on the 'why'. Bear with me. I'll email you a copy of my petition for habeas corpus, and you can read all about it there. Does that work?"

"Works for me."

She opens her straw purse and peers inside. Then she locates a lipstick, opens a compact and applies a gloss to her lips. With the help of a napkin, she blots her lips. It leaves a kiss on the napkin. She then balls it up and stuffs it into her purse. "Can't be too careful. I won't leave my DNA lying around."

"No, none of us should."

"Why, do you know something?"

I blanch. "No, I just meant...."

"Michael, Michael, I'm only fooling around. Don't take everything so seriously, Michael. Now what about your friend, here? Have you ever shot anyone?"

They're off and running. I switch off my recorder and begin drafting her affidavit as they go back and forth with more of their getting-to-know-you. I could swear she has a thing for Marcel; lots of women do.

Thirty minutes later, I look up. It's as if I've been in a dream state with my affidavit writing. Marcel has left the table, and the doctor has, too. I stand and survey the entire dining room. Nowhere to be seen. With what I already had, I'm ready to get Dr. Riddell to sign her affidavit and then talk to Cache's friends who had sex at the parties with her. After I have collected affidavits from them, I'll be prepared to file the petition for habeas corpus. My last chance to save Cache from execution.

I hunt down Dr. Riddell's office two floors below. Marcel is inside her office, and they are seated side-by-side, this side of the doctor's desk, looking at a book together. Dr. Riddell turns another page. "And this is Florence. The most beautiful silver in Italy. All of Europe, probably."

I enter the room unannounced. "Dr. Riddell, could I get you to look at this affidavit and sign it?"

"Of course, Michael. I was just showing Marcel where I was last summer. Have you heard his Rome stories? The mob has taken over the whole country!"

"I'll have to ask him about that. Here's the affidavit I need you to look over."

It's still on my laptop. She reads slowly, nodding her head and scowling at some points. "Print it out," she says. "Use my printer."

We print it out, and she signs. A clerk from the hospital business office has arrived to watch the signing and now notarizes the document. I have what I came to get.

"Marcel, I know you're enjoying talking with your new friend, but we need to go talk to some other witnesses. Are you ready?"

"Go into the hallway, Michael. I want to talk to Marcel before he leaves."

Expelled, I do as directed. Lord only knows what those two are cooking up. Marcel joins me five minutes on. "Ready?"

"Ready," I say.

I don't even want to know. My daughter is the only thing in my mind at this point.

$\sim$

We've driven up and down East Sprague Avenue at least a dozen times, each time turning around at a street sign warning that the area is an area of high prostitution and that if you're there to further prostitution, your vehicle will be impounded. I've never seen anything like that before.

We are on our twelfth circuit when we spot Inder Singh. He's standing between two young women who're wearing stilettos and miniskirts with bare midriff tube shirts. It doesn't take a Svengali to understand the setup. We park and head back up the block in his direction.

This is a run-down area of Spokane with not a lot of traffic but what there is seems to be cruising the young women strategically positioned up and down the street on both sides.

A car approaches Inder's station. One of the girls leans and talks in the passenger window, climbs in with the driver, and the car crawls away, careful to obey all traffic laws. Can't blame the driver; it would be a damn poor time to get stopped with a young woman who is probably a minor slouched down in your passenger seat. Now Inder sees my face and frowns at me.

"You're taking over my corner, is that it?" he chides me.

"I want to meet some of Cache's friends. I need your help."

"I will help Cache. I won't help you."

"That's fair. I need some introductions to a few girls who attended parties thrown by Judge Wilberforce. This would have been while Cache was living and working there."

"It's no problem. I can take you to twenty girls if you want."

"Maybe three or four. If we could get them all to meet me at a restaurant for five minutes? I'll pay each one a hundred bucks for five minutes of their time."

"Pay the man who brings them. Got it?"

"Sure."

There's a Troxell's Restaurant down on the next corner, and we agree to meet there. Inder will bring the women.

Marcel and I head up the sidewalk, when here comes a prowl car right at us, two cops giving us a long, mean look. Then they turn away and drive on. Another block and we come to an ATM. I make a large withdrawal; there are payments to be made. Marcel makes a withdrawal from his account, too, and passes his bills to me. Now the police car comes back by just as Marcel retrieves his ATM card from the machine's slot. The cops slow way down and almost stop. Suddenly their red-and-blue lights flash, sirens wail, and they are gone. Not a minute too soon, either.

"That's all we need, getting run in for solicitation, Ace," says Marcel.

"Well, we could always call Larsyn to defend us. Ten years in prison sounds about right."

"Larsyn. I'm not done with him," Marcel mutters.

I don't ask what he means by that. I don't want to know.

Then we enter the restaurant, a working person's cafe with burnt coffee you can smell as you enter. Overhead are rows of fluorescents that flicker across the ceiling like some secret code.

We find a table halfway back, large enough for eight, and order coffee.

They begin arriving, two's and three's. They aren't as young as they all looked when we were driving up and down. Or maybe they are, but the life has assaulted the clear complexions and unwrinkled faces and abandoned them behind soul-killing mascara and too, too red lips. I am sorry for them and want to help—as presumptuous as it sounds. I assuage my need to cure the world's ills by reminding myself, for the ten-thousandth time, those ills weren't created by me, and it's not my job to fix them. I'm the complete Catholic at this moment, full-on guilt and all. It will keep. Right now it's time to make my move.

They've settled around, nervously tossing back and forth Yes's and No's in response to questions about money and men. Finally, the bravest of them all looks at me and says, "Well, love, put up or shut up."

I pull out the ATM twenties and hold them up, "I need your help."

"Money first," says the tallest blond of the seven blondes. "Then we talk."

Who can argue? "Money first" is how it's done in their world. I separate the bills into seven stacks, which Marcel distributes, beginning with the nearest woman. Now we're all paid up.

"Cache Evans needs your help."

"We wanted to help like forever," says the blonde who, I'm beginning to realize, is actually a guy. "But nobody asked."

"Now we're asking," Marcel replies.

"We need to know which of you is HIV positive. If you're not HIV positive, you can leave and thanks for coming here today."

The tall one, standing up, asks, "Do we keep the money?"

"Totally. You were willing to help. That's what I paid you for."

Three workers leave. The women now number four remaining.

"I'm going to pass around a yellow pad of paper. Please write your full name and the name of your HIV doctor on the top page. I'm asking you for this because I need to talk to your doctor. Also write your cell phone number there, too. If I need you then I'll need to call you in a hurry."

"You sure you're not the police?"

"No, I'm a lawyer. And I'm Cache's father."

"Cache ain't got no father."

I smile. "She does now. Would you really think I'd claim to be her father if I weren't?"

"No."

"Uh-uh."

"Well, then. Please give up your details on the pad."

Marcel and I wait as the legal pad makes its way around the table. Five minutes later, we thank everyone and tell them they can leave.

"Fastest hundred bucks I ever made," says one.

"You mean on your feet, Roberta."

"Oh, whatever, Joanne."

They giggle and push each other in jest as they file out of the eatery.

"What do you say to some breakfast, Marcel? I'm starving."

"Do we have any money left?"

I tell him we do.

"Then order us the blue plate special. I'm going to the men's room and try to wash this place off me."

I get it. He made skin-to-skin contact with several of our visitors.

Old habits, even knowing what modern medicine says about suppressed viral loads.

~

Seven o'clock that same night finds Verona and me, plus Leo and Lucky, in front of the TV watching an animated movie about despicable something-or-others. Leo laughs uproariously, and that's all that matters. He hasn't asked about Inder Singh not even once. Marcel knocks on the door, and I let him in. We retreat to the dining table in the adjoining room of my suite.

"I made contact with all the doctors," he says. "They all helped us."

"Without releases?"

"They called the patients on their cell phones and got verbal OK's. It's all legal, boss."

"What do we know?"

"We know that three of the four women have the same virus Judge Wilberforce had."

I shake my head. "Wow. Three names that might've passed the virus to the so-called victim."

"Yes, I faxed everyone the judge's autopsy and blood studies. All matches except for the one named Mickey."

"The guy."

"Exactly. I called him and told him we wouldn't be needing him. I have an appointment to meet the rest of them tomorrow morning at ten o'clock, Troxell's Restaurant again."

"I've got the affidavit template ready. Let's plug in the names and print out the papers. You'll take them and get them signed in front of a notary."

"Where do I get a notary?"

"The hotel concierge has a notary on staff. She'll be accompanying you."

"That must've cost s fortune."

"Actually, it didn't cost a penny. This hotel is incredibly helpful to its guests."

"Amazing place."

In another twenty minutes I have all the affidavits printed and in a folder in Marcel's hands.

"Take care," I tell him.

"You know me, boss. I'll take it any way I can get it."

"Speaking of, have you seen Dr. Riddell again? Any plans?"

"Dinner tomorrow night. I think she likes me."

"I'd guess she does. What's not to like?"

"Flatter me, boss."

"One more thing, before I forget. Brent Massingill? Dean Driney?"

"Massingill teaches social studies at Serenity House. He lives about a mile west of there. Driney is listed as an Independent insurance agent in Seattle. Name, address, phone. They're both easy."

"Good. A couple more days and we'll go."

"Your call, Boss."

I smile.

"I've got a one-eyed character in goggles to get back to. Consider yourself free to wine and dine the ladies."

"All of them?"

"Yes."

"G'night, boss."

"Call me tomorrow when it's done. The habeas corpus papers will be ready to attach and have you walk over to the federal court. The game is afoot."

"Afoot? Shakespeare?"

"Gresham."

DAY 17/30 (MORNING)

Today is cloudy with intermittent rain. I am watching the clouds roll by at 5:30 a.m. and finishing the argument I'm going to say to the district court if the judge agrees to hear my petition for habeas corpus.

Basically, I'm going to be all about the conspiracy to convict my daughter of first-degree murder.

I pull away from my laptop and study the rain. It's heavier, raining at a slant, and I am finished with the keyboard. Time to see my daughter and take my grandson along. Maybe they'll let her see him one last time before the execution. I'm going to try. It's also Leo's birthday; I owe him no less than to try for a visit. Maybe even get a picture of him and mom together.

I'm still enjoying the early morning quiet when there's a loud knocking on my hotel door. I open and find Marcel standing there with his folder. He's dripping wet, but the folder was evidently carried inside his shell jacket and is dry.

"You aren't going to believe it," he says as he comes into my living room, water beading on the tip of his nose. "I talked to the women last night. Two of them told me Franklin Lemongrass came to see them during the trial. He paid them off to disappear, so Larsyn had an excuse for not calling them to testify."

"They told you this?"

"They told me they were paid off. The second half is my conclusion."

"It's probably accurate. In fact, I'm 100% sure it's accurate. We can argue your conclusion. But first, we need a supplemental affidavit for the women about being paid off."

"No need. I got on your pleading on Dropbox and opened it up. I added an extra sentence to the affidavit that now includes being paid off by Lemongrass. It's all right here, boss," he says, and he hands me the file folder.

"You're a genius. Thank you."

I read through the affidavit. The extra part he added is perfect. It's also very short and makes the point the affiant was paid off by Lemongrass to hide away during the trial. I'm excited to have it.

Marcel wants coffee. I call downstairs for a pot.

"So what do you need from me today, boss?"

"I need you to ride over to Purdy with me. I'm going to try to get Leo in to see his mother. If I can't, I'd like him to wait outside with you while I have a visit."

"Who's driving?"

"How about you. I'll ride in back with Leo and keep him involved in games and books."

"He already has games and books? You guys don't waste any time."

"Think Verona, Marcel. She's always on the front line."

"Love that woman. You're a lucky man, boss."

"What about you, Marcel? Seeing Eleanor Riddell again?'

"Tomorrow night. That's the second night this week."

"Just don't get her pregnant."

"Boss, she's fifty years old."

"Yes, but you're inordinately virile, Marcel. Keep your distance. Protected sex only, chum."

"Good grief."

Our coffee arrives, and we enjoy just sipping and looking out at the rain. We've been together a long time. I don't know what I'll do with myself when our run comes to an end. I think about that sometimes. It's very difficult because he could fall in love or decide to move away or any number of things that would take him away. He's irreplaceable, though I have a son in D.C. who I would try to enlist maybe in a new law practice. I'm working on that.

∾

The deputies manning the front office of the prison are sympathetic. Leo will be allowed inside with me to visit his mom. Ten minutes later and we're all three together as Marcel says he'll wait in the lobby. He's giving us family-space.

She starts crying the second she enters the conference room and sees Leo. But she keeps it under control for Leo's sake. He's in love with his mom and runs to her, flinging his arms out wide and hugging her for all he's worth. It's such a touching moment that I have to look away to avoid breaking down.

"Today's his birthday, Michael."

"I know it is. He's here to have you sing happy birthday to him. They let me inside with this." I open my briefcase. Inside are three Dolly Madison chocolate cupcakes I picked up at a 7-Eleven on the drive over. Also a box of birthday candles and a lighter. There will be a celebration.

She is laughing-crying with joy and comes around to hug me. This is the first time a hug has happened at her behest. I'm deeply moved. I have another kid back in the fold. Last night I talked to the three at home in D.C. and let them all talk to Leo. Exciting times for everyone.

While Leo crumbles his cupcake and piece-meals it into his mouth, I use the moment to update Cache. Her blue eyes are dazzling as she looks from me to her son as I go on. His skin is dark, like Cache's.

"So we're headed back to Spokane when we leave here, and I'm going to walk your petition through filing in the federal court and take it up to the judge and beg for an accelerated hearing."

"Is it going to work this time?"

I can only look at Leo as I answer her. "I think so. I'm praying."

"Guess what, Michael? I'm praying too. I didn't know I was a believer."

"Being on death row would make a believer out of anyone."

She lifts her son into her lap and cuddles him. I can see in her eyes that she is saying goodbye. She knows she won't see him again unless I can make magic happen. She is wracked with soundless sobs, but Leo doesn't seem to notice. He's licking chocolate goo from his fingers and pushing off from his mother's chest. Now he looks up into her eyes. "Crying, mama?"

"Just a little, sweetheart. Mama is so happy you're here."

"Me too! I love birthday cake that grandpa brought."

Did I just hear correctly? Am I grandpa now? My skin tingles. I'm a happy man.

Then the guard sticks his head inside. "Five minutes. What's the little guy got all over him?"

"Birthday cake. It's his birthday."

"They let you in here with that?"

"They did. There was a miniature hacksaw blade hidden inside the cupcake."

"Get outta here," the guard says with a shake of his head. But he does pull the door shut and gives us a few more precious minutes together.

"He's one of the nice ones," Cache explains. "He brings me books."

"What do you read?"

"Mostly lawyer stuff. I would've made a great lawyer, just like my dad."

I'm flattered. "We'll have to talk about that. It's never too late, you know."

Leo climbs out of his mom's lap and looks around at the ugliness of the room, the mint walls, the barred window, the air made fetid by the summer rain beading down the window glass. Then his face changes and he picks up the paper from his cupcake. He begins licking it.

"You made my day—Dad."

"I'm glad." It's all I can do not to break down. Dad, indeed.

The door opens and our little family hugs and kisses one last time. Then Leo turns his face to me, "Is mommy coming?"

"Not just yet. Mommy has more to do here first," I tell him.

"Don't cry, Mommy, I'll come back."

"I know you will, my precious. I'll be here waiting for you."

"Okay, bye then."

Leo takes my hand and pulls me back in the direction we came. The guard speaks into his shoulder microphone. "Guard will be right here, Mr. Gresham. They can take you out."

The four of us wait in the hallway until our escort rounds the far corner. Then Cache is taken off in the opposite direction as Leo, and I head back up the hall toward the escort.

She turns and looks back at the exact second I do. She waves. I wave back.

Then we collect up Marcel and hurry outside.

Like always when I get outside the fence of one of these places, I inhale a chest full of free air.

"How did it go?" Marcel asks.

"She was happy. Leo was happy. I'm happy. You two head back to Spokane. I'm off to Tacoma to save my kid."

It's prearranged. I have a hotel in the city where I'll be filing the habeas petition and attending court—if I'm lucky enough to get the court to hear it.

Marcel pulls over and waits until I hail a cab and am driven away. It's only fifteen miles and change to Tacoma.

It's almost two o'clock when I arrive at my hotel. I check-in then head to the federal courthouse on Pacific. It's Thursday. I have high hopes for this afternoon. I have to.

It has to work.

DAY 17/30 (AFTERNOON)

We take Leo back to the hotel. Heading for the elevator, we spy Verona and Millie talking downstairs at the Starbucks counter. They wave us over. We catch up on Cache; we catch up on Leo's birthday, and we make small talk about the drive and the weather. Then I head upstairs, alone, to print out my pleading and make copies for the court and the U.S. Attorney. I re-read everything for typos then head downstairs for a cab ride over to the district court. I'm alone; I don't need or want anyone with me. It would only be a distraction. It always comes down to this anyway: me and the judicial system. We're in for a struggle, both of us.

Every other filing is expensive. But the fee for filing an application for habeas corpus is only five dollars. They want everyone to have access to the court for habeas corpus filings. A fair first step for any inmate in the country.

Up to the clerk's filing counter I stride as if I own the place. A clerk across the secure area behind the counter sees me looking at her. I know she's a filing clerk; you can tell by how they look up when you enter the office. No one else looks up, but the filing clerks are always ready to help.

She makes her way to the counter and smiles at me. "Yessir?"

"I need to file this application for a writ of habeas corpus."

"Is this a new filing?"

"It is."

"Got five bucks?"

I hand her a five-dollar bill. She leaves it lying on the counter between us as she thumbs through my papers. It's all there, and it's thick enough to carry the weight that it does.

"What about the application for accelerated hearing I'm filing? How does that get handled?"

She smiles. "I will personally hand-carry a copy of this filing upstairs to the judges. Give me a number where I can call you."

I've rarely been treated this well in a court anywhere anytime. I write out my phone number and hand it over.

"As soon as I know something I'll call."

"What's your name?"

"Kitty Hawkins."

"I am so grateful for your help with this. Thank you."

She levels her gaze at me. "Counsel, were I sitting on death row instead of this woman I'd want someone just like me to help at this point. Getting this heard on an accelerated basis is critical, and I know that. I won't stop until it's docketed. Then I'll call you. Are you getting your five dollars worth?"

I smile. "It's a good start. We'll see what comes next."

"Wish me luck," she says and heads for the hallway. I follow her out and watch as she disappears upstairs.

Now I feel useless. What to do? Do I leave the courthouse and go back to the Davenport? Or do I wait around to see if, for some reason, the court would want me to appear in court or chambers today? I decide to stick around.

Outside, a motorist at a red light gives me directions to a coffee shop. It feels good to stretch the legs.

Down to the corner and up two blocks I go, no hurry, taking in the sights and sounds of this afternoon on my grandson's fifth birthday. Just the thought of him puts a spring in my step. The thought of him and his mother reunited, however, brings me to a sudden stop. I decide to go back where I can be closer to the court, not further away.

Retracing my steps, I feel my phone vibrate in my suit pocket. U.S. District Court calling. I answer.

"Mr. Gresham, this is Kitty Hawkins. You're on before Judge Malfi Acosta at nine o'clock tomorrow morning. You can access a copy of the order he just signed. It'll be on the court's website after six tonight. How am I doing so far?'

"Five bucks is all this cost me? This is better than Costco."

"We aim to please. See you in the a.m., Mr. Gresham. Get a good night's sleep, sir."

"I cannot even begin to thank you, Kitty."

We hang up. Using my phone, I browse to 1-800-Flowers and order a vaseful of flowers for Kitty and her office mates. It will be delivered tomorrow.

I grab a cab and set off for the hotel. In the backseat, I'm reminded, for some random reason, of Tinkerbell and Peter. "Clap if you believe in fairies," Peter tells the audience.

I clap, quietly, in the backseat. Not because I believe in fairies but because sometimes there's a Kitty Hawkins I can believe in.

The driver looks at me in the rearview mirror. "You clapping back there?"

"I am."

"Same price. Knock yourself out."

DAY 18/30

I am seated at counsel table at 8:30 on Friday morning when in walks Franklin Lemongrass and a man I don't know. Both men are wearing gray suits the color of ash and talking animatedly, stepping on each other's lines, locked in strenuous disagreement. In fact, the nearer they get, the more I realize they're having a knockdown drag-out fight.

"Morning, gents," I pipe up in a bright voice. "Did you leave the clown car parked out front?"

Neither bothers to answer. They're stewing, refusing to speak to each other and, of course, ignoring me. Which is fine. I'm after Lemongrass anyway. Marcel has dibs on Larsyn, but I've got Lemongrass, this mean little bastard from the AG's office. Right now I'd stand up and batter Lemongrass around the head if I thought I wouldn't go to jail for it, but I would. So, we'll settle this with our brains instead of our brawn.

Today I know and can prove Larsyn and Judge Maxim

greased the rails for Cache by paying off streetwalkers so they wouldn't be available for Cache's trial. It turns out Larsyn wasn't ever going to call them anyway, but it's still there, the conspiracy.

"Did you girls get my application?" I chide them. Again, no answer.

"Is this it?" Lemongrass at last replies, holding up my petition and my emergency motion. "I thought this was toilet paper you sent over as a joke."

I ignore him. "Are you planning on filing a written response? If so, how about passing over a copy before court begins."

"Oh, it isn't here yet," says the second gray suit.

"And who are you, sir?" I inquire.

"Steve S. Shofelt, Assistant U.S. Attorney. I'm appearing on behalf of the U.S. Attorney's Office. By law, we're to litigate these cases."

"And your position on the death penalty, in this case, is what?" I ask.

"Our position is that your client should be executed."

"Oh, I've never just gone along with the state like that. I have my views on these cases."

"Meaning?"

I spread my hands. "Meaning that as a trial lawyer in the Washington, D.C. Attorney's Office I've never been asked to work alongside any state attorney's in federal court. It's new to me."

"Hold on. You're an assistant U.S. Attorney?"

"I am."

"Then you have a conflict of interest in appearing here as defense counsel in the court where you're a prosecutor. A major conflict of interest. I'm going to request the court to excuse you from the case by that conflict."

My heart jumps in my chest. This had crossed my mind several weeks ago, but I had stuffed it down, ignored it. Now it surfaces again and, while I hate to admit it, Steve S. Shofelt is correct. I shouldn't appear with this conflict. There's only one thing I can do, but I wait for the court to address the issue first.

As soon as Judge Malfi Acosta takes the bench, she peers over the top of her reading glasses. "Gentlemen, the court has been called to order. We're on the record in the Cache Evans post-conviction matter. Does either side have any preliminary matters before we proceed to the merits of the petition for writ of habeas corpus?"

It's a setup. Ordinarily, a judge wouldn't ask for preliminary matters in a motion setting like this. These two gentlemen have approached her ex parte, meaning, without my participation. A very dirty and illegal thing to do. But Judge Acosta seems to have overlooked it and is now coming after me.

Shofelt is immediately on his feet. "Your Honor, we've just learned that counsel for the petitioner is an Assistant U.S. Attorney in Washington, D.C. As such, he should be conflicted out of this case."

She doesn't miss a beat. None of this is new to her—I see it now.

"How do you respond to this counsel?" Judge Acosta asks me.

That was short and sweet. She's coming after me, and I know it. First the behind-the-scenes meeting and now turning the court's eye on me. I know what I must do.

"Your Honor, just this morning I have resigned my position with the U.S. Attorney's Office. I'm here as private counsel for the defendant."

Shofelt stutters but doesn't manage to make an intelligible response except to say he'd like me to produce a copy of my letter of resignation. I say I will today before five o'clock.

He re-takes his seat. Now I've got a new angle to deal with: I'm going to have to resign from a job I've enjoyed. But the other side of the coin is that Cache's life comes first before my career. It's done, and it stays done.

"Very well, counsel, but please provide the court with a copy of your letter of resignation as well by five p.m. today. Do you understand?"

"Perfectly, Judge."

"All right, it's your motion today, so please proceed."

"May it please the court. *United States Code Title 28, Section 2254(d)* requires that a state court apply established federal law in its adjudication of a prisoner's claim for habeas corpus relief. This flows from the case of *Strickland v. Washington*, where a federal test was developed that a criminal defendant can seek relief for an ineffective assistance of counsel if he proves (1) that his counsel's performance was objectively unreasonable, and (2) his counsel's error prejudiced the outcome of the case.

"In a nutshell, if Cache Evans can show—which she can—that Attorney Kelly Larsyn's defense of her in the state court was unreasonable and that his negligence prejudiced her, she is entitled to habeas relief. On this basis, we are here today. I have attached affidavits from Eleanor Riddell, Millicent Evans, a clerk of the court, several ladies of the night, and me, which show how Larsyn did everything he could to throw my client's case, to allow her to be convicted.

"Moreover, I've proven by affidavit that Attorney Larsyn and Judge Maxim conspired to have the jury find my client guilty of first-degree murder in the death of Judge Hiram Wilberforce, the nephew of Judge Maxim, the trial judge. Judge Maxim's letter and donation to Larsyn are in the file. These are major grievances all, any one of which is grounds enough to set my client free and dismiss the case against her. Which is what we're asking the court to do. I have more I can offer, but I would ask that the court first read my complete motion and the affidavits and letter and blood tests mentioned."

Judge Acosta pushes her readers back up on her nose and clasps her hands on the desk before her. "Counsel, I have read your affidavits. And the court finds that, as a matter of law, the *Strickland* test doesn't apply in this case."

I'm immediately panicked, but I keep it tamped down and respond.

"Judge, the *Strickland* case is settled law from the Supreme Court. It cannot just be set aside in one of these cases merely because you decide to set it aside."

"Counsel, are you seriously telling me how I can run my

court and how I can make the rulings I make? Is that your motif here today?"

"It isn't, but on the other hand I am the advocate for Cache Evans, and I know, and counsel knows, and the court knows the *Strickland* Test is mandatory. It's a requirement."

"Having read the motion and all attachments, the court finds that, as a matter of law, there is not an objectively unreasonable fact situation raised by you, counsel. The matters you have listed out are all questionable, particularly the conspiracy notion. I happen to know Judge Maxim, and I know him to be a man of unquestionable honesty and integrity. He wouldn't conspire with anyone ever for any reason, and the court takes judicial notice of that integrity."

"Judge, what about the fact Mr. Larsyn did not attempt to show Judge Wilberforce's HIV could come from several other women he had sex with? Does the court take judicial notice of Wilberforce's integrity too?"

"I believe Judge Wilberforce when he says he was blackmailed by your client. What happened after that, I have no way of knowing. But, yes, I cannot find that the affidavits of prostitutes and a convicted murderer can overcome the integrity and value I place on Judge Wilberforce's claim. He just can't be overruled like you would have it, counsel. I'm not prepared to do that. I won't do it. Anything further?"

"No, Judge. I get it. I've just been home-towned. Judges looking out for other judges."

She ignores me and plunges ahead with the intention of quickly ending our session.

"Counsel for the State of Washington, anything you'd like
to add?"

"No, Your Honor."

"Counsel from the U.S. Attorney's Office, Mr. Shofelt?"

"Nothing, Your Honor."

"Very well, the court denies the petitioner's request for a writ
of habeas corpus. The execution of your client will continue
as ordered by the governor, Mr. Gresham. We stand in
recess."

I sit there, stunned.

Lemongrass and Shofelt are chuckling among themselves.
Whatever hostility that existed between them before has
dissipated. They are patting backs and allowing each other
to go first out of the courtroom until they're all but falling
over each other. I turn in my chair because, as they waltz
each other up the aisle, Lemongrass turns to me and calls
out, "Counsel, we have one ticket left for a ringside seat to
your client's execution. You can bring a date with you."

I shove my briefcase aside and turn to run up the aisle after
this insane person.

But, luckily, Marcel has come into the courtroom and
evidently observed the proceeding. From the rage on his
face, I can see he has also heard Lemongrass's insult. He
steps into the aisle, blocking me from murdering an
assistant attorney general.

"Let it go, Ace. You're gonna kick their ass before it's done.
And then you're going to sue them personally, their wives,
and their kids."

He couldn't have arrived at a better time. Marcel is a necessary ingredient in my life when the bad guys are after one of my kids.

I would kill for my family.

BRENT MASSINGILL

W e fly back to Spokane and rent a car at the airport. Marcel swings by a pawn shop. He tells me to wait in the car. He returns ten minutes later with a small case. I don't even ask.

He drives us east of Spokane. He knows the way to Serenity House, and he drives by and gives me a look. It appears to be an abandoned grade school with after-thought living quarters constructed from doublewides. There are few lights burning where the children would be housed. I check my watch. It's still early, just dark.

"Hang on. Now we're headed to Massingill's place."

"How far?"

"Less than a mile."

"Does he live alone?"

"He does. I've been out here a half-dozen times, and he's the only one out and about. It's a small apartment anyway. Wouldn't hold but maybe one more person."

I look at him quizzically across the dashboard light. "How would you know how many people it would hold? You've actually been inside?"

"Now, Boss. You know better than that."

"Sheesh. Just don't get busted."

"Now, Boss. You know better than that."

A head shake. I do know better than that.

He turns off his lights as we round the corner onto Bayonne Road. Then we travel maybe a hundred feet, up into a parking lot, where we pull into an empty slot. It's a small complex, maybe six apartments, ranch-style. The grass is high, and the cars parked around are at least ten years old.

We get out, close our doors without slamming, and head for the farthest porch light.

Marcel is lugging the small case he's purchased from the pawn shop. I have no idea what we have.

I knock on the door. Marcel rings the bell.

In less than fifteen seconds the door opens and a youngish man—maybe thirty years old—stands looking out at us, his mouth agape. "So?" he greets us.

"We're selling insurance," says Marcel.

"Don't need insurance." He begins closing the door.

But Marcel inserts his boot. "Not yet. You haven't heard our full spiel."

The man shrugs and steps back. He's outnumbered, so we simply step inside. There's a TV against the back wall and a portable air conditioner humming in the west corner. A bamboo-frame couch with a forlorn looking footstool is arranged near the tube.

"Anyone else here?"

The young man looks at Marcel. "Who the fuck are you guys? I've got a gun."

"Go get it if you want to die. You might wish you had done just that by the time we get finished. Lead me to the kitchen."

"Fuck you!"

Marcel hands me the case he's carrying. With a punch so swift it would make Ali jealous his right-hand strikes Massingill's throat. Our host immediately crumples to his knees, gasping for air. "What...the..."

"Like I said. We're going to the kitchen." He holds out a hand and pulls Massingill to his feet. We pass into the next room.

Massingill flips on the light, and I get a good look at him. His hair is buzzed, and he's wearing a wife-beater with a picture of Mickey Mouse ogling a sweet young mouse. Show Me Your Mouse? Mickey is asking her. I don't get it.

"Have a seat," Marcel tells Massingill. He looks around and sees Marcel means the kitchen table. It's small, pushed up against a wall, a chair at each end, one in the middle.

Massingill sits on the right end of the table. He still hasn't taken his hand away from his throat. He hacks and coughs, and I realize he's trying to make it appear much worse than it really is. Sympathy ploy.

Marcel opens the lid of his case and removes a portable

tattoo machine. There are three vials of ink attached, red, black, and green. "What color are you partial to?" Marcel asks. "It better be red, black, or green."

"What the fuck?" says Massingill, who by now has recovered enough pride to give off a whiff of belligerence. Exactly the opposite of what he should be doing with Marcel.

"The fuck?" Marcel mimics. "This machine right here is insurance. You bought a policy."

"What the fuck?"

"Oh, yes. It's gonna give young girls an insurance policy guaranteed to make them run from you."

"What—what—"

"You can get your tattoo free. It's either on your tongue or your forehead. Take your pick."

"What—what--"

"Forehead you say? Fair enough. Now lean forward while I do you."

"Do me? You're seriously thinking I'm gonna sit here and let you tattoo me with that thing?"

"Oh, that's right. You were going to rape me instead. Just like you raped Cache Evans. Remember her, asshole?"

"Cache Evans? Yes, I—no!"

"Like I said, forehead or tongue?"

"Neither one. I'm calling the police."

Again with a punch so fast it's a blur. When Marcel pulls his hand away, the teacher's nose is smashed off to one side of his face. Cartilage is just below the surface, and both nostrils are flowing red.

"Now lean the fuck forward, teacher!"

This time there's no hesitation. Marcel lifts the business end of the machine and begins playing the needle across Massingill's forehead."

"Boss," says Marcel without taking his eyes from his work. "How do you spell 'rape' again? Oh, never mind. I just found it right here on this asshole's forehead."

It takes almost two hours. But when Marcel switches off his machine, there is inscribed across Massingill's forehead two lines of text. The first one says, "I Rape Girls." The second line says "#MeToo."

The letters are done in black. But they are edged with a red stroke, giving them a neon appearance clear across the room. I'm standing in the doorway, and it's very clear.

Massingill looks into the mirror that Marcel makes of his iPhone. "Read it and weep," he tells his client.

Massingill opens his eyes and peers into the mirror. His mouth drops open and tears stream down his face. His wife-beater now shows a bloody Mickey beneath a shower of teardrops.

"Was she worth it?" Marcel asks, standing and coiling the machine's hose around his hand. "Did you get your money's worth?"

Massingill cannot speak.

"If I ever hear of you having sex with any human again in

your stupid life," Marcel hisses, "I will be back. You don't want me to come back."

Massingill nods. "Yessir."

Marcel motions the young man to stand up and guides him back to the other room, pressing him gently down upon the bamboo couch. Marcel bends and lifts Massingill's feet back onto the footstool.

"Comfy?"

There is only crying. There are no words.

"I think we're about done here, Cache's daddy."

The kid's eyes jerk up at me in terror. I can only smile and shake my head. Then I tell him, "Your life just developed a significant problem." I sound every bit like a lawyer. It cannot be helped.

Massingill is blubbering, looking away, tossing his head back and weeping.

"Keep it zipped up," Marcel whispers. Then he delivers a powerful fist to the guy's groin. "Zipped."

Then we're gone.

DAY 19/30

I can't sleep—not after all that.

I'm up all night drafting and fitting together the pieces of the new appellate brief, but it's still not finished. On the other hand, filing the notice of appeal and request for an emergency hearing in the Court of Appeals for the Ninth Circuit is a simple matter. Logging onto Pacer and clicking a button gets the job done within minutes. It's 6:44 a.m. when I finish.

Now I've got the whole day ahead of me to finish and file the brief itself. But I'm missing a critical piece of evidence from Cache. It's time to drive over and visit her. It's how I want to pass the day anyway, spending every minute with her that I can.

Time to get dressed; then I stop. I hear Leo crying out in his bedroom. So I head down the hallway to keep him company. Verona meets me there. "I know you want to go to Purdy. How about if we take Leo to see his mama again?"

"You know, that's a terrific idea, but I think this time I want to take my recorder and go alone. I'll dictate my appellate brief and be ready to get it typed up."

"You've asked for an emergency hearing?"

"I have. I'm praying they'll handle it on that basis. We've got eleven days is all."

"Well, we'll miss you around here, but I understand. I think I'll find a dinosaur museum and take Leo today. Something he can have fun with. He's been ignored for way, way too long and needs lots of one-on-one. When you have his mama out of prison, and back home with us, she'll need a lot of time to be with him."

"Wait a minute," I say. "Did you just say 'back home with us'?"

"I did. I want Cache to come to D.C. with us and let us help her get a new start."

"You're reading my mind."

"I know you. But I want her, too. She's our daughter. Besides, Millie's had her chance. I think Cache would be glad to be out of this place. Too many old memories. Too many slippery places. She needs a new crowd, a do-over."

My phone vibrates in my pocket, and I pull it out. It's Marcel. I don't want to talk to him right now, so I refuse the call.

I'm in the bedroom, holding Leo and making faces with him when my phone vibrates again. I don't bother to fish it out of my pocket this time—Leo and I are busy doing alligator faces.

Fifteen minutes later, I'm filling my thermos for the drive

down to Purdy when my phone vibrates yet again. Marcel calling. This time I answer.

"Where the hell you been?" he says without any niceties up front.

"Playing with Leo. What's up?"

"It's Franklin Lemongrass. He's been found shot to death in his parking garage at work. The cops are interviewing everybody. I just wanted to give you a heads-up."

"Why me?"

"The other day coming out of court. One of the deputies saw you go chasing up the aisle after Lemongrass. The deputy didn't do anything because I stepped between you two. My guess is no one around the courts much cares for Lemongrass. But that's only speculation. Anyway, that deputy remembered you, and now the FBI called me, looking for you."

"Well, I can't say I'm surprised. I'm sure I'm not the only one he's offended."

"It's the murder of a high profile victim. The FBI wants in."

"But murder isn't federal in a case like this."

"It is in this one. It turns out Lemongrass also served as tax counsel for the U.S. Trustee in bankruptcy court. That makes it federal."

I don't know what to say. Lemongrass is dead, and the FBI wants to talk to me? This cannot be happening.

Marcel speaks again. "You haven't purchased any firearms out here in Washington, have you?"

"No."

"Wait one; I've got an incoming from the agent who called me. Be right back."

So the phone goes dead, and my coffee isn't getting any hotter. I've also made a tuna fish sandwich and have made a mess of this mini-kitchen area. I screw the lid down onto the thermos. Not wanting to leave my mess for Verona, I go about cleaning up.

Phone again.

"Who was it, Marcel?"

"FBI. They've made an arrest. A guy we were seen with at Troxell's Restaurant out on East Sprague. Remember the girls we met—the ones Inder Singh brought to us?"

"I do."

"It's Inder they arrested. FBI says he wants you to defend him. He's also told them you have the kid. CPS wants the kid. What about defending Singh? What do I say?"

"Impossible. I'm not licensed in Washington."

"But you are in federal court all the way up to the Supreme Court of the United States."

"Sorry, Marcel. My daughter is the only thing I think about lately."

"I don't doubt it. So what about it? You going to talk to Inder?"

"Why should I?"

"Feds know everything. It seems he was sued for paternity

by the State of Washington to make him pay support for Leon Russell Evans."

"Leo?"

"Yes. The blood tests ID'd Mr. Singh as your grandson's father."

"Oh, hell, no!"

"Sorry to ruin your perfectly good day, Michael. But I think you need to step up for Inder Singh, mainly out of self-defense."

"I don't understand the connection. How am I involved?"

"Look, CPS told the FBI they were looking for Leo. They've declared him at risk. They'll take custody and place him."

"Place him? I'm the grandfather."

"But you're a non-resident. They won't place him with you while you're living out-of-state."

"Why not?"

"It seems Singh has got a sister here who's a physician. A pediatrician. She wants temporary custody."

"That's not going to happen!"

"Slow down, Boss. I recommend you hire an attorney. Someone to represent your interests in the juvenile case that's going to be filed today."

"I suppose you told them Leo's whereabouts?"

"Boss, I didn't. But seriously, how long do you think it's gonna take the FBI to find you in a hotel in Spokane?"

"Whatever. I'm headed out to Purdy. Wanna go along?"

"I don't think so. I'm gonna snoop around this Lemongrass thing just a bit."

"You're going to play detective?"

"Are you forgetting I used to be one?"

"I know, I know."

"You're gonna want custody, am I right?"

"You're right."

"What if you get Cache out of jail?" Marcel is testing me now.

"I'm still going to want custody. She blew her chance at custody, at least until she rehabs."

"Boss. Cache is your kid."

"So is Leo my grandson. He needs an advocate in all this. I'm just the one."

"Custody is pretty firm?"

"Yes. I can't lose him."

"Then I'm gonna dig a little bit into the background of Dr. Wanda Singh."

"Inder's sister?"

"One and the same."

"You're one step ahead of me on everything this morning, Marcel."

"Isn't that what you pay me for? See, your money's well-spent, Boss."

"I've never worried about that for a second."

"Have a safe trip, Boss."

We end it. I go in to kiss Verona goodbye. Leo holds out his arms, and I swoop him up. He pats my face. "Did you shave?" he asks.

"Where did you hear that?"

"I don't know."

"I'll see you later, okay?"

"You see my mama?"

"I am. Yes."

"Take me, please, grandpa."

"You're going to do something fun with grandma today."

Tears roll across his eyes. But I'm resolute. I do need to dictate on the drive down. Marcel could've helped with that.

"Let me hold you," Verona intercedes. "Do you want to see a dinosaur today?"

"Yes!"

"Let's find out if Spokane has a dinosaur museum, shall we?"

"Jurassic Quest is in town. I looked when I had my coffee earlier. This was bound to come up."

"Then that's where we'll go. Oh, Leo, dinosaurs that move and growl!"

Leo can't stop smiling. All is well here. So, I'm off for Purdy.

I'm an hour northeast of Purdy when my phone startles me. I've been dictating into my handheld—the best fifty dollars I've ever spent on devices, incidentally. I hit STOP and take the call.

"Michael Gresham here."

"Mr. Gresham, this is Warden McCann calling from Purdy. Have you got just a minute?"

"I do."

"I'm calling about your daughter. She's stopped eating. She refuses water and coffee. Won't take anything by mouth. I went down and talked to her. She says she's done fighting, that she wants to get it over with."

"The execution?"

"She wants us to accelerate it. She says it was a good idea, to begin with, and she wishes you'd lost in court. She wants to die today, Mr. Gresham. That's not going to happen, but she is on suicide watch. I hate to see a prisoner have such terrible last days."

"What, you've seen prisoners who had good last days? Happy last days? What are you talking about, 'terrible last days?' They are terrible!"

"I just thought you should know, sir."

"I'm sorry. Just upset. I'm on my way there now. I'll talk to her."

"No need to apologize. I've never been in your shoes. We're not here to make her unhappy."

This stops me. What in the hell doesn't she understand about "execution"?

"Look, Warden McCann, you're not there to make her unhappy, we know that. But you are there to kill her, and she knows that. It's no wonder she's withdrawn. It's no wonder she won't take the food you're giving her."

"Just one more thing before we hang up. Cache said something that was relayed up the pipeline to me. She was sitting in her cell, talking to one of the guards, when she said 'Don't tell anyone, but I'm not going to let you people murder me. I'm going to do it myself before it's your turn. I'm outta here."

"Is there any possible way she could kill herself?"

"She's on suicide watch, so, no. Well, not unless someone passed her a knife or something. Then she could. But that's not going to happen."

"You can guarantee that?"

"Almost."

"Goodbye, Warden. I'll see her soon, and we'll talk."

"'Bye, Mr. Gresham."

∾

Cache is already waiting for me in the conference room when I arrive. The guard says Cache was brought early just to give her a break from the monotony of her cell. Besides, she says, everyone likes her and wants her well-fed; maybe the changeup will help.

When I walk in, she stands up—no waist chains, no ankle chains—and steps to me. "Give me a big hug," she says. "Don't ever let me go."

I whisper to her, "I'll never let you go. Ain't gonna happen."

She buries her face in my shoulder. Then we take a seat. Someone has given her a pack of cigarettes. I see when she goes to light up that she even has a BIC. I wonder if this is common, the guards plying her with gifts and comforts before their employer murders her? Is it their guilt compelling them to bestow favors? And I thought she was on suicide watch—a cigarette lighter? Really?

"How are you doing? Not so good, I hear."

"Not very good, Michael. I just want to get the whole mess over with. They told me Inder got arrested and they were going to place Leo with Wanda. She's a witch, and I do not want my son with her. She's always gone all day. I don't want Leo around that, never having anyone nearby who loves him. Do you blame me?"

"No, I don't blame you. I want Leo with me. Especially now. No sudden changes after we've spent the last week with him and he likes us. Plus, we've brought him here to see you; which he wants to do again."

"And she won't do any of the things you and Verona do. She works from six in the morning until ten at night. Where does Leo fit in that? It's depressing."

"Is that why you won't eat? You're depressed over Leo?"

"Wouldn't you be?"

"I would. But I also wouldn't be willing to give up the fight. I heard you've told them that you just want to get it over with. You want the execution moved up and done with. Does that sound like what you've told them, Cache?"

"I'm done fighting. Every day that I don't win, I lose. I can't take more losing. Every day doesn't feel like one step closer to my execution. Every day feels like ten days. It's excruciating. Please, just let them end it, Michael. I'm begging you to step aside and let me go."

She's looking at me with those big, pleading eyes that have melted me since I first met her. She is getting harder and harder to turn down the longer I sit here. Dammit, she doesn't have all that much to live for in her view. But I also know that I can give her a life worth living by helping her get resettled one day at a time, getting her little boy back one day at a time as she rehabs, and just being there for her. That's what she needs more than anything, is someone in her corner. That someone who wants to be there is me. I would do anything to help."

"Do this for me, please. Try to turn this case over to me. Just let it go. Just walk away. Just say to yourself that your dad is here and he is going to get you out of here. Continue with mealtime, eat what they give you, exercise when given a chance. And take advantage of those hot showers. Anything you can do to make Cache feel better, do it. While you're busy with all that, I'm busy with getting you out of here."

"Really? You honest-to-God believe you can get me out?"

"I really, honest-to-God do. Washington is just like the rest of the U.S. There are honest people running the systems out here, and they vastly outnumber the idiots like Lemongrass and the creeps like Larsyn. We're just about to call out for help to three of them on the U.S. Court of Appeals, and I think those men and women are going to see the kangaroo court you've been subjected to and they're going to turn you loose. Down deep in my heart, I believe this. Please believe along with me. I'm going to make it happen, Cache. Good will finally prevail."

"Holy shit, I hope your closing argument is that good," she suddenly laughs, a complete turnaround from the depressed woman I walked in on just a short time ago.

"Good, huh?"

"Mister, you can speak night into day with all that. All right, you got me. Let's win this and give Leo back to his mom."

"We'll talk about that last part. First, we deal with you, Cache. Then with you and Leo."

"Lead on."

"No need. You're staying put right here while I go to Seattle and do my thing at the Court of Appeals. Then I'll come back for you, and we'll go home together."

"Wow. You are almost having me believing all this."

"You can take it to the bank."

"But what if you're wrong? What if the absolute worst happens?"

My mouth is dry. It had to come to this point, didn't it, given the topic.

"What if your execution proceeds? Then I will be there

with you, holding your hand, praying for you, carrying your love for Leo in my heart and making sure he knows your love is still alive in the world for him. He will know his mom."

"All right, then. I'm gonna go eat. I could eat a cow."

"Tell them, don't tell me. I do law, not cows."

"You do freedom, Michael. I'm believing in you."

"You won't regret it."

As I'm leaving the prison a half-hour later, I'm regretting the whole conversation. I may have just told my daughter the biggest lie of her life.

But I tell myself I didn't have any other choice.

The BIC lighter was taken away as soon as she left the conference room. So at least they're keeping track—as far as I can tell. I don't feel entirely safe about Cache; you can't ever feel safe about someone in prison. There's just no such thing.

I leave the prison in my rearview mirror, and I'm quite sad as I go. I say a prayer and leave it alone. But then at the first stoplight, I'm rubbing my sleeve across my eyes.

I love this kid, and this is killing me, if not her.

I pull into the first coffee shop I can find. The waitress plops a plastic menu in front of me and asks, "Coffee?"

"With cream," I tell her. I already know how bad it will taste —I could smell the burn just as soon as I walked in the door.

But I have calls to make and burnt coffee is better than no coffee just now.

Seattle is where the Court of Appeals is located. It will be Cache's last hope and my last opportunity to save her. I make a call. The Hyatt in Seattle has room for us all. I'm able to reserve a suite with two bedrooms on the same floor as the swimming pool. Leo is going to enjoy this one.

Then I open my laptop and log into my travel account. Two tickets, one for Verona and one for Leo are purchased, Spokane to Seattle. We're changing our area of operations. The war has moved west.

Verona has been awaiting my call. What about Lucky? She'll call the airline and get back to me about Lucky.

Ten minutes later, she calls me back. It's our lucky day: dogs fly free.

I down my coffee—not so bad after all—then I place a call to the jail where Inder Singh is being held. He's very grateful I've called him—at least at first. But then I break the bad news: I cannot represent him because he and I have a conflict of interest: we both want custody of Leo. I think he understands why I can't ethically represent him in his criminal case while I'm duking it out with him in the custody case. It just isn't going to happen. He asks me whether I have any recommendations for another lawyer. For just a moment, I consider giving him Kelly Larsyn's number, but he must already have that. Good luck if that's where he turns next.

Then I head out to Seattle.

I've got an oral argument to prepare for in the Court of

Appeals. It will have to be the best presentation I've
ever made.

And it will be. I've been around long enough to know I can
make that happen: in fact, I can already hear most of what
I'm going to say running through my mind.

I think we've got a shot at winning.

DAY 20/30

L ast night I worked until after midnight. Verona was in
a deep sleep by the time I slid in beside her. Then I
was out.

I awaken in Seattle. It's impossible to tell what time it is—
Verona closed the blackout curtains last night. My watch is
on the nightstand. I check the time. No wonder it's dark in
the bedroom: it's dark outside, too: 5:14 a.m. Time to
make hay.

This is day twenty. Only ten days left for Cache, according to
the State of Washington. I have lots to do, so I climb out of
bed, pull on my robe and traipse into the living room of our
suite. The red light on our room phone is beeping. I dial the
access code for the message.

It's the Court of Appeals, Clerk's office. Oral argument on
my appeal is set for tomorrow at one o'clock in the afternoon. A bolt of excitement shoots up my back. This is actually going to happen.

It can't come soon enough.

I make coffee. One of those things that only makes two cups at a time. But it will do. I notice my coffee standards are getting lower the closer I get to the Court of Appeals.

Over at the desk, I place a call to Marcel. He's been working up the background on Wanda Singh, the pediatrician who wants to take Leo away from us. Marcel doesn't answer. Too early for him? I can only guess. Or maybe off with Dr. Riddell? Who knows with this guy? One thing about Marcel is that ladies love him. He's never been without the company of a woman when he wants one. Which is often. So who knows where he spent the night? I leave a message to call me.

Now I crack my laptop and wait for it to come online. No emails of any import. It's time to file my brief, which I finished last night. Filed. Next, I write out my oral argument —an old habit, so I don't leave anything out. I do this also to make sure I can support every sentence of what I'm going to say, with reference to either a case or a statute to support what I'm telling the court. This exercise will take half the day; the second half will be taken up by researching and differentiating all of the cases that are against me.

The U.S. Attorney will have a jillion cases that they drag out and use against prisoners over and over in cases like mine. But my job is to anticipate what those will be and be prepared to explain to the court how those are different than my case and thus shouldn't control the outcome. I'll also Shepardize all cases, both pro, and con. This means tracing each case to determine if it's been later overturned or changed by a subsequent case that refers to it. Shepardizing is tedious and time-consuming, but it's also where you can lose your butt if you rely on a case in your argument only to have the other lawyer gleefully tell the court that your case has been overturned. That's disastrous and cannot be allowed to happen tomorrow. Finally, I will also Shepardize the State's case to see whether I can set the same trap for them by finding one of their key cases that's been later overturned or modified by a subsequent case. Two can play the same game.

~

By two o'clock in the afternoon, I'm about halfway through my review of the State's cases, when my phone rings. Marcel calling.

"Hey, Boss. Guess what I'm doing."

"I hope you're dredging up dirt on Dr. Singh that we can use against her to keep Leo with me."

"Better than that," he says, and I can hear the intrigue in his voice.

"All right, I'm clueless. Fill me in."

"Guess who has a dinner date with Dr. Singh tonight."

"Who?"

"Me, Boss."

"You're kidding me. What did you do, get her to agree to an interview?"

"No, I told you, I have a dinner date with her. She thinks I'm a new psychiatrist she met in the doctor's lounge at the hospital."

"Marcel, you amaze me. How did all this happen."

"Easy. I bought a doctor suit at the local doctor store."

"Come on; you stole some scrubs somewhere. Right?"

"That might be more accurate. Then I followed another doc into the lounge and waited. I had made an appointment with her. She finally showed, a half hour late."

"Typical. That's the usual wait to see a doctor."

"Anyway, she shows up, and I introduce myself. We start talking."

"How did you know she'd come to the lounge yesterday?"

"That's where it becomes an art form, Boss. I called her office and told the receptionist that I was opening a practice in town. Then I let it be known that I would like to meet with her to discuss back-and-forth referrals."

"Referrals?"

"Yes, I'm a new psychiatrist in town, and my specialty is kids. She's a pediatrician. She jumped at the chance to meet me. So we set it up for yesterday afternoon at three when she would be making rounds at the hospital."

"Amazing."

"So we chatted. One thing led to another; she agreed to take my referrals and agreed to refer back to me, as well. We exchanged business cards—I only had five cards, printed off my computer. Long story short, we're meeting tonight for dinner. It turns out she's single, I'm single, so we'll see where it goes."

"And you're looking to get dirt on her, am I right?"

"No, Boss. I'm just nosing around to see what her life is about. If something comes up that we can use, so be it."

"Well, I can't say I approve, but I'm amazed at your ingenuity. Plus, I have to say, Leo is going to stay with me no matter what."

"My thought exactly. So how about I call you after my date?"

"Perfect. Don't get crazy on me, but if you turn something up, I'm happy."

"Exactly. Later, Boss."

"Later, Marcel."

We end the call. I can only sit here and shake my head.

Back to my computer. Miles to go before I can join Verona and Leo out at the pool.

I start laughing as I try to refocus on my work. Marcel, a psychiatrist?

Dr. Singh never had a chance.

DAY 21/30

I'm up early the next day. It's argument day. My last chance at saving Cache. I'm so effing nervous I could scream. And stress. It's seeping into my joints and inflaming all muscles and ligaments.

I leave the hotel at 11:30 by taxi. It drops me off just before noon. Very little traffic. The court building is unimposing— two American flags out front and two sets of stairs.

Inside, I head upstairs to Suite 420, the office of the Clerk. At the counter, I check my courtroom and time.

Federal courtrooms are locked until a half-hour before the session starts. So I find a not too uncomfortable bench down the hall where I'll pass the next half-hour. My plan is to study; but, I find, my mind is racing. I meant to be much calmer at this point, but I'm not.

At 12:30 the bailiff opens the courtroom doors. Then I'm inside and headed for counsel table.

Cases scheduled for oral argument are usually assigned

twenty, or occasionally thirty minutes per side. Our case allotment is twenty minutes. We've been told that the judges have the briefs and excerpts of the record and they will be familiar with the facts and issues of our case, so there's no need to waste time with a factual introduction or summation. Instead, we are to spend our argument time clarifying issues and responding to questions raised by the judges.

Forty minutes later, we've begun. I'm into it, clarifying the difference between one line of cases of ineffective assistance of counsel that favor the State and another line of cases that favor Cache. Suddenly, Judge Crittenden, a rickety old jurist who looks like his expiration date was a year ago, raises his hand and motions for me to stop talking. He levels his gaze at me, and I can see piercing blue eyes that are steady and look very much alert and alive.

"How, Mr. Gresham," he asks me, "are we to believe it wasn't possibly your client who infected Judge Wilberforce? As I understand the facts, her strain of HIV and the judge's strain of the virus match perfectly. The women's affidavits prove that three more women have the same virus. So maybe the odds are one-in-four your client was the carrier who infected the judge. But that doesn't mean the jury couldn't have found it was her, period. In fact, they did find it was your client, and this court cannot overturn what the jury said is a fact."

"Well, I—"

"No, wait, Mr. Gresham, I wasn't finished. According to your client's affidavit, she was put upon by Judge Wilberforce, and she infected him only when she was forced to have sex with him. Isn't that it?"

"Yes, Your Honor. That's the gist of it."

"But what proof, what hard evidence, do you have that changes the outcome? The *Strickland* case says her lawyer was ineffective only if he did something or didn't do something that would definitely have changed the outcome of the trial. Give me that something, please."

"Her affidavit is very compelling."

"That's what you say. But I'm not convinced."

"The other women's affidavits are also compelling. Taken together, the four lines of testimony could very well have changed the jury's mind."

"That's argument, not objective fact."

"Can we come back to this?" I finally ask, the last gasp of the drowning man. "Maybe the affidavits can be modified. Please."

"You're saying you need time to change the facts again? I'm sorry, Mr. Gresham, but the self-serving affidavit of Cache Evans isn't enough to make me consider overturning the jury's verdict. You don't have my vote, sir."

The other two judges are nodding with him.

Then I remember Dr. Riddell. "What about Dr. Riddell's affidavit? She says Cache's virus was suppressed with drugs."

"That's what a doctor says who wasn't called by your client's lawyer. The affidavit she gave you, that testimony may or may not have changed the outcome. Again, we can't say for sure. You needed to prove to us your client didn't even have HIV, Mr. Gresham before I'd be compelled to take action on her behalf. You haven't and cannot do that. I'm sorry, but there you are, sir."

"Well, according to what you're telling me, my case is unwinnable no matter what I do. Is that it?"

"Mr. Gresham, Dr. Riddell's affidavit shoots down your theory. There's just no certainty that she didn't infect him. I think you're a little too close to your case, Mr. Gresham, and you don't have a clear view."

At this point, the judge to his right leans over and speaks into Judge Crittenden's ear. Judge Crittenden nods then looks up at me and adds, "Mr. Gresham, I've just learned that the prisoner is your daughter, I'm sorry for you, sir. And for her. But I cannot support you."

I look at the two other judges. I only need two—but they're nodding in agreement with Judge Crittenden. It's all over for me. It's all over for Cache.

I don't have an answer. The U.S. Attorney jumps onto the court's line of reasoning and drills me further into the ground. At the conclusion of our forty minutes, the judges thank us and tell us their decision will be forthcoming in seven days. That's forty-eight hours before Cache is scheduled to die. Not enough time to do anything at that point even if there were anything I could do. But there's not.

The taxi ride back to my hotel is like a dream. I am detached from reality; I am in a feeling state that is so strong, so overwhelming, that I see nothing of the world around me.

I have drowned.

～

Verona is adamant that I keep a promise to Leo and join him in the hotel swimming pool. So I change, grab a couple of towels and take him by the hand. We head toward the end of the hall and the entrance to the pool.

As we walk along I'm wondering whether we'll ever do this again, my grandson and I. Or if we'll ever do anything together again.

He's chatty and tells me about the poolside dives he can do and asks if I'll watch him. I tell him of course I will, that the only reason I'm going to the pool is to watch him. Now his face lights up, and I see what an effect having a man pay attention to him is having. No discounting Verona and maybe Cache, but this little guy is just lapping up everything about being with a man who's interested.

We get to the pool and wade in. I find that Leo can swim pretty well. I have no idea who taught him or when, especially since he was living in a pimp hotel when I paid to take him away. But there you are, he's swimming to beat the band, and I'm following along behind, cheering him on.

Now he wants to hit the hot tub—he's cold. So we move the party into the hot tub, and he shows me how well he can swim in hot water, too. I tell him it's fantastic that he can swim in both cold and hot water. He beams; we're already in love with each other. My only prayer is that somehow I get to keep him with me and raise him to be the man he can be.

Which is the exact moment Verona comes into the pool area, carrying my phone in her outstretched hand.

"Marcel," she mouths.

I dry my hands on a towel and take the phone from her. She

leaves us there, apparently not wanting to interfere in the grandpa-grandson moments. Leo continues splashing around as I take the call.

"Marce," I say, calling him by the nickname I use, "what's up?"

"Sorry I didn't get back sooner, Boss. But I've got some news."

"What's that?"

"It turns out Dr. Singh and I hit it off pretty good. I stayed over last night."

"Did you practice any child psychiatry on her?"

"No, we got way down the road past that. In fact, we got so friendly that I told her who I was."

"And she threw you out."

"No, she said nothing would surprise her about her brother and the kid and Cache. She was resigned to the fact anything could happen."

"So what did you find out?"

"There was an old doctor by the name of Henry Easter. Henry was a pediatrician, too. He had a practice out at Liberty Lake, fifteen miles east of Spokane."

"Go on."

"He practiced out of his home/medical clinic. The town wasn't big enough to support a regular office, so he kept it small and built a clinic along the front of his house. Something like fifty years he practiced there."

"As a pediatrician."

"Yes, but he did colds and flu and sprains and allergies, that kind of stuff with adults, too. But mainly he doctored little kids."

"So where's this going, Marcel?"

"It turns out that he doctored Cache at one time. Dr. Riddell sometimes let him use an examination room in her office to meet patients who couldn't come all the way out to Liberty Lake."

"Hold on. Why would a Liberty Lake doctor be treating a Spokane minor child? How does that work?"

"Because he had a sub-specialty in infectious diseases, HIV being one of those."

"Okay, so what?"

"He examined Cache after the trouble at Serenity House. He was on call at the hospital that night."

"He examined her after the rape, okay. Then what? Did he follow her case after?"

"He did. He ordered the first blood draw, and it was negative. Then he ordered another one ninety days after—maybe more—and it came back HIV positive. On the second blood test, she had contracted the disease."

"So she got HIV from the boys who raped her. Didn't we already know that?"

"Here's the good part. Dr. Easter also tested the boys who raped Cache. None of them was HIV positive."

"Oh, my God!"

277 Days of Justis

"That's right. Cache got HIV somewhere else."

I'm thinking, thinking, my mind is running a hundred miles an hour. This fits with what Dr. Riddell was suggesting might have happened. Unlike her possibilities, however, this new development is based on facts.

"You're saying—"

"I'm saying we've got our smoking gun. Cache caught the HIV from Judge Wilberforce. She was clean when she went to work there, a couple of months later she's HIV positive. The only thing that's happened in between is Judge Wilberforce raped her."

"Hold it. How do we prove Wilberforce raped her?"

"Simple. She has the same HIV virus he has. That's the only history anyone knows. On top of that, don't forget at trial the testimony was that Wilberforce did have intercourse with her, the claim being that she blackmailed the poor, innocent old guy."

"Where is Dr. Easter?"

"He's dead. A car crash on icy roads."

"Where are his records?"

"Wanda doesn't know. I can only guess they're still at his home in Liberty Lake. Assuming the doc's widow is still living there. And assuming she didn't burn all his records after he died."

"I could hug you right now, Marcel."

"That's not why I called. Your hugs mean more to other people than me, Ace."

"I'm on my way to Spokane in an hour."

"Call me when you land. I'll come pick you up."

"Yes. And tell Wanda thank you."

"Who?"

"Wanda."

"Oh, her. See, we already broke up. She doesn't want anything permanent and, well, you know me, Boss."

"See you at the airport, Romeo."

"Marcel is close enough."

"Marcel, then."

We disconnect. I am stunned. I cannot even move across the hot tub. Leo is lying on his stomach in the water, his arms outstretched, holding onto the side of the tub, kicking his legs like a wild man.

I grab an ankle and pull him to me.

"C'mon, my boy. Grandpa has to run."

"Why are you running?"

"Actually, I'm flying."

"Which is it, grandpa, running or flying?"

He laughs, and I haul him up out of the water.

The court of appeals absolutely has to know about this.

There isn't a moment to spare.

∽

Spokane is less than an hour by air tonight. The plane lands, and I deplane and, sure enough, Marcel is waiting just outside the terminal. He's rented a white Highlander with blackout windows. "How's it look on me?" he asks me once we're inside and belted in, surrounded by a wavelet of red leather.

His dark skin and vacant eyes look me over as I formulate an answer. Everything looks good on Marcel, and nothing looks good on Marcel. He's an enigma. Attractive to the ladies, yes, but doesn't seem interested in long-term. He likes hopping from job to job for me and solving ridiculously complicated cases with his massive experience and quick mind. As well, nothing escapes Marcel. He's never been anyone's chump, has never been gamed, and is the first to know when the fix is in. He's literally saved my life maybe a half dozen times, and he's saved my professional life maybe fifty times with all the cases he's turned into wins for me. I love the guy like a brother, but Marcel's not the kind of guy you want to say that to. Between us, we just know what we know, and that's that we're a good combination. We fit. If it were man/woman, you might say it's a marriage of convenience. With an overlay of trust and caring. Except don't tell him that, at least not the part about caring. It's okay that it's there, but it's not okay to discuss it. Not with Marcel.

"So you've found the pediatrician's widow?"

"I have. Eva Easter lives in Liberty Lake on Sprague Road. Right across from the golf course. She looks like she's not hurting for anything. But no, I haven't approached her yet."

"Good." He would ordinarily leave the approach to this kind

of resource in this kind of case to me. It's just the way
we work.

"What do you say we drive on over and talk to her tonight?" I
ask, more than a little panicked by the few days left to
rescue Cache.

"She's eighty-years-old, Boss. Tonight wouldn't be good.
People that age hit the hay pretty early. Let's drive over in
the a.m. And we should call her first."

"Fair enough. I'm having trouble restraining myself, that's
all. Cache needs something done like yesterday. I've got my
fingers crossed on this one."

The next morning, I'm up before the sun and ready to go. Marcel gets me calmed down—breakfast first in the hotel restaurant--and at seven o'clock we drive out to Liberty Lake. It's an old house, 1970's probably, set back from the road on a circle drive. The front windows are two stories tall—you can look right inside. There are no cars in the driveway, but there is a garage. I'm thinking she's got the car in there. So we hop up on the front porch and ring the bell. We ring it several times, and there's no response. Knocking hard on the wood frame produces no results either. Marcel tells me to stay put and heads for the backyard. I can see him reaching over the gate and opening from the other side. Then he's inside and disappears around the back corner of the house. So I wait.

Five minutes later, Marcel is back. His shoes are muddy and his hair mussed.

"I tried to crawl in through a basement window, but it's got electronics."

"Meaning there's an alarm system?"

"Exactly."

"Well, what the hell were you doing trying to break in any way?"

"She's your kid, Boss. I'd kick down the gates of hell to save her."

He's got a point. Anything goes, I decide. But first, I'm going to try the neighbors and see if they can help.

Next door sits another house maybe half the size of Eva Easter's place. I step up and ring the bell. This time, there's an answer. A stooped little man standing with the aid of a walker peers out through the screen door. "What can I do for you?"

"I'm looking for Eva Easter, next door. I'm wondering whether you have any idea how I might get in touch with her."

He squints at me. "You kin?"

"No, I'm—I'm a lawyer."

"She's not in trouble, is she? Eva's rock solid so I'd be surprised."

"No, no trouble. Dr. Easter treated a patient who's a client. We're trying to track down some old medical records on her."

"Eva's probably burned all his stuff. She said too many memories. Not like a lot of old people like me. She cleaned house after Henry died. I think she probably threw out all his files and stuff. There was a huge fire out back, and she

was throwing clothes on it, books that belonged to him—
everything. That was back when you could have fires, back
before the goddam fools at city hall made everything illegal
on your own property. Can't even have a fire. They'll arrest
you if you do."

My heart has sunk to a new, all-time low. The image of Eva
Easter burning Cache's medical chart is just too, too
depressing.

"Thanks for that. I'd still like to talk to her, sir."

"She's back in Rye. Got a son there. He never amounted to
much—teaches junior college. Probably couldn't get into
medical school. That's my guess."

"Do you know his name?"

He squints even harder at me. "Are you okay, son? His
name's Easter, just like his ma and his old man. Easter. Rye,
New York. There you go."

The door begins closing.

"Wait! Do you have any idea how we might get inside
the house?"

The door opens up again.

"Sure do. I've got the key."

"Please, let us in!"

"What for?"

"We need to look for Dr. Easter's files."

"No can do. Those would be confidential. If they even exist
at all."

"Sir, this is a matter of life and death. My daughter is going to die in five days if I don't get those records."

"Who's that?"

"Cache Evans. You probably have never heard of her."

"I can read. She's the one got sent to jail for killing Hiram Wilberforce? That the one?"

"Yes. Can you help us help her?"

"I never was one to cotton to criminals. No matter what their excuse is, they're all rotten."

"Mr.--"

"Sylvester Hammerstein. My friends call me Sly."

"Mr. Hammerstein, let me be blunt. I'm going to get inside that house with or without you."

Marcel steps closer to the screen door. "Listen, Sly; you need to help us. I don't know what might happen if you don't step up and do this girl a good deed. Are you following me, Sly?"

I catch a sideways look at Marcel. The eyes are slit like he gets before he strikes. I want to reach out and pull him back but don't.

Sly Hammerstein begins closing the door again.

"Leave it open, or I'm coming inside open or not. Now you get up off your couch and get us inside, sir."

"I'm calling the cops. Get the hell off my porch."

"Sir, you are not calling the cops," Marcel says through gritted teeth. "I'm going to count to five, and then I'm coming in. I'm going to make it look like you attacked me so when

they come for your body they'll know I was the victim.
One, two--"

"All right, all right, all right. Jesus, man. What's got
into you?"

"Your nasty attitude, that's what. Now you be a good boy and
get that key and take us next door and let us in. Three, four--
"

"I'm looking right now. There, I've got it in my pocket on my
keychain. Eva wanted me to have it. I guess she figured I'd
need it if there's an emergency."

"Put it in your book, Sly. This is an emergency."

"How's that?"

"If you don't take us next door this minute we're going to
have to call for an ambulance. To haul your sorry ass to the
hospital."

He pushes open the screen door and comes out onto the
porch. Sly Hammerstein must be ninety-years-old. I'm
feeling half-bad for letting Marcel scare him witless, but the
other half of me is grateful Marcel's here.

The three of us cut across Eva's front lawn. Up on the porch
we go, Marcel extending a hand to pull Sly up, too. He
hands the keychain to Marcel. "It's the brass one," he says.
"On the separate ring from the others."

"Jesus, Sly, how come so damn many keys?"

"Everything's locked up. My garage, my lawnmower shed,
house, garage. I might even have a boat I've forgotten about.
Don't get old, fellas."

Marcel tries the key and the door swings open. Sly enters a code into the security system's keypad. "Street address," he says with a wink. "That's the code."

We're inside and already rushing throughout, looking for something that might be holding files. Nothing on the ground floor, so we head downstairs to the basement.

And there, spread across one wall, is file cabinet after file cabinet. I count seven file cabinets in all. Maybe
—just maybe—

Marcel is opening and closing drawers, high-speed.

He reaches the last file cabinet then turns to me. "All empty, boss. Must have been the fire."

"But why would she still have all the filing cabinets? Doesn't add up."

Marcel looks at Sly, who shrugs. Then he asks the old man, "Does she have a storage locker anyplace?"

"No, but she's got the garage. We ain't looked in there."

Back upstairs we double-time, then through the kitchen and out into the garage.

Empty. Not even an automobile. We've struck out here.

"Now what?" I ask Marcel. Locating evidence is his specialty.

Sly pulls out a pipe and packs it with Prince Albert. He doesn't light up, just sticks the stem between his front teeth. Then he removes it. "Maybe Junior's got them. Ever think of that?"

"Why would Junior have them? He's clear the hell back in New York teaching community college."

"Nope, that's Russell. You haven't asked me about Junior. He's a pediatrician in Coeur D'Alene."

Coeur d'Alene is just across the Idaho/Washington border.

"It's not thirty minutes from here," Sly adds. "Why not just trot over and ask him?'

"Seriously?" says Marcel. "Were you going to tell us about Junior?"

"It's not like you asked," Sly says, biting off the words. "You can't ask me to do your job for you, Mister."

"C'mon," Marcel tells me. "We're going to Idaho."

We leave Sly Hammerstein to lock up behind us. He's still fiddling with the front door as we drive off in a great rush, headed east.

～

As we're driving east, my phone chimes. The prison at Purdy is calling. They are calling collect. It can only be Cache, of course. I accept the call without hesitating.

"Hello?"

"Michael, it's your daughter, Cache. They're being terrible to me here!"

"Okay, what are they doing?"

She's crying now; sobbing. I close my eyes and try to think, try to imagine where she is as she's calling. Probably a pay phone down the hall from her cell. I can see the spiral of silver wire connecting the phone to the wall. I can see the airborne transmission of her call to my cell tower, then to me. I can see these things because I am her father and I'm trying to keep a connection to her through all of this. I haven't been able to release her from my mind not even for a second. This call is my reward.

Again. "What is the problem?" Besides the fact they're going to kill you if they can.

"They want my organs and my skin and my eyes and my bones."

"I don't follow."

"They make sure I'm dead first. Then they harvest my body so other people can live. They want my kidneys and liver and lungs, too."

"Oh, my God. I'm so sorry, Cache. How did this come up?'

"The social worker came to my cell. She said she had something very important to talk to me about. I didn't know what, so I said sure, go ahead."

"Okay."

"So she starts telling me about all the people who will probably die in hospitals the same day I die because their liver failed or their dialysis no longer worked. All this terrible stuff about dying people. Then she asked if I would like to try to save some of them. I didn't know how I could do that but I said sure, I'd like that. So she had papers for me to sign. Organ donor papers."

I didn't know they want organs from HIV-infected donors. But that's not the point here, so I let it go.

"I'm so sorry this happened, Cache. Nobody called me about it first."

"Well, should I sign? I want to help those people. But I don't want to die either. How can they want parts of me to live but not all of me?"

What can I say? It becomes a jumble in my mind because I don't have an answer and I realize I'm too close to her to be objective. Should she sign? Can I even answer that? I don't want my dead daughter's body sliced up by a bunch of do-gooders. It revolts me. I shiver; Marcel eyes me from behind the wheel. "Boss?" he inquires.

I'm shaking my head. Then, to Cache: "Tell them there's no need for that conversation because your dad says you're not going to die. Tell them to ask someone else for a heart. Tell them to check back in about sixty years. Never mind all that. Just tell them no." I'm as honest with her as I can be, but I also know one sad truth about myself that I don't want her to know: If they were to ask me, once her heart has stopped beating, I would tell them yes, take what they can use. Her mother—the health sciences graduate—would want them to harvest as well. And I, the eternal do-gooder, would want that too. I can tell her none of this and don't. Now I've got a secret from her, and she's already made me promise always to tell her the truth. Oh, my Sweet Jesus. Now, what do I do?

I just lied to her, is what I did. It's only been three weeks since I promised I wouldn't lie and here I am already back to my old deceits.

Now she's crying uncontrollably, weeping into the phone. I can hear a stern voice calling out. I can hear her being ordered to hang up, that her three minutes are up. Then the line goes dead. Just like that, and she is gone.

"What is it, Boss?"

"They want to harvest her organs after they murder her."

"That's probably a good thing, Boss. She could help a lot of people."

"Don't tell me that, Marcel. Never tell me that again."

"Sorry, Boss. It's a different case this time since it's your daughter."

"Tell me about it."

We ride along without another word until we reach Coeur d'Alene. Marcel neatly drives us right up to the doctor's street address. We park at a long, low new building just outside the other end of town. It has the windswept design of a B1 bomber, and I'm guessing the doctor, and his cohorts own the place. One day they will sell it off, add the profits to their 401k's, and leave for Florida. Or San Diego. Whatever.

Marcel leads the way inside. Large waiting room, plenty of tables piled high with Fisher-Price for the pediatricians' endless string of clogged noses and ear infections. The walls are slathered with cutouts of yellow chickens and white ducks. Plus, children stretched across mothers' laps as well as posted at the kiddie-accessible tables until names get called, and they hurry away. What follows, of course, is a week of antibiotics and a re-check. I would hate to work here.

"Dr. Easter, please. We need to speak with him," Marcel is saying to the woman behind the glass barrier. She doesn't respond directly. Just gives him a puzzled look.

Then she says, "Are you the parent of one of our patients?"

Marcel turns to me, so I step up. "I'm the parent of a child who Dr. Easter treated fifteen years ago."

"You must mean Dr. Easter Senior?"

"That's right."

"And you want to see his son?"

"That's right. It's critical."

"What can I tell him it's about?"

"I just told you. About my daughter fifteen years ago."

"I'll check with his nurse. I know he's booked all afternoon."

I look down at my watch. It's only eleven in the morning. Might we have to wait here until the close of business? So be it.

"My daughter is going to die in eight days if I don't get to see Dr. Easter right now."

"Goodness."

"Yes. Please ask him to come up here immediately."

"I will, sir."

She disappears into her headset, back turned to us. Then she turns back around.

"He's coming. He just has to finish up with an earache."

"Of course."

"Let me take you into the kitchen. He'll be right along."

We're led down a short hallway to the kitchen, which is a

small room with two metal tables, a soft drink dispenser, and a coffee pot that smells of very burnt coffee.

"Don't, boss," Marcel says when he sees me eyeing the coffee pot. "Please."

We settle at one of the tables just as a doctor wearing a white lab coat strides inside.

"Dr. Easter. Melanie says it's an emergency? What's up?"

"I'm attorney Michael Gresham, and this is my investigator. We need a file from your father's records."

"Who was the patient?"

"Cache Evans. She was probably between thirteen and seventeen."

"Your relationship to Cache?"

"I'm her father."

"Wait just a minute. Let me go to my office and check our database. Help yourselves to some coffee. There's water in the refrigerator, too."

That latter sounds good; Marcel grabs two chilled bottles, and we drink up.

Dr. Easter doesn't take five minutes to return and give us the news.

"Unfortunately, her records have been destroyed. But I'll tell you who might have copies."

"Who would that be?"

"Spokane Health Department. It looks like the file contained an infectious disease badge. That would've involved Spokane Health."

"All right, doc, thank you."

He abruptly turns on his heel and leaves us there, water bottles in hand, our next clue resonating off the walls.

Marcel touches my shoulder and guides me out of the room. It's a fair thing to do: I've almost succumbed to the feeling this isn't going to happen for Cache. But then I buck up as soon as Marcel touches me and we leave the office, out to our Highlander.

By the time I'm sitting down again, I'm feeling dizzy and light-headed. Air intake is slowed way down, too. Now what?

"Eleven-thirty, Boss. Time to head back to Spokane."

"Floor it, Marcel. No time to waste!"

We roll into Spokane at twelve-ten and follow Marcel's phone GPS to the county health department. Inside we go, hurrying to the front desk, where we are met by a young man with a thin mustache. His black hair is swept back in a very smooth pompadour like the old pictures of Valentino. Very today.

"What can I help you gentlemen with?"

"We need access to the health records of a young lady by the name of Cache Evans. The records would be about fifteen years old. I'm her dad, and she desperately needs certain medical records out of her file."

"Goodness, let's make that happen. Fill out this form, please, and I'll send it back to records. What you're looking for may or may not be restricted from all eyes. Plus, I'll need to check the birth certificate we have on file for her and confirm that you are in fact her father. What is your name?"

"Michael Gresham."

"Be sure and include that on the form."

"Wait, you don't understand everything yet. I'm her father, but her mother left me off her birth certificate."

"Now why would she do that?"

"Please, that doesn't matter. I just know I'm not on it."

"Then you'll need to bring your daughter or your wife here to obtain those records, Mr. Gresham."

"We were never married."

"If she's the mother we don't need to worry about marriage and such as that. If she can confirm her identity and it matches the birth certificate, then you've got the records. They belong to your child, and that means the parent has access. Have I helped you?"

I have to admit he has. Another hurdle to jump, but we're very close. I can almost feel the papers in my hands.

We turn away from the window.

"All right, I can drive to Purdy and pick up Millie. We can't make it back before this place closes, but we can be here first thing in the a.m."

"Drop me at the hotel and hit the road, Marcel. And thanks."

We climb back inside the Highlander. He winks at me, we back away from the curb, and we're headed for the Daven-port Hotel. I'll spend the rest of the afternoon swimming with Leo, hanging out with Verona, and drinking Starbucks out of politely small carafes.

But there will be no relaxing. Tonight, when everyone's asleep, I'll climb quietly out of bed, go to the desk, and spend the rest of the night re-writing the amended appeal I'll be filing tomorrow with the Court of Appeals.

Then I fall asleep upright in my seat, broad daylight. This has never happened to me.

I force my eyes open. I shake my head.

I want to say something to Marcel.

But I don't.

M illie took the room next to mine at the Davenport late last night.

Now, she's up early, rapping on my door—but not loud enough to wake Verona or Leo. I'm wearing cutoffs and a sweatshirt so I can let her inside immediately. A quick hug hello and we pull apart to face each other as the parents of a child about to die for a crime she did not commit.

She's all business. "Marcel told me what you need. What time do they open?"

"Eight o'clock."

"That's two hours. How can I help in the meantime?"

"Do you have your phone?"

"I do."

"Then I'm going to email you the amended appeal I'm working up. You can proofread."

"Email away. I'm all over it."

I send the document to her email and moments later we've both gone our separate ways, in a mental sense, no longer aware of each other. At seven-thirty my watch's haptic alerts me; it's time to go to the health department and do whatever it takes to claim our daughter's records.

I message Marcel, who's knocking on my door moments later. Downstairs we go, stop at the coffee station, then outside, where we pile into Marcel's rental, and off we go.

It's July 26, and I can feel the time ticking away in my bones. No one needs to tell me the date; my subconscious is keeping tabs on that. My subconscious is playing games with me, too, sometimes counting the number of breaths a person takes in a day and multiplying by her remaining days. A parent should never know the number of breaths a child has left. It's not right.

We pull into the spot right next to the sidewalk. We're so early the lot is nearly empty. We fidget and make small talk until precisely eight o'clock, when we head for the entrance, hurry inside and rush to the counter before anyone else— there's no one else here—can beat us there.

The same young man as yesterday greets us from his side of the counter.

"This must be the mother," he says with a polite smile.

"I am," says Millie. "I'm here for my daughter's records. I have my passport, my driver's license, and my Social Security card. Where do you want to start?"

It's only a matter of minutes before Millie has clearance to review the entire file. We're led back to a carrel area, where Millie can sit down and begin reviewing Cache's records on

a visitors' computer. The young man—whose name is Tom
—stands at Millie's shoulder and helps her find the beginning of the file. Then we're off and running. Millie is
intently poring over records screen by screen when she hits
pay dirt.

"Oh my God, here it is!"

I'm looking over her shoulder and see the same thing.
Cache's first visit with Dr. Henry Easter is viewable. We
speed read. It appears Cache first saw Dr. Easter in 2002. He
examined her at the hospital following the rape by the three
boys. He worked up the rape kit, took a blood draw and took
another about ninety days later. Both were negative for any
virus. As an additional precaution, he also tested the blood
of the three criminals who raped my daughter. Their results
are posted in her file although their names are redacted.
The smoking gun—first smoking gun—is that all three
tested negative for HIV. They weren't infected, in other
words. So the prosecuting attorney's case, which was linked
to the three boys as the presumed source of Cache's
presumed infection with HIV just evaporates.

The prosecutor had no case; he only made the jury believe
he had a case. Even better, Cache returns for another blood
test six months after going to live in Wilberforce's house—a
common safeguard to follow-up on the previous tests—and
now she's HIV positive. The only thing that's changed in the
interim, according to her history, is the rape by Judge
Wilberforce. Given her history, and given the results of her
three blood tests, the judge is the HIV carrier who infected
my daughter. Millie looks up at me, tears in her eyes.

"They all lied," she says in a voice that breaks off.

I lay my hand on her shoulder. "They did lie. Here's the smoking gun. Now, why didn't Dr. Easter report the new finding, the HIV infection, to CPS? Wouldn't they have moved Cache out of that environment?"

Millie, ever the scientist, answers me. "Maybe he did report it. Maybe CPS just failed to act."

I'm scanning further down the doctor's entries. "Ah, here we are. It appears that he told CPS. June DeWitt got back to him and told him she was going to change Cache's place-ment. According to the doctor's next note, she advised Dr. Easter that she had informed the court authorities of the infection. Evidently, they ignored her, or her message got lost because nothing happened after that."

Marcel speaks up. "Or maybe they were already protecting Judge Wilberforce. Maybe that's why nothing happened."

"Good grief." I can only close my eyes and let this sink in. My gut tells me that Marcel is right. I've seen entire athletic teams of young girls sexually abused by their team doctor, and the entire thing gets covered up while the abuse is allowed to continue. The whole idea just sickens me. Cache's case is just one more.

"What do we do?" she asks. Her voice is small and far away.

"We show this file to the Court of Appeals. Then we walk our daughter out of the Purdy prison."

She throws her head back, and a long cry of joy fills the small room. Tom comes to see that everything's all right. We tell him which records we need and he inputs a passkey and prints them out for us. Two sets. She has hers, and I have mine.

"Now I need to go back to my room, to my computer. And I need you two to leave me alone to work. In the meantime, so that it's quiet around there, do you suppose that you, Marcel, could figure out something to entertain Leo while he and Verona give me some space?"

"Done, Boss. That river running through town. I think I'm taking Leo fishing."

"Excellent. Millie?"

"If I'm done here then I'm going back to Purdy. I'll bring Cache up to speed on what we've found. That should give her some hope, something to hold onto."

I tell her I agree and we load back into Marcel's Highlander. Then we're headed back to the hotel. Valet parking takes over the vehicle while the three of us rush for the elevators.

There's no time to waste. I have no idea if the court will even entertain having a look at this newly-discovered evidence, but considering the fraud that was perpetrated on the jury and considering that a life hangs in the balance, I don't see how they can refuse. I know that I couldn't if it were me sitting there in a black robe. I'd just have to look.

Now to write the motion to amend the appeal—newly-discovered evidence with Dr. Easter's records attached.

A half-hour later, Verona and Leo are walking out with Marcel, who hasn't yet told my grandson where he's going, only that he has a great surprise for him. Verona's only condition is that they stop in the gift shop downstairs for sunblock. She is already taking care of Leo like one of her own. He is, when you come right down to it. He is by default. There's just no one else.

Millie follows them out the door, telling Leo that she'll see him again soon. Leo is somewhat quizzical; it's clear he's not entirely sure who Millie is. Attribute that to Cache's refusal to see her mother in the past. But Millie, God bless her, is trying. She tells Leo she's going to see his mother; is there anything Leo wants to tell her? "I miss her," says the little boy. "I need to see her real soon."

Alone at last with my laptop, I pull up my motion to amend the appeal. It's a relatively simple job to plug in the new information and follow that up with what I hope is a compelling legal and humanitarian argument in favor of the Court considering what we've found. Before long, I'm buying my own argument; I don't see how we can lose.

When I'm ready, and everything's set to file, I log in to the Ninth Circuit Court of Appeals website and upload my new filing.

It's not five minutes until I receive a call from the same court, office of the clerk.

"Mr. Gresham, we've received your electronic filing. We're wondering whether you've heard the news about Judge Crittenden?"

The elderly judge; the one who said he couldn't support my case.

"What news?"

"He's had a stroke. He's in Mercy Hospital. No one can tell us what his condition is."

"Well, that's simple enough, right? They just assign another judge, right?"

"Yes, but that will have a definite impact on your daughter's case."

"How's that?"

"We're all pulling for your daughter around here. We want her to succeed. Judge Wilberforce's reputation had spread as far west as Seattle. He was a nasty man. But there will be a delay now. A delay that could take longer than your client has to live."

"Can't we get my new filing heard on an emergency basis?"

"I'm going to try. I'm going to walk it through and see if we can expedite. But there's no guarantee, Mr. Gresham."

She has my full attention. More than ever in my life.

"What's your name, ma'am?"

"I'm Suzanne Crosby. You can call me Suze, everyone does. I'm going to give you my cell number where you can get through to me, Mr. Gresham. And you can rest assured that I will update every time there's a development."

"Is there anything else I can do to expedite the hearing on my motion?"

"Not really. Just let me do my thing now. I'll try to let you know something in the next twenty-four hours."

"All right. Then I'm finished, I suppose."

"I believe you've done all you can for your client, Mr. Gresham."

"Is there any possibility the court will need me for oral argument?"

"Their practice in cases like this is to rule by abstract. They'll either say yea or nay. There won't be oral argument."

"Then I'm safe to go to Purdy and see my client? There's not going to be a last-minute demand I appear in court?"

"Ninety-nine times out of a hundred, no. I can't say positively; I can only tell you how I've seen it done the past twenty years."

"That'll have to do, then. Thank you, Suze."

"You're welcome. Goodbye, Mr. Gresham."

I terminate the call. I'm left staring at the blinking cursor on my computer screen. Who else has the authority, the official power to save Cache?

The governor, Jackson L. D'Nunzio? He does, but he's a known quantity. Governors always have the power to stop executions. But Governor D'Nunzio has already shown himself to be a man more concerned with appearances than with substance. He cared more about who handled this case than what the case was about. So in the time remaining, I am convinced the governor is not my final recourse. I am convinced he won't lift a finger to save my daughter. Not a finger.

Color me crazy, but I decide to visit the hospital where Judge Crittenden is treated. I have nowhere else to turn.

I catch a flight to Seattle and check into the Hyatt.

~

I can't locate the judge. No one will give me the name of his hospital. I understand; if it were my loved one, I wouldn't want them bothered by desperate appellants either.

So I turn to the one last place I know to turn. The press. A newspaper reporter by the name of Sari al-Hatari. She's the one who wrote today's *Seattle Daily* article about the judge, his illness, and his hospitalization. I'm confident she will have the particulars. I'm praying she'll be willing to direct me to him.

The *Seattle Daily* is an online newspaper with a vast number of viewers. Nearly lost among a tsunami of staff writers is Sari al-Hatari, whose regular beat is the City Desk. I call the online news outlet's main number and ask for her. She isn't long coming to the phone; I am very thankful when she takes my call.

"Ms. al-Hatari, I'm the attorney for Cache Evans, presently on—"

"Death row in Purdy. I wanted to do a series on her, and my editor nixed it."

"Nixed it? Why?"

Her voice is hushed. "I think the so-called victim had a lot of juice around here."

"Meaning he was protected?"

"I didn't say that."

"Of course you didn't."

"What can I do for you, Mr. Gresham?"

A thought crosses my mind. The judge is dead now. Maybe—

"Cache Evans is not only my client, but she's also my daughter."

Long pause. "That would make an amazing story. I'd love to run with it."

"Then let's meet. My entire case, my life, Cache's life will be open to you. I mean it, there's nothing you can ask that won't be fully answered."

"What are you doing right now, Mr. Gresham?"

"I'm in my room at the Hyatt. With Judge Crittenden down, I'm out of ideas."

"How about meeting with me for a few hours? Let's see where this might go."

One hour later, we're ensconced along the pier where a seafood eatery keeps its outside tables.

"Cache is twenty-eight, I believe?" asks Ms. al-Hatari. She's something else. Her skin is mahogany, her hair is styled in a short, choppy black cut, and she wears a thin gloss of lipstick that contrasts with refrigerator-white teeth. A beauty, and charming.

"She is twenty-eight. Unmarried, I believe. She's the mother of Leon Russell Evans, my grandson. He's four, and he prefers 'Leo.' He went fishing today with my investigator. Leo is now determined his life's work will be bass fisher-man. A fait accompli, one could say."

"He sounds adorable." She studies the folder I've placed on the table between us. "You brought papers with you?"

I look down at the manila folder in which I've tucked Cache's chart from Dr. Easter. "I've brought records. I made this copy for you."

"What am I looking for?"

At this point, I explain to her the dates, the years, the allegations by Judge Wilberforce, the truth of Cache's records. Sari takes it all down. She has asked if she can record me and I've agreed. Ordinarily, I'd say no to the press recording a private conversation, but this isn't ordinarily. This is life and death.

As Sari slowly reads through the records, I take the opportunity to excuse myself, turn my back on her, and call Millie. She tells me she's seen Cache and she's never seen a more demoralized child than what was left of her after she heard about Judge Crittenden's hospitalization. She understands how a delay could kill her. She's beset at all sides, too, as the social worker was back today looking for an answer about body parts. I cannot even imagine how Cache feels right now. I only want to take her up in my arms and give her a long hug. She needs that, I believe; so do I. My shoulders sag. It is all spinning out of control.

Sari clears her throat behind me, and I turn back around after ending the Millie call.

"So?" I say.

"This is unbelievable. It's like a huge ball of yarn that you've been unraveling ever since you found out you have a daughter named Cache."

"Oh, then you read my file memos, too. Now you know our history."

"I do. I'd like to run with the story. And I'd like to ask my readers to start making calls to the Court of Appeals, demanding action on your motion. It's the least I can do. It's also the most I can do for now. But be certain that as I see openings along the way I'll do everything I can to help Cache's case. No one should die for this raft of lies."

"I thank you and Cache thanks you."

"Michael, one more thing. Do you think I could get a video crew into the prison to record an interview with Cache?"

"I have no doubt we could do that, especially if we convince the warden we're videoing a deposition."

"That would be incredible. If we can do that we've got a first-page story on our hands."

"Call your people. Let's meet tomorrow at Purdy."

"Noon work for you?"

"Noon is perfect," I tell her.

We say goodbye, and she hurries off to make her preparations. I hang behind, indulging in a paper plate of fried clams and french fries before I hit the road for Purdy. As I finish eating, I get a call from Verona. First comes the bass fishing update starring Leo. Then we talk about Judge Crittenden's condition and my hurry-up trip and video session back down in Purdy. We hang up after just a few minutes; she knows how anxious I am and how little time I have left. "*Vaya con Dios*," she whispers. "Be safe, my love."

DAY 24/30

I t's eleven o'clock when I'm finally allowed to speak to Warden McCann in her office. They've been telling me she's in a conference, but when I enter her office, there's no one else coming out or hanging back. She's alone; I'm not; I have Sari al-Hatari at my side. Introductions are made, and McCann studies al-Hatari.

"You're on *Seattle Daily*, am I right? I've read lots of your stories. Welcome to Purdy." She extends her hand to shake with al-Hatari. She doesn't offer me the same courtesy, and I don't give a damn.

"I've been with SD four years now. Before that, it was the Post. So I've got Seattle down pretty good."

"Why are you here for a deposition, Ms. Al-Hatari? This is a legal moment, not a news moment."

"I asked Mr. Gresham if I might tag along and he had no objection. So here I am. I do hope the State of Washington won't object to my presence."

"Oh, not at all. Please feel free. Mr. Gresham, we have our press room reserved for noon for your session. It's not all that large, but I think you'll find it works for you."

So. We're going to be allowed to go ahead with our video session. I'm very relieved. We spend maybe five minutes more with Warden McCann and then we're shown to the door. The secretary in the outer office hangs up the phone on her desk. "Security will be here in five minutes. They'll escort you to the press room so you can set up."

Sari says, "I'll alert my team. They're in the main reception area. Will you let security know they're to be brought to the press room as well?"

"Done. Give it ten minutes, and you're all together."

It's a huge relief, and I take one of the black vinyl chairs for a minute. What do we hope to do today? We're going to capture Cache's version of the Judge Wilberforce era. We're going to get the news out that she was raped by Judge Wilberforce and tested HIV positive not long after. There's no one from the other side here; we didn't want anyone else. This also looks like a deposition to be used in court so far as the warden knows. In truth, it's a news story with video.

I lean forward, hands on knees, and shut my eyes just to collect myself. The significance of what we're about to do isn't lost on me. I feel it through and through, and I'm anxious yet again. At just this moment I'm aware there's a dark shroud being pulled across my brain, and I pass out.

DAY 25/30

"Exhaustion," Verona says, standing far above me, looking down at my face.

Ever so slowly I fight to understand. Then I see. I'm in a hospital bed. I struggle to shift upright in the bed. Something has gone terribly wrong.

Verona stoops to place her hand on my forehead. "Easy, Michael, don't try to sit, please."

Two nurses are off to my left; one I can see and one I can only hear, but I recognize the sound of vitals monitors recording and reporting my condition.

"Where?"

"St. Anthony Hospital. You passed out, and they've been worried it's a stroke. We're waiting for test results."

It begins returning to my mind. "What about Sari and Cache? The video?"

"Sari went ahead and got the story. I've spoken with her. Amazing woman."

"What about the court?"

"The story ran last night on the *Seattle Daily* online news. Marcel took a call on your phone. The Court of Appeals has listened and heard. They've set oral argument on your motion for the day after tomorrow. But you won't be there."

"Like hell, I won't. Wild horses can't keep me away."

"Doctor's orders. You'll be here several days until they release you."

"How is Cache?"

"I went in last night," a voice says from my right. I try to move my head to the right to see, but it doesn't move. It feels locked up.

"Millie?" I manage to say. "Is that you?"

"It is, Michael. I saw our daughter last night. She's doing better. She was quite rattled when I watched the video on the *Seattle Daily* website. But she's doing a lot better now. Just really worried about her dad."

Her dad. That resonates in my heart. I miss her and know I've let her down. I try to raise my hand, my right-hand, to push up and out of bed, but my right-hand doesn't work. Then I realize I might have a string of saliva running out the right side of my mouth. I sense that it's there more than I feel it. What the hell is going on with me?

"Michael," Verona is leaning down again, "you've had a mini-stroke. They did an MRI, and they've done blood tests. But you're going to recover a hundred percent."

"I've got to get to court. Cache is counting on me."

"You're not going to court. Now lie back and rest."

Now a white-frocked doctor sweeps into the room. She scans my entourage and says, "Whoa, who are all you people? Mr. Gresham needs rest right now."

"I'm the wife," says Verona. "So, I'm staying."

"I'm the almost-wife," Millie says with a tone of sarcasm. "I'll be leaving."

The doctor smiles and pulls up a chair to my bedside. "I'm Linda Fox. Do you know your name?"

"Howard Hughes."

"Seriously?"

"Michael Gresham."

"Well, Michael, you've had an incident. I'm calling it a mini-stroke. A TIA. Now, what month is it?"

"January."

"And what state are you in?"

"Disappointment. And pissed at my body."

"State, please."

"Washington. State of."

"Month, for real?"

"July."

"Do you remember where you were when you passed out?"

"Prison at Purdy. We were getting ready to take a video interview."

Dr. Fox looks to Verona, who confirms my answer with a nod.

"I have to be in court, doc. The day after tomorrow. This is no BS. I'm going to be there."

"No, you won't be there unless you leave the hospital AMA. Then I can't help you."

"There's no one else. My daughter is on death row. I have one last chance to convince the Court of Appeals she was railroaded. I've got to be there."

"Your cognition is excellent. That's a good sign."

She didn't reply to what I just said. She simply changed the topic. Nice.

"I need to see Marcel," I mutter.

"Marcel's with Leo downstairs," Verona tells me.

"Please get him up here. We need to talk about one last thing I need for Cache's case."

"Michael," Millie says from my right, "you want to see Marcel to plan an escape. You're not fooling anyone. Now instead of insisting on going to court, start thinking about a lawyer to fill in for you. That's what you need to be doing."

"I concur," says Verona.

They should know this can't be done. "I don't know anyone. I don't practice here so I don't know a soul. Doc, I'm a little bit tightened up in my right arm. How long until that goes away?"

"With a TIA you're talking several hours to a day or two."

"Do I have to stay here with a TIA?"

"Ischemic stroke patients can usually leave in three-to-six days. TIA, at one end of the scale, maybe two days."

"If I'm out by tomorrow night, why wouldn't I be able to appear in court the next day?"

"Michael, you've been under a huge amount of stress. And the worst thing for stroke victims to engage in is worry and stress. Stress can precipitate another incident; next time maybe worse. So you're going to need to listen to me and humor me. When and if you leave here tomorrow, it won't be with any hope of you going to court. That would be against medical advice. AMA. Now hang in there. I'll be back later to see how you're doing. We can talk more then."

"Okay."

Ever so slowly, now, the assault begins from Verona and Millie. Explaining—very slowly, so the stroke victim understands—my future if I insist on going to court. They are stressing me out with their words, so I stop listening.

My turn to change the subject. "I need to see the court order setting the emergency hearing. Can someone get that for me?"

Verona sighs and crosses the room. A long, countertop runs along the windows. She lifts my laptop from it and brings it over. She takes the chair the doctor had occupied and flips open the laptop. "Okay. Where do I sign in."

"It's called Pacer. I've got a bookmark on my toolbar. Click that. It will automatically enter my user ID and password."

She takes a minute or two and then says she's ready.

"What to do next?"

I explain the search feature for a Pacer case, and she executes it flawlessly. The court order appears onscreen.

"Read it, please," I ask Verona.

She reads. It's very short and to the point. The court has granted my motion to amend Cache's appeal and to allow follow-up argument. The argument is less than forty-eight hours away. Counsel are ordered to attend.

"Marcel. Please get him." I say this to the ceiling. Whether Millie goes and watches her grandson while Marcel comes up here, or whether Verona goes doesn't matter. I just need Marcel. "It's part of finding someone else," I add. This pleases Verona, who raises a hand to Millie.

"Let me go see Leo," Verona says. "You must want to say some private things to Michael about your daughter."

Millie doesn't respond. With Verona gone, the room is hushed. I can hear Millie's breathing.

Now she says, "I apologize for keeping Cache from you. I'm crying inside and horrified at what I've done. You may never get to know her and I could never forgive myself for that."

I wave her off. "Forget it. It is what it is, and there's nothing fixable about that. But apology accepted. I understand. I wasn't all that stable when we had our little fling. In fact, as I remember, I was bouncing off the walls. You took a chance with me, Millie."

"I did, but you were too good-looking not to take a chance.

Besides which, you were my first white man. I was curious. Isn't that horrible to admit?"

"Not really, because I can say the same thing," I tell her.

"What, I was your first white man, too?"

We laugh. The air around us is considerably cleared, and I feel right about Millie again. It's the first time since I got here. The truth is, I've been furious over what she did over all those years. I was cheated—no, it's worse, because something was taken from me—and the truth is that I'll never be able to trust Millie again. Forgiven, yes. But trust? Not again. But that's just between me and me. No sense in telling her.

Now it's quiet again. We have nothing else to say to one another. Our past has diverged.

Marcel hurries into the room, a worried look plastered on his face that might indicate I'm in much worse shape than what Dr. Fox just told me.

"Relax," I say to him. "I'm going to live."

"How much of you is going to live?"

"All of me. I can wiggle my fingers on my right hand already."

"That's good news. And the other good news: we got a new hearing for Cache. Congratulations, Michael."

I close my eyes and think about that for a minute. He's right. I did do it—but only with Marcel's help, and I tell him. "You were there with me every step of the way, Marcel. Fifty percent goes to you."

"You're back in court on July thirtieth. Less than two days. Can you make it?"

"Millie," I say, "would you excuse us now while we talk?"

She leaves, shaking her head as she goes. She knows what I'm going to need to do.

"Promise me, Marcel, that you'll have me at the courthouse, seated at that table, when it's time to argue. Will you promise me that?"

"What, bust your sorry ass out of here? Kidding. I'll do it, of course."

"No matter what Verona or any doctor says to you?"

"No matter. I'll have you there, rain or shine,"

Now I can rest.

~

Hours later. Four in the morning and someone is taking my blood pressure. No, it's the cuff has tightened but there's nobody here. Maybe it's on autopilot. Whatever it is, I come awake. I'm feeling much stronger now. I test, and I can move my right arm. And leg. Not completely but better.

"You awake?" Verona says from somewhere in the dark room.

"More or less. Where's Leo?"

"Back at your room with Millie. My stuff's there, too."

"How's Cache?"

"They wouldn't let Millie see her. She called ahead. So she didn't go. She's with Leo."

"Thanks for being here."

"Thanks for not dying, Michael. I think we need to talk about your future and the practice of law."

"We'll have to do that at some point. But not tonight; not until I'm well again, okay?"

She sniffs like some wives do. I know what it means,

"I love you, Verona, Thanks for being here."

"I love you too, Michael. And I'm distraught."

"Don't be. I'm ready to get a full physical and see where I am."

"That's a start."

"It's necessary."

She sighs. "Marcel is taking you to court tomorrow?"

Long silence. She knows. Did she intuit? Did Marcel tell her?

"Yes, Marcel is taking me."

"I knew you wouldn't listen. Well, two things. One, don't die."

"What's the other?'

"Two, don't lose."

They release me the next afternoon. Marcel drives us to the Hyatt. I'm feeling like fifty percent of my old self. Not whole, yet, but I'm feeling pretty good. Maybe a little hitch in my right leg but no one notices. Or no one says anything.

We ride upstairs to our room. The three of us enter and find Millie asleep on the sofa with Leo seated in front of the silent TV working with his Legos. Millie is instantly awake and sits up.

"You again?" she says to me.

"Disappointed are we?" I reply,

"Grandpa!"

Before I know it, Leo has jumped into my arms and is hugging me around the neck. This one is easy to love.

Millie and Verona have some plan in place because they gather up their purses and advise us that Marcel and Michael will be watching Leo for a couple of hours. It surprises me, but the activity in transferring from the hospital to the hotel has worn me down just a bit. Marcel winks at me. He's got this.

Two hours later I open my eyes. I've drifted off, but Millie and Verona have returned and are talking to Marcel,

"Casket," I hear Verona say. "About five-thousand for the preparation and burial."

Now I'm wide awake and sitting up.

"What are you talking about?" I ask Verona,

"We went and found a burial plot and a casket."

"Just in case," Millie says and turns away.

"Well, stop payment on the check," I tell them. "We won't be needing any of that."

I'm angry. I also remember I've been told to avoid stress and upset.

I get up and go in on my bed. I plan to sleep the rest of the day, wake up tomorrow, put on a suit, and go save my daughter's life.

That's my plan.

DAY 27/30

I attend court in a wheelchair. Verona has pleaded with me to find co-counsel, just a warm body to read my short motion and amended brief to the court and let it go at that. But no, I've resisted her—and Marcel—who has joined with her. So, Marcel has requisitioned a wheelchair from the Hyatt and hauled me to court.

We're just five minutes away from the start time by the time he has me wheeled up to counsel table, and I've spread my papers—my notes to argue—before me. He then goes back on the other side of the bar, and I'm alone at the table. On the table at my right, there is a woman, alone, who neither looks my way nor speaks to me. Fair enough, she looks sickly in her summer suit, even frail and skinny. I determine that I will overwhelm her.

Now the three judges file in; Judge Crittenden is not among them. Instead, there's a new face, a female judge who, of course, I don't know and whose name I probably won't know until I read the court's written decision sometime after today. The court is brought to order, the case is called, and the chief judge turns to me and nods. "Your motion, Mr. Gresham. You may proceed."

Suddenly I feel very insignificant, confined to the wheel-chair. I'm accustomed to standing and using my height and bulk to convince the court that I am vital, believable and that I deserve to win. A lot of what I do is about attitude. I find that being confined to a wheelchair robs me of some of that and I'm uneasy from the gate. But I push on.

"May it please the court, what we have here today is a simple *Strickland* case."

My train of thought has evaporated.

I lean forward in the wheelchair, toward counsel table, and appear to be searching for notes. What I'm really doing is trying to remember what was so important before. It must be said today, now. I want them to clearly and thoroughly remember what they've read in the new records I submitted. I can continue.

"Cache Evans has shown beyond all doubt that Attorney Kelly Larsyn's defense of her in the state court was unrea-sonable and that she was prejudiced." I lose it again. So I merely add, "Cache Evans is now entitled to habeas relief. Her grievances are major grievances all, any one of which is grounds to set my client free and dismiss the case against her. Which is what we're asking the court to do. That's all I wanted to say here today. Thank you for your forbearance and this opportunity."

I quit prematurely. I am covered in sweat, and my head is spinning. I'm asking myself what in God's name I was thinking by insisting I be the one to appear in this case today and not someone healthy, someone coached by me from my sick bed.

But my thoughts, my doubts, are cut short.

Alisa Edmundson, the U.S. Attorney assigned to argue the case today, slowly climbs to her feet. She catches my attention out the corner of my eye even as I sit and shake and sweat. I make her out to be frail and probably inhibited, and I'm hoping her presentation is short and weak like mine.

Fifteen minutes later, my case lies smoldering at my feet. Ms. Edmundson has not only turned out not to be frail; she's turned out to be a hurricane. It has taken her less than seven minutes to demolish the facts that I've brought before the court, and to argue that Cache's infection from the three boys was merely delayed, or, alternatively, that there were other people she could've had sex with in any case, and that the assumption the jury made in finding her guilty is the kind of assumption juries always make where circumstantial evidence is involved. At the end of her summary of the evidence, she adds, "As Henry David Thoreau once said, 'Some evidence is very strong. Like when there's a trout in the milk.'"

Then she spends another seven or eight minutes reviewing what she says the *Strickland* case really means and how I'm misrepresenting it here today—on purpose—in my effort to mislead the court.

To my surprise, she then adds, "I hate the death penalty personally and would gladly join in counsel's motion if I found it compelling and an accurate statement of the law. But I don't. So I have to ask the court to leave the execution warrant untouched."

After sucking all the oxygen out of the room, she finally sits —much to my enormous relief. I'm allowed three minutes for rebuttal, but I can only flail away and sound almost incoherent. I'm rattled, and everyone knows it. Plus, I'm getting weaker by the minute—even woozy, perhaps on the verge of passing out. I remember Dr. Fox's warning about stress and then, in spite of my commitment to Cache to fight until I'm dead if it takes that, I have to sit back in the wheelchair and tell the court I'm finished.

The court takes the case under advisement. I want to cry out, "When can we expect to hear from you?" but I know better. Attorneys don't cry out at judges. Especially not when attorneys have just handed their child's life to them. So I sit in my chair, my eyes closed, trying to slow my heartbeat. And it works. After just a few minutes the thumping pulse in my neck has retreated and my heartbeat has slowed.

The judges have cleared out. The U.S. Attorney is packing her briefcase. Then she turns to me. "I really wanted you to prevail," she says. "I hate this goddam case."

"You should have told them so," I tell her.

She flattens her mouth into a scowl. "But then I wouldn't be doing my job. And if I don't do my job I can't pay my rent. I hate this goddam profession. I'm working in clay, Mr. Gresham. I'm trying to learn how to throw pots and move to Taos. I'll sell my crockery and smoke peyote."

"What the hell?" I mutter.

"I'm sorry you lost. But you did."

"Thanks. I'd buy one of your pots, just for that."

Marcel comes up behind me. I can feel his hands grip the wheelchair.

Ever so gently he says, "Ready, Boss?"

He knows, damn, he knows.

I blew it. I shouldn't have tried this. I should have turned over all the stones and found competent appellant counsel to represent Cache here today. My thoughts weren't clear at any point, and my voice was weak. Even my right hand won't stop shaking. What the hell is that about?

"I'm ready. Wait. How bad was it?"

"I think you did fine, Boss."

"Thanks, Marcel. You never fail me, do you." It isn't a question. We both know what I mean. He's constant, and he's loyal to a fault. But he did try to talk me out of coming here today. He did tell me he was hoping I'd let him interview a couple of appeals lawyers and pick one that would be aggressive and intelligent on Cache's behalf. The winning ingredients. But I wouldn't let him do it. I objected and pitched a fit and said I was going to defend Cache, that no one else could do it like me.

Wrong. Just about any first-year law student could have outdone me here today.

"Okay," Marcel says and wheels me back from the table, swings us around, and begins pushing me back up the aisle. At the doors, the last remaining bailiff, who has been waiting patiently for us to clear out, pushes open the door and gives us a kind smile.

"Good luck, Mr. Gresham."

"Thank you."

Then we are outside, where it is overcast and rainy—gloomy to the point where I seriously think about just getting on a plane and going home, unable to face Cache and admit how I've let her down.

Marcel opens his umbrella and shields me from the heavens.

Lord knows I need it.

DAY 28/30

After court yesterday I returned to the hotel and collapsed into bed. I was whipped, and I was ashamed of how I'd let my ego run away with me and maybe sent my daughter to her death. I was complaining about Larsyn's negligence when my own might have just been enough to finish her off—a horrible thought.

Early today, Marcel took Millie and Leo to Purdy in an attempt to let Leo visit his mom for what will be the last time. Verona tells me this as she's bringing me orange juice and a danish. I have no appetite and beg her not to open the drapes when she turns to them. "I can't stand the gray Seattle skies today," I tell her. I know I'm depressed and wonder when I'll see the sun again. Right now, a week in Scottsdale sounds very inviting.

I'm avoiding. Who wouldn't? Yesterday's gone, however. Somehow I need to get off the pity pot and pull myself together.

Verona stands beside the bed, looking down at me. I'm wallowing in self-hatred, and she knows it.

"How are you feeling?"

"I've been better."

"I mean your arm and leg, the side of your face. Is it getting any better?"

I test those limbs; I test my face, moving my mouth side-to-side and feeling my cheek for drool. There is none, and my leg and arm and hand seem to be functioning as meant.

"I think I'm all systems go. Except I don't want to go."

"Well, save your energy today. Because the day after tomorrow you have to go. You have to be there for Cache when she leaves us."

"Oh, my God."

"You're her dad. You did everything you could. I'm sorry it went so bad, Michael. But also, we tried to get you to find another lawyer. I need to say that to you, as your wife. You wouldn't listen to reason. You were self-will run riot. Now Cache pays the price. There, I've said it. I've been honest with you. Now let's get started and build you back up again. You don't deserve to suffer for this. You did so much. You tried your heart out, and it finally put you in the hospital. No one could ask any more of you. So let it go, Michael. Let yourself rest and recover now."

"Where's my phone, Verona, in case the court calls?"

"Did you hear anything I just said?"

"I did. I've taken it in. But I'm just going to have to live with much of it for a long time and work through it. I can't just let it go, as you put it. That doesn't work for me."

"You need to beat yourself up, is that it?"

"Seriously, where's my phone. They could call at any minute, and I've got to answer."

"Your phone is right next to you on the nightstand. I've got it plugged in, so it's fully charged. We love you, Michael, all of us. We want to be there for you. And we have been."

"All right. I think I need to stop talking now and just rest."

"Eat your pastry, Michael. Drink your OJ."

"I would like some coffee and a big glass of ice water."

"I have coffee in the other room. It's still hot. And we have ice. Marcel brought us a bucket earlier. He knows you pretty well, Michael. You've got yourself one hell of a pal there."

"Please. Just let me have some coffee and water. I'm drained right now."

"Okay, message received. I'll shut up."

"And the TV clicker. I'd like to watch the news."

"It's on your nightstand, next to your phone. Can you reach it?"

"Okay. I can. Let's talk again later, Verona. Thanks for being gentle with me."

"I don't know what horse you're used to riding, mister, but that wasn't gentle. That was truth-telling time."

"Okay. We'll talk later. Thanks."

Everyone will need to have their say. Starting with Verona.

And ending with Cache.

DAY 29/30

S till no word—the court hasn't called. I don't know any
more today than I did the minute I was wheeled out of
court two days ago. And it's driving me insane.

Purdy did allow Leo to visit his mom. She cried the whole
time and didn't try to hide it from Leo. All restraint is gone,
Millie reports. She also reports that Cache is very subdued
and very pale-looking. As if the blood has drained out of her
skin. She's ghostly, to use Millie's words. Naturally, she's very
worried about her daughter's health. I'm not going to point
out the irony. I won't even go there.

Today I call Cache and get put through. I explain the whole
process—my getting sick, the court, what happened in
court, and how I see it coming down. I don't pull my
punches. She deserves to know the truth.

"Michael," she says when I've run out of things to say. "Don't
ever hold any of this against yourself. Promise me that.
You've done a fantastic job for me. No regrets, father."

"Thank you, Cache. I'll try to take that to heart."

We chat on as if there's nothing unusual going on. Except, oh yes, she did tell the social worker they could have organs, skin, whatever they can use. She told them to take what they want. She has no regrets and is pleased with her decision.

I spend the day in blue jeans and a thin sweatshirt. My moccasins brush noisily on the carpet as I move around the suite looking for something to do. I am every bit as much in prison as my daughter. There is just no escaping the horror of knowing your loved one is going to die tomorrow. And that—that—you couldn't make it stop even though you had the chance.

Later in the day, everyone helps me down to poolside, and we order sandwiches and iced tea. It is warm today and sunny— a beautiful day for August 2. Thirty hours until they take Cache away from us. I try not to think about it.

Good luck with that.

DAY 30/30

Her guard brings me up to speed while I wait for them to bring Cache to the family room the next morning.

She wakes up at 6:16 a.m. They allow her to take a hot shower in the guards' locker room, under heavy security measures. They allow her to blow dry her hair and apply makeup they keep for the last day death row prisoners. She uses the blow dryer and applies the makeup sparingly. She studies herself in the mirror. "Is there a toothbrush?" she wants to know. One of the guards fetches a new toothbrush from the commissary. It's still in the wrapper—paid for by the guard herself. I want to reimburse her. She gives me an angry look.

They feed her a breakfast of eggs over medium, English muffin, Canadian bacon, a small T-bone, a twist of orange, and tomato juice. She is ravenous, she tells them. But then she picks at it.

A priest comes. She refuses to see him. A counselor comes; she agrees to see her. The guards hear it all. She asks the counselor to tell us what she wants for Leo. First, I'm to have custody of my grandson. Second, she wants him home-schooled if possible. She thinks it will be too hard for him to attend school and have to explain why he's living with his grandpa. Kids are death on other kids, she tells the counselor. The counselor is gentle with her and tells her she's writing it all down, that she's sure her wishes will be carried out. Then she dictates a letter to Leo to be opened by him on his twelfth birthday. While the letter was being taken down, the guard had to make rounds on the floor, so she missed out on what was said. I can't even begin to guess.

At 10:00 a.m., they move her into the final staging area. A physician arrives to examine her. It is the same physician who will insert the needles into her flesh and who will pronounce her dead minutes later. I am told Cache is friendly with the doctor and even jokes to him about which veins to use as she's been an addict and the heroin needle has all but destroyed the common veins. They're scarred, she tells him. She also tells him she was finally able to get on the methadone maintenance program and is proud that she had six months off the black tar heroin until her arrest. I know the black tar heroin is the cheapest heroin available on the street. In my twisted frame of mind, I'm sorry she couldn't get the better grade of the drug, the stuff with fewer impurities. How close am I to going over the edge?

At noon they are going to allow us to spend as much time with her as we want. They have the family room set up for this purpose. It's a replica of a typical living room in a typical three-bedroom tract home, complete with couch, loveseat, two straight-back chairs, and a wet sink overseen by a Keurig coffee maker. There are K-cups and donuts in the room. And there is a menu of dishes that can be requested at any time in any amount. This is very different from what I've seen before. It's almost humane...but not quite, given the overarching reality that death will follow our get-together.

Throughout the afternoon and the evening, we laugh, and we cry. Leo needs a nap, and he's put down on the loveseat, where he sucks his thumb and falls asleep under Millie's cotton sweater. His mother sits beside him, stroking his hair while he dreams his dreams. I would love a picture of this for him, but there are no cameras allowed. Even our phones were taken from us when we passed through security. If the court calls me now, I won't be able to take the call on my phone. Out of a deepening sense of frustration, and growing fear, I ask to see the warden.

She comes to the room and knocks. I'm asked to speak with her in the hallway. She's wearing a suit of expensive blue slacks and blue coat. Her shirt is white, and there's even a necktie, one of many more colors than most men would wear on such an austere day. She's dressed to talk to the press after the execution. I get it. She has to look good for the public. I don't hold it against her; it's her job.

"What about a last-minute call from the court?" I ask her. "Are they able to connect with you on a minute's notice?"

"They are. I've called the chambers of the chief judge. They are talking, but the chief judge's courtroom deputy doesn't expect a last-minute call. That's the message I have for you tonight, Mr. Gresham. I'm so, so sorry."

What can I say? It's unacceptable. I can't say it's okay, that I understand because it isn't. None of it is okay, none of it is understandable.

At 7:00 p.m., Cache is returned to her holding cell. It's time
for her to be alone with a priest or counselor—they're going
to try again to salve their collective conscience by making
humanitarian services available to the walking dead.

We wait in the prison cafeteria, a small group gathering,
huddled around a wood table in a room where only one
overhead panel of lights have been illuminated for us.

Time drags, and we've run out of things to say.

At 11:50 p.m., Millie and I are escorted to the room where
Cache will die in ten minutes. The procedure is explained to
us; they expect our daughter to feel no pain. Millie is
weeping as they explain about the straps to hold Cache
down, even though a paralytic drug is introduced after the
sedative drug. I can't hold back any longer, either. I am
reduced to a tear-stained father with nothing to hold onto.
When it's come down to it, none of my religious preferences
and beliefs, none of my half-assed belief in the judicial
system, can take away my terror and my pain. I don't know if
I can do this.

At 11:55 p.m., we're moved into the viewing area. Millie and I
are seated in the front row. Millie takes my hand in hers and
holds on tight.

The U.S. Attorney—the not-so-frail Assistant U.S. Attorney
who destroyed my case—comes into the room. She looks
every bit as frail and pallid as she did in court, despite the
fact the room is dark, and the only light comes from the
windowed room where Cache will finally die.

The warden suddenly comes in and leans down to me. The
court has called. The execution is to proceed.

Cache is brought into the room moments later. She is strapped to the table. There is a rustle and a cry behind me but I cannot tear my eyes away from my daughter. A door behind me opens and shuts rapidly. Someone has left the room. I can only imagine it's the U.S. Attorney's representative; she's finally unable to be a participant in the death she helped bring about.

Needles are inserted. Cache doesn't wince. She is dressed in a short-sleeve prison jumpsuit gray in color. She looks at the ceiling; she doesn't look at her mother and father.

Then the door opens behind us yet again, and the lights come on. The warden once again approaches me. She bends down.

"Michael," she says, using my Christian name, "the U.S. Attorney has reversed field."

"Meaning?"

"She just came out and told me to stop the execution. She called the court of appeals. She joined in your motion and your appeal. She said to tell you she'll think of you when she makes Taos. The court reversed and remanded. Cache's writ of habeas corpus is ordered. She's to be released, and the charges against her dismissed. Congratulations."

Millie slumps against me. She is openly weeping. So am I. The room is clearing, noisy yet hushed. I wipe my face and look for Cache. The needles have been withdrawn, the straps are unbuckled, and she sits up. She looks through the glass panes at her mother and father.

Finally, her parents, together with her.

The warden has entered the glassed room. She speaks to

Cache. I watch her lips move. I watch my daughter collapse back against the table, rolling onto her side, her knees pulled up to her chest in the fetal position.

Call it being reborn. Call it whatever you might.

It looks like a rebirth to me.

~

My daughter and grandson return to Washington, D.C. with us the next day. She is going to join our family and be with us while she sorts her life. There is no plan; there are no expectations. She is simply going to live now. She has her do-over.

Cache's guard, the woman who stood outside her cell month-after-month-after-month, has written me a note. I unfold it on the plane and read.

 Mr. Gresham.

You did Justis.

Thank you from all of us.

EPILOGUE

Six Months Later

It is now six months to the day since Cache escaped the needle. Escaped by two minutes. The technician's log reports 11:58 p.m. as the exact moment her hand was removed from the switch. I know this because I have sued the State of Washington and everyone and every entity that came within ten feet of Cache's court case and imprisonment. The lawsuit has brought a pickup truck load of documents and court filings and medical records to my home office where, nowadays, I work on her case. My only case.

I don't think her case will be my last. I'm finding I want to search deeper and deeper into the how's and why's of wrongful convictions and wrongful sentences in the criminal justice system, especially regarding those inmates on death row. 100% certainty is the only acceptable standard for that place. Maybe I have one more case inside me for the innocent imprisoned and sentenced to death. Or maybe not. I'm still suffering great tiredness from my mini-stroke. Most days I tire before noon and have to turn away from my work.

Afternoons are for watching over Leo, whose mother is now attending junior college. I'm no match for this boy. At three in the afternoon, I'm nodding off in my recliner while Leo builds with his Legos and suddenly blasts my ears with his walkie-talkie. I need two of me, one dedicated 24/7 to Leo. We've also had his blood tested twice—negative for HIV both times.

Cache has announced her plans to attend law school. Today, as I sit and develop her case in my head, she's attending a junior college class in biology—the delicate task of separating a frog into his component parts with a scalpel. She still has her nose pierced. The lip ring has been removed, but the neck tattoo remains, of course. Who doesn't like looking at Harley roses on his daughter's neck? The real truth? She can pierce away and tattoo away her entire geography; I'm just happy to see her alive and living maybe her first dream ever. She is also connecting with Leo in a way I can tell was absent before. He's loving every minute of having his mom home and managing his 1000-questions-per-day habit.

Mikey and Dania and Annie—my other at-home kids—haven't broken stride since the newbies came onboard. Their lives have continued unfettered from all care and shortages and fears. Mikey's constant disturbance in his equilibrium is that, as a first-grader, he has so many school days yet ahead. A playground friend explained they were all looking at eleven more years, and Mikey has been downcast ever since. Until he remembers his new friend Leo is waiting to explore the world outside our new home in Liberty Lake. Then he's a happy young lad.

Dania looks more like her mother, Danny, with each new

day. She is lengthening and achieving the willowy *Vogue* look every day. She has no interest in boys, yet, though she did complain last night about Daniel J. Stevens kicking the back of her chair all through reading studies yesterday. Maybe the assault of the citadel has begun? I shudder to think.

While the two younger kids are dealing with school and extreme youth, Annie, my second-most-recent daughter (by adoption) is now part-timing for the City of Spokane police department. She profiles criminal cases that have stumped the detectives. It's paying off, too: a string of sexual assaults has ceased thanks to Annie's work on the case where she was given the profiles of twenty parolees. Working backward, Annie was able to rule out nineteen of the twenty, leading to an arrest that coincided with the cessation of sexual assaults against women in late-night parking lots. I applaud Annie and keep her close; we need each other more than any of the others need either of us. The apple of her dad's eye, it might be said. Or the genius under my roof, it might be even more accurately said. She is happy and becoming better adjusted. Her penchant for swallowing coins and batteries has ceased since her one-year stay in a hospital where such behaviors got sorted. She still calls me "Michael," so, in my worldview at least, we haven't arrived yet, the two of us. But we shall.

Marcel's life has taken a turn: he spends his mornings with me, assisting with Cache's lawsuit. Then he spends his afternoons writing his memoirs. So far he's refused all my requests for a preview. I don't blame him. I'm a harsh literary critic, especially the cops and robbers stuff. An interesting development, however: he has been out on several dates with Eleanor Riddell, the pediatrician who offices off

East Sprague in Spokane, the doctor who treats all the runaway girls. She just turned fifty-one—we all attended her birthday dinner—and Marcel, as per my wishes, still hasn't impregnated her. I know; I'm kidding Marcel. A man after my own heart.

Oh yes, one more note about Marcel. An *Instagram* page for Kelly Larsyn was opened. A hundred photos or more of Mr. Larsyn in bed with an unidentified woman was posted on his page. He is seen in the most outrageous poses with the woman, various fruits and utensils and crude sexual positions. The pictured subjects are all nude, of course. The *Instagram* link was emailed to all clients and family and the entire Spokane Bar Association. The links had been sent from his laptop computer using his Contacts file. It is said his business is evaporating and the Bar Association has begun an ethics and decency investigation. They are trying to establish just why he would post such an outrage for everyone he knows. Larsyn is experiencing such sweet bliss in the photos his eyes are shut. I can only wish him well.

Some friends who follow my legal exploits have grown increasingly outspoken about the after-effects of some of my younger dalliances. That's right, some who know me well know about my conquests and subsequent defeats by my own hand. I'm talking about unwanted pregnancies and unwelcome affairs of the heart. As time has passed, my roving eye has settled down for what looks like a long, but warm, winter beside Verona, the love of my life. She has remained true to me in word and in fact. She is my north star, my *sine qua non*, my fellow traveler, and my friend. She is also my lover; advancing age and familiarity haven't quelled that inferno one bit. For which I am grateful. And so is she.

What remains, for Cache, is a lifetime of choices. Happily, these will be choices she makes rather than choices someone else makes for her.

There remains only this one comment to Millie: it was a mistake all those years ago, but it's no longer a mistake today.

One afternoon I answer a knock at the door. Lucky, asleep beside my feet, opens his eyes and looks up at me. We pal up and open the door. It's UPS. The driver, wearing brown shorts and brown shirt, holds a box up for me. It's about the size of a world globe. I accept the delivery and retreat inside.

The mailing label has my name handwritten as the recipient. It says it's from Taos, New Mexico. I rip it open and find, inside, submerged in bubble wrap, a green bowl such as you would use to serve baked beans out on your patio at noon in August. There's a note inside, handwritten. I read:

DO YOU THINK I CAN SELL THIS SHIT?

THE END

AFTERWORD

The Death Penalty raises serious philosophical questions and quick arguments on both sides. People become angry talking about the death penalty and rightly so. Both sides make sense to this author and yet neither side makes sense. A total conundrum.

However, this book is not a tract about the death penalty. The author is a writer, not a priest or rabbi or politician or philosopher. Each individual will deal with the reality of the ultimate penalty in his or her own way.

In this book, which takes place in the State of Washington, there is a moratorium on the death penalty. Despite that, literary license was taken to make the story what it is.

There is no purpose intended for this book. I'm not out to change anyone's mind. I only wanted to tell Cache's story, the story of a young woman completely of my imagination.

Finally, it's the story of a death row inmate who has been wrongly convicted.

It happens.

What that might mean to you is your own private concern. I practiced criminal law for forty years. While my health and stamina allowed, I felt like I was doing my part in all this.

That's the thing about law, and courts, and juries. We seldom know for sure what's what.

That's how it goes for the lawyers on both sides of the fence.

This book is for them.

ALSO BY JOHN ELLSWORTH

THADDEUS MURFEE SERIES

THADDEUS MURFEE

THE DEFENDANTS

BEYOND A REASONABLE DEATH

ATTORNEY AT LARGE

CHASE, THE BAD BABY

DEFENDING TURQUOISE

THE MENTAL CASE

UNSPEAKABLE PRAYERS

THE GIRL WHO WROTE THE NEW YORK TIMES BESTSELLER

THE TRIAL LAWYER (A SMALL DEATH)

THE NEAR DEATH EXPERIENCE

SISTERS IN LAW SERIES

FRAT PARTY: SISTERS IN LAW

HELLFIRE: SISTERS IN LAW

MICHAEL GRESHAM SERIES

THE LAWYER

SECRETS GIRLS KEEP

THE LAW PARTNERS

CARLOS THE ANT

SAKHAROV THE BEAR

ANNIE'S VERDICT

DEAD LAWYER ON AISLE 11

30 DAYS OF JUSTIS

PSYCHOLOGICAL THRILLERS

THE EMPTY PLACE AT THE TABLE

ABOUT THE AUTHOR

John Ellsworth 2016

USA TODAY Bestselling Author John Ellsworth practiced law in Flagstaff and Chicago. As a criminal defense attorney he became expert in defending state and federal criminal defendants. Some of that experience and knowledge led to his writing this book.

Since 2014 John has been writing legal, crime, and psychological thrillers with huge success. He has been a Kindle All-Star (Amazon's selection) many times and he has made the *USA TODAY* bestsellers' list.

Reception to John's books has been phenomenal; more than

1,000,000 have been downloaded in 40 months. All are Amazon best-sellers.

John lives in Southern California where he makes his way around his small beach town on a yellow Vespa motorscooter.

He is married and has lost count of how many grandchildren his five daughters have produced.

ellsworthbooks.com

johnellsworthbooks@gmail.com

Cover design by Nathan Wampler.

Published by Subjudica Press, San Diego.

First edition

Ellsworth, John. *30 Days of Justis*. Subjudica House. Kindle Edition.

EMAIL SIGNUP

If you would like to be notified of new book publications, please sign up for my email list. You will receive news of new books, newsletters, and occasional drawings.
— John Ellsworth

Made in the USA
Middletown, DE
03 March 2018